Deadly Truth

SM Dougan

http://smdougan.com

Deadly Truth is a work of fiction. The incidents, names, places and characters are the product of the author's imagination and any resemblance to actual persons, living or dead, businesses, locations or events are completely coincidental.

Copyright © 2013 SM Dougan

All rights reserved.

ISBN: **0973938552**
ISBN-13: **978-0973938555**

This book or portions thereof may not be reproduced, scanned or distributed in whole or in part by any means or method with the prior express written permission of the publisher.
Please do your part in preventing piracy of copyrighted works

Printed in the U.S.A.

1

Leslie Harrison brushed back her long blonde hair and removed an earring to answer the phone. Her voice was young and sultry as she spoke, "Hello."

There was a moment's pause on the other end before the voice of an older male with an Australian accent responded, "Hello, Leslie, do you have a moment? I'd like to talk to you."

Leslie's laugh sounded more juvenile than its twenty-five years, "Certainly. I thought you might call. What can I do for you?"

The male spoke in a controlled manner, "I received your message. What can I do to stop you from sending that package?"

The cocky smile on her face could be heard through her voice, "As I said in my message, pay me three million dollars. You are the last holdout. Everyone else has come through. It would be a shame that they should all go down because you didn't pay. I don't imagine they would be very pleased with you. If the three million dollars is in my account by 2:00pm tomorrow all of this will be over. Otherwise, the package arrives at its destination. I am pretty sure that is not something you would want, am I wrong?"

There was a long moment of silence before he spoke again, "How do I know that once you get your money, you won't come back for more?"

Leslie giggled unpleasantly, "You don't, but I am a woman of ethics and integrity. You can trust me."

The man chuckled, "Somehow I don't take comfort in that guarantee."

Leslie was serious, "You really don't have any choice, now do you?"

He was silent for a moment, "Very well, three million dollars. How did you manage to get an account in the Caymans, anyway?"

Leslie laughed, "What, don't you think pretty little ol' me paid attention to how all you good ol' boys do things? Don't be silly."

Her voice became instantly hard, "Enough chit-chat. I am a busy woman. You have until 2:00pm tomorrow, period. End of discussion. I suggest you don't be late."

Leslie abruptly returned the handset to the cradle. The evil smile looked out of place on such a beautiful young face. She nodded with satisfaction as she returned her earring to its proper place. She retrieved the small flash drive from her housecoat pocket. It was still early but she had no intentions of dressing further than this for the rest of the day.

She looked at the flash drive for a moment before giving it a gentle kiss and placing it on the end table beside the laptop computer. She smiled broadly as she turned and walked to the kitchen. A teacup sat on the counter waiting for the water in the kettle to boil. Beside the cup sat the teapot. It was already warmed and had two tea bags waiting inside. She loved her tea and even if it was just her, she would drink it from one of her pretty china cups and saucer. She didn't believe that special occasions were the only time for good china.

With the tea now steeped and her cup full, she walked into the living room and curled comfortably on the couch facing the television. It was already on and was halfway through one of her favorite movies. Her mood was bullet proof and she could not think of anything that could spoil it.

The movie ended and Leslie stretched. A few tear stains showed on her face as a reminder of the more emotional parts of the movie. She reached for the remote and turned the television off.

As it fell silent there was a knock at the door that surprised Leslie.

She was not expecting company. Cautiously she made her way to the door and peered through the peephole.

She didn't recognize the face, but the uniform was familiar, "Yes? Who is it?"

The voice on the other side of the door spoke instantly with a hint of delight, "Leslie Harrison? I have a package for Leslie Harrison."

Leslie was suspicious, "A package? Who is it from?"

The man behind the door glanced at the package he carried as he responded, "Er... It says it's for Leslie Harrison, and ahhh, the shipper is, ahhh Prentice... Bartholomew Prentice."

Leslie stood taller and smiled, "Prentice, really? I wonder what he would be sending me?"

She unlatched the chain from its slide and released the two dead bolts on the door before opening it.

In front of her stood a man in the brown uniform of a known messenger service. In his hand he held a large package and Leslie smiled as she reached her hands out.

She hadn't noticed the 9mm pistol the man held under the package with his free hand. A silenced round struck her in the abdomen and she went down hard to the floor.

He quickly followed into the apartment and closed the door. He took a moment to scan the room. His voice was rough and unpleasant, "Where is it?"

Leslie lay on the floor clutching her stomach. The pain she felt was expressed on her face. The man pointed his weapon at Leslie's head and spoke, "You are alive. You will live. Tell me where it is and I will leave. Your call"

She shook her head lightly, "I don't know what you are talking about?"

The man shook his head, "Do you really want to die? Is it worth dying for? Tell me and I leave."

Leslie looked at the man for a moment and then spoke frantically, "There, on the table. The flash drive. Beside the laptop. That is it, I swear. I won't say anything to anyone."

He saw the flash drive on the table and in one motion, he grabbed it and put it in his pocket. As he did, he heard Leslie moan.

He returned his attention to Leslie and raised the weapon again. With a smile, he put a round in her forehead. He took a moment to remove the silencer from his weapon before putting both in separate pockets in his brown jacket.

He looked back towards the television area of the room and noticed the empty cup on the coffee table. He smiled as he turned and walked into the kitchen. He took a fresh mug and quarter filled it with tea and returned to the living room. He placed the mug on the far end of the table. Then he carefully wiped the mouth of the mug with his right hand.

He took one more look around the room before nodding satisfaction. Then he picked up the laptop and placed it in the package he had been carrying before continuing towards the door. He slowly opened the door to inspect the hallway. Satisfied, he walked out of the apartment, closing the door behind him.

Once he was clear of the building, he pulled a disposable cell phone from his pocket and dialed 911. He performed his best concerned citizen voice as he reported the sound of gunfire in the apartment building, and mentioned the apartment he believed the shots had come from. Before the operator could press him for more information, he hung up, powered down the phone and tossed it in the nearest dumpster before continuing up the street to his waiting car.

He drove immediately to a quiet stretch of the river. He quickly looked around to see if anyone was nearby. Satisfied he was alone, he reached into his pocket and tossed the gun and silencer into the river.

***

Detectives Williams and Davidson arrived at the apartment to find the usual entourage of uniforms on the scene. One stood at the doorway of the apartment watching the hallway and a few others were inside. The two detectives are as much a contrast in appearance to each other as they are to the officers in the apartment.

Davidson's grey hair was extra short and the brown tweed jacket he wore looked as though he had owned it all his life. The tie around his neck was loose and the top button of his white dress shirt was undone.

Williams on the other hand was much younger and wore his hair a bit longer. His attire was more carefully put together and looked far more professional than Davidson. The detective's respective personalities were perfectly captured in their attire.

Both detectives nodded politely to each officer in turn as they entered the apartment. Leslie Harrison still lay precisely where she had fallen. Williams shook his head, "What a waste of a beautiful woman."

Davidson looked down at the victim, "Yeah. It is a shame. It's always a waste."

The look on Williams' face was less disconnected than it should be and Davidson noticed it, "You seem a little out of sorts today. You and what's her name have a falling out?"

Williams was immediately angry, "Her name is Barbra. Barbra. Not that it matters anymore."

Davidson nodded knowingly. His voice was almost sympathetic, "Sorry, Williams. This job is not particularly conducive to long term relationships. That is why I never get involved in them."

Williams laughed sarcastically, "Yeah, that's why. That's the only reason why, right? Yeah, I'm thinking there are a whole lot of reasons for all sensible women to stay away from you."

Davidson smiled as he continued to look around the room, "It certainly doesn't look like she was hurting any. Money wise that is. This is a nice place."

Williams smiled knowing that Davidson had deliberately changed the subject. He nodded approvingly as he walked around the room. His movements were deliberate. He slowly checked the scene from several different angles. Davidson stood by the body and looked in the direction she was most likely facing when she was shot. Then he looked in the opposite direction. The expected blood splatter verified his theory, "Well it is pretty safe to say she was facing the door. There are no signs of forced entry, so either she knew the killer or it was someone she didn't consider a threat."

Williams spoke up, "Yeah. There are two cups on the coffee table. One is china the other a coffee mug. That would suggest they knew each other. I'm guessing she used the china cup and the mug was used by a male visitor. The question is, if that is the case, why did he wait until he was leaving to shoot her..." He pulled on a pair of latex gloves and touched the side of each mug in turn, "They are still a little warm."

Davidson nodded, "The 911 call came from a cell phone. No ID on the caller. If I were a betting man, I would suggest that it was the killer calling. He wanted to be sure the body was found in a timely manner. He certainly is a courteous slime ball."

The forensics team arrived in the apartment. The first one in the room was a man Davidson's age; easily in his late fifties. He took a deep breath as he crossed the threshold, "There are certain smells that once experienced are never forgotten; Fine tobacco from a pipe; alcohol on the breath; burnt gunpowder; and death." His attention left the body and was directed towards Davidson, "Hello, Sam. Looks like you have a cute one for me."

Davidson laughed sarcastically, "Really, Frank, really?" He shook his head, "I think even you would conclude that it is probably the bullet in the forehead that did her in."

Frank smiled, "One has to maintain a sense of humor to do what we do, Sam. As for the GSW, it is only an assumption until I get her on my table."

Sam sneered, "Of course, Frank, how presumptuous of me. She may well have died from a nasty cold and the bullet holes were an attempt to kill the bug before it could spread."

Sam had known Frank for a great many years and was fully aware of how absolutely meticulous he was at his job and never assumed anything, no matter how obvious it seemed at first glance. He always let the victim lead the way in his investigations. Nonetheless, he couldn't resist poking a little fun at him.

Davidson turned his attention to Williams, "Okay, kid, I think we have everything we need." Sam looked back towards Frank, "Don't forget the two cups on the table. I know how your memory is at your age. They may be important."

Frank shook his head, "Piss off, Sam."

Davidson smiled as he and Williams walked out of the apartment. Williams slapped his partner on the shoulder, "I really wish you would stop calling me kid, old man. We have been partners for a while now. I know it makes you feel important, but really, you aren't that important." Williams laughed.

Davidson grinned half heartedly as the two split up and walked in opposite directions. Uniformed officers were already knocking on doors and questioning the neighbors. Davidson approached an officer down his end of the hallway, "Hey, George, how's it going?"

George turned to Davidson and smiled, "Hi, Sam, nothing yet. No one heard or saw anything."

Davidson nodded, "Yeah, I'm thinking the perp probably used a silencer. It looks like a hit in some ways, which makes a silencer likely, but it also looks like a sloppy kill in other ways. This may be an interesting one."

Davidson looked around the hallway and noticed a black dome on the ceiling, "Well, isn't that convenient."

George looked up to the place on the ceiling that had caught Davidson's attention and chuckled, "A surveillance camera, sweet."

Davidson nodded and smiled, "We may have just caught a break already."

Davidson started to walk in the direction of the elevators, "George, give my best to Beth will you."

George smiled, "Sure will, Sam. She misses you, you know. You really should come for dinner some night. I know Beth would really love to see you again."

Davidson nodded, "I'll do that George. Get your people to give my people a call and set something up."

George laughed, "Ya, ya, I get it. You are married to the job and she's high maintenance. I get it. Still, pop over anytime. You know you don't need a formal invitation."

Davidson looked back to George and nodded sincerely, "Thank you, George. I would really like to take you up on that. We'll see how it goes."

He nodded again and turned back towards the elevator. Davidson spotted his partner further down the hall, "Hey, Williams, you gonna stand around visiting all day or are we gonna do some of that investigating stuff?"

Williams spun to face Davidson and saw him pointing at the camera mounted on the ceiling. Williams smiled and quickly walked to catch up with his partner.

The elevator stopped on the main floor and the detectives walked immediately to the concierge desk. The uniformed man in his early thirties looked up with a half interested look on his face. Williams spoke, "Do you happen to have the footage from the surveillance camera on the seventh?"

The concierge bit into the apple he was eating, locking it between his teeth as he typed into his keyboard. After a moment or two he spoke through the apple, "Yup. I have the footage recorded for the last twelve hours, why?"

Davidson shook his head. The sarcasm in his voice was unmistakable. "Would it be too much trouble for you to make a copy of it for us. If you have the time, of course?"

The man didn't notice the inference and simply nodded, "Yeah, sure. Give me a minute. Everything is digital now so this will take just a sec."

Williams chuckled quietly as he looked towards Davidson. Davidson looked back at Williams and smiled but shook his head. Williams tried to squelch his amused expression.

True to his word, the man handed a DVD to Davidson, "Here you go."

When Davidson took the disc, the young man removed the apple from his mouth, "If you need anything else let me know. How long do you think you guys will be working up there? Some of the tenants are complaining about the noise."

Davidson put on his most sincere face, "I am very sorry for the inconvenience. Some people have no manners in where they get killed. We'll do our best to get out of here as quickly as possible. I apologize to your tenants."

The man didn't miss the sarcasm this time and was not pleased. He nodded angrily as he picked up his apple and returned his attention to the newspaper he was reading.

Williams slapped Davidson on the shoulder again, "Sometimes I think you are an even bigger ass than me."

The two detectives laughed quietly as they walked out the front door to their car.

***

Angela and Connor Shea had been at sea for two weeks and were now on their way back to their homeport. They had had near perfect weather the whole trip. As the sun shone above their forty-six foot sailing yacht, Conquest, Angela held the wheel. Connor stood directly behind her, holding her around the waist. His graying brown hair was almost too short to be teased by the wind, but Angela's flowed freely.

This was the first time this year that they had been able to spend any significant time on Conquest, and even longer since they had spent a significant amount of time alone, without their daughter. Although it has been a fabulous vacation and as much as they had enjoyed themselves, both were looking forward to returning home.

Janet Elaine Shea was born three years ago and with both Angela and

Connor semi-retired, they had been able to be there to enjoy watching her grow. Two of Angela's most cherished people lent their names to their daughter. Janet had been Angela's closest friend since they were in high school and to this day they are still closer than even sisters.

Elaine, of course, was from Angela's mother. No matter what happened in life, Elaine had always been there; not just for Angela, but also for Janet and anyone else important in Angela's life.

This vacation away for Angela and Connor served as an excellent opportunity for Elaine to spend some quality time with her granddaughter. This had not been the first time, of course, but it was the longest stretch for some time.

The Conquest was still a day and a half out of port and the weather was expected to hold. They hadn't seen land for three days now and had not missed it. There is a certain appeal in being alone with someone dearly close to you far from the reach of any other human.

They had made a point of not bringing their cell phones or computers on this trip. The only electronics onboard were for navigation, safety, and emergency communication. This was a time for just them.

Angela leaned her head back and rested it between Connors neck and shoulder. Although he was several years older than her, one would be pressed to guess his age. Angela looked up at his face and spoke softly, "I love you, Connor. I have so enjoyed these couple of weeks."

Connor turned his head just enough to give Angela a light peck on her forehead, "I love you too, my dear."

Angela stood back straight, released the wheel and slid away from Connor's grip, "I am going to put something together to eat, Captain. Can you handle her on your own?"

Connor laughed, "Yes, number one. She is the only lady that will follow my commands."

Angela chuckled as she made her way inside the main cabin of the vessel. Connor watched her descend out of sight. Connor loved her without doubt and just the sight of her warmed his heart.

He saw his bride's long brown hair teased and flowing magically on the air as she moved. Her shape stirs the man in him at every glance. He considered himself very lucky and they were very happy in their life together.

He now had a full grip on the stainless steel wheel and confirmed his heading on the compass. Even with all the electronics onboard, he still liked to do things the old fashioned way. If nothing else it confirmed what the electronics were telling him, but more importantly the manual work with compass and chart kept his skills sharp. Electronics can fail but a compass and sextant don't.

Forty minutes passed before Angela called up to him, "Dinner is ready, darling."

Connor smiled, "I'll be right down." He confirmed his course one more time and let in some of the sails. Speed was not something they were concerned about and frankly neither was the course. As long as he was headed in the general direction that was close enough for now.

When he was satisfied the vessel was safe and secure, he headed down the steps to the cabin and his meal. Angela had removed all but her bikini and smiled teasingly as Connor made his way to the table.

Connor shook his head lightly. The scars on her body from years past could still be seen, but Connor didn't notice them. A lustful smile crossed his face, "What?"

Angela giggled like a schoolgirl, "Eat up. I want to get on with dessert."

Connor laughed openly and changed his course from the table to Angela, "How about we take care of dessert first."

Angela giggled again and started running for the bow of the cabin and to the master's suite. The smile on Connor's face broadened as he walked quickly after her. His shirt came off as he went. When he passed through the cabin door, he closed it behind him.

Angela was already on the bed. Connor wasted no time joining her and taking her in a long, deep kiss. Angela pushed back slightly, "The boats okay, right?"

Connor laughed, "Okay enough. It won't flip or anything. I can fix everything else later." He returned to his passionate embrace of Angela.

***

Williams and Davidson were sitting in front of the computer monitor on Davidson's desk watching the video supplied by Leslie's building. They had fast forwarded the video to the time they believed the killing took place.

From that point, they ran the video forward as they watched for anyone approaching Leslie's door. Given the time of day, there was little traffic in the hallway so it was easy for them to run the playback more quickly. Finally they came to the approximate time of the murder and someone appeared on the screen.

Williams pointed to the screen excitedly, "There, there. Pause it there."

Davidson reached for the mouse to pause the video. He slowly reversed this part of the disk until the moment when this person had entered the picture. Davidson stopped the disk again and repositioned himself to get a better view of the screen. Williams slid a little closer as well. Davidson started the video again in slow motion.

Williams nodded, "Okay, it looks like a courier with a package."

The man in the brown uniform stopped in front of Leslie's door and knocked on it with his free hand. When he put his hand down, the man looked up and down the hallway, being careful to keep his head low so the bill of his cap hid his face from the camera. It appeared the man was satisfied and pulled a pistol from his pocket and held it under the package he was holding.

The video didn't have sound so Williams and Davidson couldn't hear what was being said. However, it was obvious that a conversation between the man and Leslie was taking place. The man had obviously been convincing enough as a few seconds later the door opened and a flash from the gun could be seen.

Williams blurted out, "Beretta, 9mm", as the man entered the apartment and closed the door behind him. Davidson chuckled at Williams as they continued watching the video. At this point they wanted to determine how long it was before the man came back out.

Time elapsed very slowly as the two detectives waited. Finally their patience was rewarded as the man exited the apartment slowly with the same package under his arm. He walked briskly down the hall towards the elevator and was gone.

Williams sat back in his chair, "Damn. Not one decent shot of the bastards face; nothing."

Davidson chuckled sarcastically, "The video doesn't tell us who he is, but it does give us an exact timeline, and a general description. It is also pretty clear that Ms. Harrison didn't know him, but it does confirm that he was not someone she would suspect. It is also obvious the second mug was planted for some reason or other."

Williams nodded, "Yeah, that is interesting for sure. Obviously there is a reason for it. It is pretty obvious he knew the camera was there too. He knew we would get this video and see how it all went down and we would know the mug was a plant."

Davidson nodded agreement, "Exactly. That mug means something to the shooter and is meant as a message for us."

Davidson took his pen and notepad, then positioned himself to start writing notes, "Okay, so what do we know." He cleared his throat, "We have a Caucasian male. Based on the standard height of a door frame, he is about six feet tall. We saw a bit of his hair and it is dark brown salt and pepper. The way he moved and the hair suggest that he is probably in his mid to late forties and in decent shape. His frame suggested he is around one hundred and eighty pounds."

Davidson reached forward and backed the disk up and watched the timestamp, "Okay. He arrived at her door at sixteen hundred twelve hours and left at sixteen hundred twenty-two hours. So everything he did took ten minutes. Ten minutes. That is a significant amount of time for just a hit. He made his kill and went into the apartment and remained for ten minutes, so the hit wasn't the only reason he was there. He should have left much sooner than that. So he was looking for something. The place was not trashed and he wasn't there for that long, so it is safe to say that he found what ever it was relatively quickly. Whatever it was must be small as he didn't appear to be carrying anything other than the box he arrived with." Davidson nodded his head and sat back in his chair.

Williams smiled and spoke in a sarcastic tone, "See. I told you. All you have to do is listen to me and you will go places."

Davidson looked over at his partner and laughed lightly, "Sorry is there anything I missed? Is there anything I got wrong?"

Williams shook his head, "No. That is about right. I would have made the same conclusion if I could have got a word in edgewise."

Davidson chuckled, "Tell you what, why don't you check her phone records and see if there is anything interesting there? Also, give Frank a call and see if he has a preliminary for us."

Williams nodded, "What are you going to do?"

Davidson smiled, "Me? I am going to grab another cup of coffee and put my feet up until I hear from you."

Davidson rose from his chair and slapped Williams on the shoulder as he walked to the coffee room.

When he returned to his desk, he had brought a coffee for Williams, too. Williams was just hanging up the phone when Davidson was passing him his cup, "Frank says Ms. Harrison died of her gunshot wounds. The belly shot was first and was not fatal. It was the head shot that killed her.

"Of the two cups on the table, one belonged to the dearly departed. The other mug has gunpowder residue on the rim. The conclusion is that our shooter rubbed the rim with his shooting hand. They also found a partial on the mug. They are running that now. That could take awhile."

Davidson nodded, "Shocker, she died of gunshot wounds. Guess that's why Frank gets the big bucks."

Williams laughed, "Yeah, I know. As for telephone records, it appears there was a call from a Bartholomew Prentice thirty minutes before the shooting. The call lasted less than a minute. That was the only call in or out all day."

Davidson smiled, "Less than a minute, eh. Interesting."

Williams nodded agreement as his phone rang. He spun around to his desk and answered, "Williams!"

As he held the phone to his ear he nodded and made notes. After a few seconds he hung up and turned to Davidson again, "The uniforms finished talking to the neighbors. No one heard or saw anything today.

"Ms. Harrison has lived in the building for about three years but no one recalls seeing anyone visiting her and no one seemed to have any idea what she did for work. Apparently Ms. Harrison was a bit of a loner."

Williams shook his head, "How does someone like her manage to go completely unnoticed and remain below the radar in a building like that? The busy bodies in there seem to know everything about everyone else."

Davidson chuckled, "A talented young woman to be sure. That is unfortunate for us though. It would be nice to have a list of associates to chat with."

Davidson thought for a moment, "Alright, I think we need to look a little deeper into Ms. Harrison's life. We need to look at her bank records, credit cards, cell phones, and vehicles. Absolutely everything and try to piece together who this woman was and what she did for money."

Davidson sat at his desk and picked up his phone. Williams nodded to the back of Davidson's head as he spun back around to his desk and picked up his phone. He knew that it was going to be another long night. He chuckled lightly as he thought about his recently ended relationship. Perhaps Davidson was right, 'This is not a profession conducive to long term relationships'. He wanted to call Barbra and talk to her. He was going to do just that, only it would have to wait for a bit.

2

Connor had been up for a couple hours and was sitting on deck to watch the sunrise. It had been as spectacular as usual. He enjoyed sunrises at sea as they were always far more beautiful than on land. On the water there were no hills, mountains, trees or buildings to take away from the pure beauty of dawn breaking. The light and colors rise quickly as if a curtain was being pulled up on a new day. There is a sense of beginning that can't really be duplicated in any other way.

Now with the sun claiming the sky, Connor checked his instruments for position, heading, and speed. The night had been kind to them. They were only slightly off course and far closer to port than he had expected.

He smiled as he made slight adjustments to the sails and modified their heading. He could sail Conquest by himself to virtually any destination. That freedom was worth the price he had paid for her.

Angela came up the steps from the main cabin. She had not as yet commenced her morning reconstruction ritual. Her hair was a strewn mass, there wasn't any makeup on her face and overall she looked like someone that had just crawled out of bed after a busy night.

Connor smiled when he saw her. He loved to see her this way. It is the most natural she looked all day. She was a beauty in his eyes no matter what state of disrepair she considered herself in. His eyes only saw her in that one special way.

Angela saw the smile on his face and spoke teasingly, "Are you laughing at me, Connor? Cut me some slack, I haven't had my coffee or brushed my hair yet."

Connor chuckled, "I wasn't laughing at you my dear. You are always beautiful to me."

Angela smiled as she walked and gave him a warm kiss before sitting next to him, "How are we looking, Captain?"

Connor was slightly more serious, "We are looking pretty great actually. We should reach port by mid afternoon - provided the winds and currents behave."

Angela was a little shocked, "Really, that soon? I thought it would be well after dark before we got in. That's wonderful. I hate docking at night. Or rather I hate sitting back and watching you try to dock at night. It is very nerve racking for me."

Connor laughed, "Yeah, I'm sure it is. The white of my knuckles is really just out of sympathy for your apprehension."

Angela laughed, "How's your coffee, darling?"

Connor looked quickly at his cup, "I would love a fresh one, thank you. The pot should still be warm."

Angela nodded as she took his cup and headed down the stairs to the cabin. As usual, Connor watched her every step. His mind quickly flashed back to four years ago. They had only just begun their relationship and he had almost lost her.

She had been held prisoner by that psycho, Alice, and her daughter. They were on a killing rampage, bent on killing all of Angela's half brothers and sisters out of revenge for the death of Dwayne Smythe. When they were finally killed, the location where Angela was being held captive died with them.

Connor recalled how helpless he felt trying to find her. When he finally did, he recalled the absolute and complete joy. He hasn't been able to let her out of his sight for more than short periods since then.

The mental trauma Angela sustained took years to overcome. She still has nightmares every now and then. Her disposition and manner softened considerably and her appreciation of every single moment of life became her new mantra.

Connor vowed to always take care of her and protect her from the world and Angela has become completely committed to letting him. The bond between them was stronger than anyone could imagine and while such closeness would choke most relationships, theirs thrives because of it.

***

When Williams arrived, Davidson was already at his desk reviewing last evening's information. Williams shook his head as he passed his desk and continued on to the coffee room. It wasn't until he returned to his desk that Davidson acknowledged him. "How very nice of you to join us this morning, Mr. Williams, I assume you slept well?"

Williams nodded sarcastically, "Yeah, yeah, slept like a baby thank you very much. All five hours of it. How long have you been here?"

Davidson didn't lift his head from the documents he was reading, "About thirty years, give or take."

Williams shook his head, "It is way too early for that, Sam. Way too early. You come up with anything interesting or was your night a complete waste of time."

Davidson smiled, "I stayed here last night and slept on the couch, and yes, it has been a very productive day so far."

Davidson turned and Williams saw the dark bags under Davidson's eyes and shook his head. He is always surprised when he gets these unexpected reminders of just how run down Davidson is becoming.

Davidson frowned, "Yes, I know. I look like hell. So what? Anyway, I have been going over all of Ms. Harrison's financials. She doesn't have any credit cards, none. Not even one for a clothing or a shoe store. You saw her place; I can't believe she doesn't like to shop."

Williams chuckled, "Yeah that is strange."

Davidson ignored him as he continued, "Her bank account shows a balance of four hundred thousand dollars. Records indicate that she only makes deposits under nine thousand dollars, always cash and always spread out through the month."

Williams sat up, "Smart."

Davidson nodded, "Forensics got back to me a few minutes ago. They finally managed to get into her laptop. There wasn't much on it, but it did show a bank account in the Cayman's containing a nice round one million dollars."

Williams whistled in amazement, "That is a lot of cash to have stashed away. How does a pretty twenty-five year old manage to accumulate that much cash?"

Davidson chuckled, "Oh, I'm not done yet. Her computer was set up with TOR. TOR is The Onion Router, if you haven't heard of it. It is modeled after one of the governments international communications systems. So what the hell would she be doing online that required that kind of security and anonymity?" Davidson shook his head, "Whatever it was that she was doing, she wanted to be sure it couldn't be traced."

Williams computer made the sound of email arriving. He turned in his chair and opened his email client. He read the message and snorted, "Well, isn't that just freakin' wonderful. Apparently our little Ms. Harrison didn't even exist three years ago. Every trace and check they could do came up empty prior to three years ago. They are running her dentals and prints now to see if they can figure out who she really was."

Davidson shook his head, "I was sorry to see such a pretty young thing gunned down like that. I wondered what kind of beast could have done such a thing. You would think that after all these years nothing would surprise me anymore. However, I can't imagine anyone legitimate needing to go to such lengths to become invisible and stay so far below the radar."

Williams nodded, "There is really not much to go on here so far. Without more information about her it is going to be a nightmare to get a list of suspects. It will take them a bit of time to get anything back on the dentals and prints. The only thing we have is this Bartholomew Prentice. I think we should have a chat with him."

Davidson smiled, "Way ahead of you. The search warrant should be ready now. We can grab it on the way. We have enough to validate him as a person of interest. Hopefully we can get something solid to go with it."

Williams stood and smiled, "Let's hope."

***

It took two rings of the doorbell before a man in his mid-forties with dark brown salt and pepper hair answered the door. He wore a bathrobe with all the appearance of a man who had just risen from bed. He was immediately confused when the door opened and he saw the two detectives and the small entourage of uniformed officers, "Ah, can I help you?"

Davidson handed his business card to the man, "Good day, I am Detective Davidson and this is my partner Detective Williams. Are you Bartholomew Prentice?"

The confused man at the door scratched his head and nodded, "Yeah. I'm Bart Prentice. What do you want?"

Davidson smiled, "We would like to ask you a few questions if you don't mind. May we come in?"

Mr. Prentice opened the door wider, "Yeah, sure, come in. Has something happened?"

Deadly Truth

The group entered the foyer of the large home and the uniformed officers spread out immediately to begin their search.

Mr. Prentice became instantly angry, "Hey, what the hell is going on. I said you could come in, I didn't say you could just wander around the place."

Williams donned a cocky smile as he handed Mr. Prentice a folded piece of paper, "This is a warrant to search your premises."

Mr. Prentice grabbed the paper from Williams and opened it in one movement. He read through it quickly before refolding it and tossing it to a side table, "What are you looking for? What is going on?"

Davidson spoke stoically, "Mr. Prentice, where were you between 3:00 o'clock pm and 8:00 o'clock pm last night?"

Mr. Prentice's eyes shifted their focus to the right, "er, I was in the mountains. I have a cabin up there. I was up there for a few days. I got home last night... around 11:00pm, I think. Something like that. Why? What's this about?"

Davidson continued, "Can anyone verify that you were there?"

Mr. Prentice shook his head, "No. That is the whole point. I go there to get away from everything. Is my wife okay? Should I be calling my lawyer?"

Davidson didn't change his manner, "Where is your wife, Mr. Prentice, I would like to ask her a few questions as well?"

Mr. Prentice shook his head, "She is away with some friends on a girl's vacation. I don't expect her back until tomorrow."

Before Davidson could ask another question, one of the officers in the den raised his arm to summon Davidson. In his hand was a large manila envelope. Davidson caught sight of it and turned to face the officer. Then he looked back at Mr. Prentice, "Please stay here, I will be right back."

Davidson and Williams walked to the officer. When they were close to him, Davidson noticed the framed pictures that sat on a table in the corner of the room. One of the pictures he recognized as a wedding photograph of Angela and Connor Shea. The sight of it surprised him.

Mr. Prentice had followed him into the room and saw what Davidson was looking at, "Yes, I know the Shea's. I sometimes play at the Too Shea with Connor and his band. I have been a friend of his for many years. In fact my wife is one of Angela's sisters through the sperm bank. I met Leigh Ann at their first anniversary party."

Davidson nodded as he opened the envelope that was now in his hands, "I know the Shea's. They are good people." He pulled the contents out of the envelope and viewed all the pictures one by one.

Mr. Prentice looked confused again, "What do you have there, Detective?"

Davidson finished looking through the pictures and handed them to Williams who immediately rifled through them as well.

Davidson turned to Mr. Prentice, "Do you know a Leslie Harrison, Mr. Prentice?"

Mr. Prentice thought for a moment before he shook his head, "No. I don't believe I have heard that name before. Why? Is that what this is all about?"

Williams nodded, "She was shot to death in her apartment yesterday. Are you sure you don't know her?"

Mr. Prentice's brow furrowed as he shook his head, "Positive. Why?"

Williams handed a few of the pictures to Mr. Prentice, "Are you sure, Bartholomew? It looks like you two were rather close."

Mr. Prentice's eyes opened wide in surprise, "I have never seen these photos before. How did they get here? What is going on? I demand some answers!"

Williams spoke again, "Do you know the woman in the photographs?"

Mr. Prentice nodded, "Yes. Her name is Valerie. I don't know her last name. She approached me a couple weeks ago. She offered to do some consulting work for me. I met her for lunch and we discussed her services. I wasn't interested, so I left. I have not seen or heard from her since."

Williams nodded and handed the rest of the pictures to Mr. Prentice, "Those photos suggest that you did a little more than just discuss business, Bartholomew. I wonder what your wife would say if she saw these pictures?"

The shock on Mr. Prentice's face looked genuine, "I don't know what these are. I mean, I know what they are, but it is not me. I swear. I have never slept with that woman. We met for lunch, we talked for less than fifteen minutes and I left. That was it. That is not me in those pictures."

Davidson's cell phone rang. He nodded a couple times then hung up and looked first at Williams then at Mr. Prentice, "So, you have no knowledge of what transpired at Ms. Harrison's apartment yesterday. Is that correct?"

Mr. Prentice shook his head, "Nothing. Like I said, I don't know a Ms. Harrison and if that is the woman I know as Leslie, I have never been to her apartment. What is going on?"

Davidson cleared his throat, "Mr. Prentice your phone records show that a call was placed from here to Ms. Harrison's apartment about two hours before she was killed. We have confirmed that it is only a twenty minute drive from here to her apartment. A partial fingerprint was found at the scene and it traced back to you. Do you own a 9mm pistol, Mr. Prentice?"

Mr. Prentice realized where these questions were going, "I am not saying another word until I talk to my attorney."

Davidson smiled, "That is probably a good idea. We are not charging you with anything at the moment, but I think you need to come downtown so we can continue this conversation. You should probably put some clothes on. You may be there awhile."

Williams stepped forward to escort Mr. Prentice to his bedroom to change.

Davidson turned back to the officers, "Keep searching. Let's see if you can find anything else he knows nothing about. We need anything that can tie him to Ms. Harrison, or Valerie or whoever she was. There should also be a 9mm around here somewhere. Find it."

***

Connor double-checked to ensure the last of the lines were secured before he again boarded Conquest to help Angela gather things up. There wasn't much they would be taking back to the house at the moment, but there was assorted garbage that needed to be cleaned up before they locked up. Connor would have someone come later to deal with cleaning the boat and addressing the various holding tanks.

The two of them could easily handle those tasks. They have done it every other time they returned from a trip, but today they wanted to get back to Angela's mother's house to see Janet Elaine. Angela was sure her daughter had a wonderful time in their absence. Grandma always spoils her. Still, Angela wanted to get back and see her and hear all about it.

With the last of their personal possessions taken to the Porsche, Connor returned to the Conquest to secure all the doorways and hatches. They were moored in a secure area, but he still took all the necessary precautions to lock the boat.

Satisfied, he returned to Angela waiting in the car. They gave each other a kiss before driving off to the house.

Elaine and Simon had many discussions after they were married as to whether or not they would keep Angela's childhood home. They had purchased a condo in the city and spent most of their time there. The weekends were always spent in the old house.

At the last minute Elaine decided she couldn't part with it. There were too many memories of the years Angela was growing up. Besides, now that there was a grandchild in the picture, she decided the house was something they needed. Elaine said it was to ensure Janet Elaine had solid roots and somewhere safe to play, but everyone knew that was only a very small part of the reason. Janet Elaine was simply a convenient excuse.

No one minded. Elaine and Simon are financially secure, especially since Elaine sold out her business interests. Maintaining the house in the country and condo in the city was simply the way of things and it was a burden Elaine was more than happy to accept.

Angela and Connor had discussed the possibility of buying the house and living there themselves. Angela loved the house and it was a way to ensure the house remained in the family. Of course Elaine wouldn't hear of it. There was no way she would accept money from Angela and Connor. After much discussion, Angela and Connor agreed to live in the house full time while maintaining an area of the house for Elaine and Simon when they came out on the weekends.

While Angela and Connor had been away, Elaine has been staying at the house so that Janet Elaine could remain in her familiar comfort zone. Simon stayed at the condo in town most nights during the week, but would make the trip out to the house whenever possible.

Every weekend he stayed at the house with Elaine.

As far as families go, they would be considered very close. The events surrounding Angela's kidnapping and the past murders of her siblings have pulled them closer as a family. They are far closer than they would probably be had those horrible events not occurred.

3

Williams and Davidson stood looking through the one-way mirror in the dark observation room at Mr. Prentice sitting at the table in the interview room.

Davidson shook his head, "Look at him. He is anxious, fidgety and completely stressed out."

Williams nodded, "I know. He looks more like an innocent man than a guilty one. Is it possible he didn't actually kill Harrison?"

Davidson knew the question was rhetorical, "We have no choice but to follow the evidence. The evidence doesn't lie. The evidence doesn't know how to lie. It simply is what it is. Whether he is innocent or guilty, only the evidence can say."

Williams smiled and was about to speak when the door to the observation room opened. A uniformed officer leaned in, "His lawyer is here."

Davidson nodded, "Thanks, bring him down."

Williams immediately turned to the video camera and began setting it up as Davidson walked out of the observation room and closed the door behind him. Mr. Prentice's lawyer came walking towards him and smiled.

Davidson knew this lawyer well. Nolan McGuire is the criminal partner at Jackson, Solomon and McGuire. Davidson stuck out his hand to McGuire, "Nolan. Good to see you again. Bart Prentice is one of yours?"

McGuire took Davidson's hand with genuine friendship, "Not mine personally. He has been a major corporate client of our firm for many, many years. Frankly, I am not sure why he would be here. This is totally not something Bart is capable of. He is a decent man. Way more decent than one would expect from someone that has amassed such wealth as he."

Davidson chuckled, "Yeah, how many necks did they step on to get where they are?"

McGuire chuckled, "Exactly, Sam, but this man simply isn't like that. It is so out of character for him. Let's go in and have a little chat and see if we can't straighten this whole mess out."

Davidson nodded and turned to the door that led into the interview room. He held the door for McGuire to pass through first. He followed behind and ensured the door was closed. When McGuire was seated, Davidson placed the file folder he was carrying on the table and sat in the chair facing both of them.

McGuire spoke first, "I assume you have a camera rolling back there."

Davidson simply nodded as he turned on the microphone on the table and opened the file folder. He took a moment to review the material it contained before he proceeded. "According to your statements at the house, you were alone at your cabin and didn't return to your home until approximately 11:00pm, correct."

Prentice nodded, "Yes, correct."

McGuire had his pad of yellow legal paper on the table now and was making notes and listening carefully to every word Prentice said and every question Davidson asked.

Davidson looked at Prentice for a moment before spreading the Harrison crime scene photos out on the table facing him, "So, Mr. Prentice, how long have you known Leslie Harrison?"

Prentice started speaking but McGuire stopped him, "Don't answer that Bart."

McGuire looked at Davidson with genuine disdain, "Really? Are these tactics necessary? Mr. Prentice is not some low life off the street. He is a highly respected member of this community. We are cooperating as much as we can with you, Sam. This is supposed to be a nice friendly chat. I'm afraid that if you prefer to interrogate him, you'll need to either charge him with something or we are out of here."

Davidson smiled, "You know full well, Mr. McGuire, I can hold Mr. Prentice without charging him. This investigation is ongoing. I am giving your client the opportunity to clear his name before things go any further."

Before McGuire could answer there was a knock at the door and Williams entered quickly. He bent over towards Davidson's ear and whispered. Davidson grunted as Williams stood up and backed away.

Davidson reached to the photos scattered across the table and gathered them up neatly and returned them to the file folder.

Prentice and McGuire watched the procedure for a moment before McGuire spoke, "Something you would like to share with us, Detective."

Davidson looked at McGuire first and then to Prentice, "Mr. Prentice, I really hate being lied to. I have done everything in my powers to be opened minded and fair, and this is how you treat me?"

McGuire looked towards Prentice with confusion.

Davidson continued, "A couple officers took a drive up to your cabin, just to have a little look see. It turns out that a group of teenagers were in there. Apparently they have been partying for several days. By the way, we can charge them with trespassing and vandalism if you wish."

Bart looked to McGuire, "I don't think charges are necessary, but if there is damage I do expect that to be paid for."

McGuire nodded, "I'll have someone look into it."

Davidson shook his head, "Ah, excuse me. What is important is that it is pretty clear you were not at your cabin like you said, Prentice. The issue with the kids is pretty minor right now, don't you think?"

Davidson paused a moment before continuing, "Bartholomew Prentice, you are under arrest for the murder of Leslie Harrison. Williams here will give you your rights on the way down to booking. I'm pretty much done with you."

It was clear how angry Davidson was. It was unlike him to not proceed with an arrest himself. McGuire knew that and stood as Davidson left the room. He waited a few moments as he listened to his client's rights being read. When Prentice acknowledged that he understood, McGuire smiled to him, "I will come see you after processing to go over a few things."

Before Prentice could reply, McGuire left the interview room to follow after Davidson. He spotted Davidson sitting at his desk looking through the file and quickly made his way to him.

Davidson saw him coming and raised his hand in front of himself, "Save it counselor. I thought there was a chance your man was innocent. I do not feel the same way now. I intend to go after him with everything I've got."

McGuire smiled courteously, "I understand, Sam. I still think this a mistake. I know this man. He could never do something like this. I don't care what evidence you have that says otherwise, he did not do this. You saw his reaction about the kids. He was more worried about that than the murder charges. Do you really think that would be the case if he was actually guilty?"

Davidson nodded, "Everyone is innocent until proven guilty. I am satisfied I have done that. If your beliefs are contrary to the evidence, then feel free to prove me wrong."

McGuire spoke again in an attempt to get his point across, "Sam, you don't have a weapon and you don't have a motive. All you have is this carefully orchestrated set of circumstantial evidence, and I do mean orchestrated."

Davidson fought to keep from exploding, "Nolan, as you are well aware, I have gotten convictions with far less. You want to protect your pay check that is your business, but I have little doubt that he did this thing. I don't care why and I don't care where he tossed the weapon. She was killed with a 9mm and that just happens to be the same type of weapon Prentice has registered.

"It is a little too convenient that no one seems to know where that gun is at the moment. All we can find is a half empty box of cartridges. I'm done. The evidence is aligned in a perfect little arrow pointing directly at your client's head. Sorry Nolan but that is all."

McGuire smiled and nodded as he turned away from Davidson. His client was being processed for this crime and he intended to stay in the building until that was finished. He needed to see Bart again. They would go over every detail very carefully and do so without the detectives breathing down their necks.

***

Connor pulled the Porsche up to the front door of the stately house. Angela was out of her seatbelt before the car came to a stop, and was out of the car, heading towards the door, before Connor turned the engine off.

Connor chuckled lightly as he watched her. When the car was off and the brake set, Connor got out, grabbed their bags and headed into the house. As he crossed the threshold he saw Angela holding Janet Elaine in a full hug.

Janet Elaine saw Connor and smiled broadly as she spoke excitedly, "Hi Daddy."

Connor smiled back at her and dropped the bags just inside the door, "Hello, princess. Did you miss us?"

Janet Elaine smiled and nodded in the cutest way. Elaine came into the foyer from the back part of the house, "Hello you two. Welcome home. How was the trip?"

Angela was still wrapped around Janet Elaine and Connor spoke with a smile, "It was fabulous. It was so nice to get away for awhile." Then he pointed towards Angela and Janet Elaine, "But it is also good to be home."

As Elaine reached Connor, she gave him a friendly embrace. Then she turned towards Angela who had just released Janet Elaine. Angela stepped into a warm hug with her mother, "Thank you so much for taking care of her for us."

Elaine smiled, "It was absolutely my pleasure. I love having some alone time with my granddaughter. She is such a sweet child."

As they split apart, Janet Elaine was already in the air, flying towards Connor. Angela always held her breath when Janet Elaine flew like that, or when she did anything adventurous, for that matter.

Connor laughed at Angela as he caught Janet Elaine in his arms, "Hello there princess. I missed you too. I hope you were a good girl for grandma."

Janet Elaine nodded into Connor's neck, "Yes, Daddy. I am always a good girl. Grandma said so."

Connor laughed, "I'm sure she did."

Connor put her back on the ground, "Why don't you take Grandma and Mommy into the kitchen for some tea. Daddy is going to take care of our bags."

Janet Elaine nodded gleefully and turned to Elaine and Angela. Taking each by the hand, she escorted them through the house to the kitchen. Connor hesitated a few moments to watch the three leave before picking up the bags.

The maid entered the foyer from the living room and smiled, "Welcome back, Mr. Shea. I can take care of those for you."

Connor smiled, "Thank you, Mildred, I will carry them out back."

Mildred nodded and smiled, "Thank you, Mr. Shea."

Connor walked to the laundry area of the house with Mildred following close behind. Mildred has worked in this house for more than ten years. She is an attractive woman in her early thirties without a family of her own. It was hard for Connor to get used to the fact that she lived with them full time and was available around the clock. He made a point of trying to do as much as possible himself, while at the same time ensuring she had plenty of work to be busy at.

That generally wasn't a problem given the size of the house. Still, Connor had more empathy for her than the ladies of the house. For many years Connor lived in a small suite in his office. He was the only one that took care of his needs. The building staff took care of his office, but the suite was all his. An appreciation for the work required to maintain a space grew from that.

After dropping the bags in the laundry room, Connor walked to the kitchen to join the ladies. Janet Elaine and Angela were sitting on the stools pulled up to the counter with Elaine fussing with cookies and tea.

When Connor entered the kitchen, Elaine looked to him and smiled, "There is a fresh pot of coffee Connor."

Connor nodded and smiled, "Great. I haven't had a really good cup of coffee in a couple weeks. I love my boat, but there are a few things it just can't duplicate."

Angela was stroking Janet Elaine's hair when Connor joined them at the counter with his coffee. Angela turned to him, "Mom was saying that Simon is working a bit late this evening and asked if we would like to go into town and have dinner with him."

Connor nodded, "Sure. That would be great, if you three are up to it, that is."

Elaine spoke sincerely, "Most definitely. I need to get back to town anyway, so what could be more perfect. When we have finished our tea, Angela, why don't you come up and help me get packed."

Angela nodded, "I'd love to, Mom."

Connor gave Janet Elaine a loving tap on the shoulder, "Little missy here can get me caught up on all her doings for the last couple weeks."

Janet Elaine smiled broadly as she picked up her cup of cocoa and tried to finish it more quickly.

***

Bart Prentice was finished being processed, and McGuire joined him in his cell, "Okay Bart, what is going on? Where were you yesterday? Detective Davidson is a good and fair man. You have pretty much blown any chance of getting him on your side."

Prentice nodded acceptance but remained silent.

McGuire stared at him for a few moments longer before speaking again, "Are you having an affair? Were you with a woman?"

Prentice immediately snapped his head towards McGuire, "No. Never, I love my wife. I would never do anything like that."

McGuire nodded, "Okay. Good. So where were you?"

Prentice dipped his head into his hands, "I don't know. I have no idea where I was. I can't remember anything. I remember leaving the house to go up to the cabin. I remember stopping at a rest area; the same rest area I always stop at on the way up. Next thing I know I wake up in my bed at home with the cops banging on the door. I was scared. I know I didn't do this, I know it, but there is absolutely no way for me to prove it."

McGuire sat back to think, "They have to prove it, not you. Don't worry about that. Did anyone see you... anyone? Maybe there was someone at the rest area or at a gas station... something? Did you buy anything with a credit card or bank card?"

Prentice just shook his head, "Nothing. I keep the cabin stocked so I didn't have to stop. The caretaker was away on vacation, so I thought this a perfect time to go up there unnoticed."

McGuire was concerned, "It is exceedingly difficult to get them to believe you lost your memory and that you had nothing to do with this. Especially now that you have added this lie to the situation."

McGuire shook his head a few times before giving Prentice a couple quick friendly slaps on his knee, "Alright, Bart. Try to relax and stay calm. I am going to leave now and see what I can find out. Are you sure there isn't something else you can tell me, anything."

Prentice shook his head, "I didn't do this, Nolan. It wasn't me. This Leslie Harrison woman is not who they think she is. I don't know her as Leslie. When I met her, the name she gave me was Valerie. There has to be a reason for that too don't you think? Find out who she really was and that will probably help figure out why this is happening to me."

McGuire nodded as he stood and called the guard to let him out. "I'll come back tomorrow, Bart. Get some rest and try to think of anything else that could help us. There has to be something."

Prentice nodded as he lay down on the mattress.

***

Jack's has been the favorite restaurant of Angela and her family for a great many years. At least it was their favorite for the years prior to Angela marrying Connor. Now, the pub they own, Too Shea, is Angela's favorite. Still, she loved to eat here from time to time simply because it wasn't Too Shea.

Jack's is the polar opposite in atmosphere to their place. Here the style was more finished and clean with a high end look. Too Shea, while also located on the beach, has a far more relaxed, cozy feel. It was a place people returned to over and over because of that feeling of warmth and family.

The four of them were seated at their usual table overlooking the outdoor deck and ocean as they waited for the arrival of Simon. He had sent a text message to Elaine moments ago to say he was on his way.

As they waited they engaged in light conversation over glasses of wine. The wine they consumed was a vintage they held dear. This label was one they purchased by the case each year for themselves and to share with their closest friends.

Soon Simon arrived. He saw the family seated at the table and smiled as he made his way to them. His imposing size and frame looked almost out of place in this space, but the tailored, dark pinstriped suit he wore kept his appearance appropriate. Standing over six feet tall and weighing in at the better part of two hundred and fifty pounds, one would be hard pressed to find much fat on his body, even at his age. He prided himself in staying in shape and it showed. It gave him a visible air of strength and trustworthiness.

Deadly Truth

As soon as he was seated the server came over to take his beverage order. When his drink arrived. He took a few quick sips from the glass before turning to Angela and Connor. His face was dressed in a solemn expression, "You two know Bart Prentice, right?"

Both nodded but it was Connor who spoke, "Of course we do. He plays in my band sometimes. He married Leigh Ann. What about him? Something happen?"

Simon nodded, "He was arrested this morning for murder. A colleague of mine, Nolan McGuire is representing him. I wasn't sure if you had heard."

Connor smiled, "Well, we really haven't gotten around to catching up on the news yet. We are still in holiday mode."

Angela spoke softly, "Who is he accused of killing?"

The memories of her past came forward in a rush. With them came a cold flush through her body.

Simon looked to Angela caringly, "No Angela, not Leigh Ann. It wasn't anyone of your siblings. It was a young woman by the name of Leslie Harrison. They aren't one hundred percent sure that is her real name, though. Of course Bart is denying any involvement in the murder. I know Bart too, and he is one of the most ethical and moral men I know. I have a hard time believing he could have done this."

Connor nodded, "I agree, Simon. Something like this just isn't in his nature. I have to talk to McGuire. I have to know what is going on. I don't know what evidence they have against Bart, but they are dead wrong. It is absolutely impossible that he could have done anything like this. He just isn't wired that way."

Simon nodded, "That is what Nolan was saying too. I figured you would want to talk to him. Nolan has agreed to meet for drinks after dinner."

Angela turned to Connor and gripped his arm with her hand, "Connor, no, please. We are retired now. We have a family. We can't go back down that road and churn up those memories."

Connor patted the top of Angela's hand, "I'm just going to talk to him, that's all. I love you, Angela, but the Prentices are important to both of us. I have to know what is going on. You know that."

Angela stared into Connor's eyes for a moment before she reluctantly nodded and turned to face Simon. It was clear she was not pleased with him. "What about Leigh Ann? Does she know?"

Simon saw her expression, "I'm sorry, Angela, but I know how much they mean to you two and I know how much Connor would want to help if he could. I also know you wouldn't forgive me if I didn't tell you." He took a breath before continuing, "Leigh Ann is away with some girlfriends for a few days. She has been contacted and she'll be back tomorrow. It is the earliest flight she was able to get."

Angela shook her head, "Poor Leigh Ann. She is going to be an absolute mess."

Connor nodded compassionately and picked up his menu, "I think it would a good idea to change the subject and order something to eat."

Angela shook her head, "I'm not hungry."

She got up from the table and walked out onto the deck. She leaned against the railing and stared out to sea as the waves crashed ashore.

Connor was about to go after her when Simon put his hand on his arm. He spoke in an almost fatherly voice, "Leave her, Connor. She needs a few minutes to herself. She'll be fine."

Connor smiled and nodded as he relaxed in his seat and returned his attention to his menu. He kept looking passed it at Angela. He believed she needed some time, but at the same time he didn't like the idea of her out there by herself.

Elaine spoke angrily as she stood, "Oh for heaven's sake."

Simon reached his hand to Elaine's arm. She promptly shook it off, "Don't say a word, Simon. My daughter needs me." Elaine turned and joined Angela outside.

Simon just smiled and shook his head. Connor did the same and looked towards Janet Elaine, "So my dear, do you know what you would like to eat?"

She looked back to Connor with concern, "Is Mommy okay?"

"Yes, darling, Mommy is fine. She is just worried about a friend, that's all."

"Can I go outside and worry with her, Daddy?"

Connor put down his menu and quickly glanced at Simon and then back to Janet Elaine, "Yes my dear. I think Mommy would like you to be there with her."

Connor then looked to Simon, "I hope you weren't hungry. This may take awhile."

Simon smiled, "Yeah, I probably should have waited until after we ate. Sorry about that."

Connor chuckled, "It's okay. She has come a long way, but there are times when she seems to just fall right back into the funk. Sometimes even the littlest things spark it off. I'm sure Elaine will be able to drag her back."

Connor looked over the menu again, "I think I'll just order some appetizers for now. That may be all anyone wants, but if that changes we can always order dinner later."

Simon nodded, "Yeah that is probably a good idea."

Connor signaled the server who responded immediately. Connor and

Simon discussed the options for a moment before ordering and the server was off again. It wasn't long after that the girls returned to the table.

Angela placed her hand on Connor's arm and smiled warmly, "I'm sorry, darling. I was being childish. Of course you should do whatever you can to help. You are very good at that sort of thing and God knows something like this requires all the help it can get."

Connor put his hand on top of hers and gave it a loving squeeze, "I have to do what I can. I will be careful."

Angela nodded cautiously and the appetizers arrived at the table. Reluctantly everyone helped themselves to the dishes. Janet Elaine on the other hand was hungry and she gratefully devoured the food in front of her.

Angela watched her and smiled at the pure innocence of her daughter. The world can be a cruel place and she wanted Janet Elaine to grow up strong in the face of it.

4

Nolan McGuire arrived at the restaurant a few minutes after 9:00PM and took a table in the waiting lounge. He summoned a server and ordered a drink. He also requested she let Simon know he had arrived. The server nodded politely and left.

A few minutes later Connor and Simon joined him at the table. Nolan stood as the two arrived and Simon proceeded with the introductions before all three men sat down. The girls had already left for the evening. They went back to Elaine's condo in Simon's car. Connor would drive Simon home later and pick up Angela and Janet Elaine before returning to the house.

Connor didn't waste any time, "Simon tells me you are working with Bart Prentice. Bart and I go way back. What is going on?"

McGuire chuckled, "Well, as I'm sure Simon has already told you, Bart has been charged with the murder of a young woman. He swears he doesn't know anything about it. Unfortunately, he has no recollection of where he was during the time the murder took place, and his gun is missing. They found a partial print at the scene that has been identified as Bart's.

"A phone call to her apartment was made from his house before the shooting. They have video of someone entering and leaving her apartment. The body type and build of the suspect is similar to Bart's.

"They found a ball cap in his closet that looks like the one in the video. The icing on the cake is they found photographs of him with this woman. The shots that show his face are taken on the street and others of them in a restaurant. The sex shots don't show his face, but the build of the male is close enough to Bart's as to not rule out the possibility that it was indeed him."

Fresh drinks for all three men arrived as McGuire finished talking.

Connor sat back in his chair and picked up his drink. He took a few mouthfuls and ordered another before the server had left. He was deep in thought for a few moments before he spoke. When his new drink arrived he leaned forward, "I know Bart very well. I have known him for a very long time. He is a good man. Do I believe he is capable of killing someone? I really doubt it. Do I believe he is capable of cold blooded murder? Not a chance in hell. That alone tells me he didn't do this. So, where does that leave us?"

Connor took a smaller drink from this glass before continuing, "The only answer is that this has to be a frame up. The question then is who is framing him and why are they framing Bart, of all people?"

Nolan shrugged his shoulders, "I have no idea, Connor, none. My problem is how I am going to defend him. If I didn't know him, the evidence they have would make me believe he did it."

Connor nodded and took another mouthful of his drink. Then he looked McGuire in the eye, "I am not sure what Simon has told you, but I have, er, let's just say resources. Frankly I haven't had to use them in years, but I have not forgotten how. I would like you to give me a copy of everything they have on him and everything he has told you."

McGuire smiled, "This is an open case and an ongoing investigation. The police don't take kindly to citizens sticking their nose into open cases. Believe me, I know."

Connor chuckled, "I do too; tough. Call me your investigator or whatever. I don't care. Who are the detectives on this, anyway?"

McGuire didn't hesitate, "Williams and Davidson. Both of them are decent and fair. I trust them, but at the same time, their hands are kind of tied on this. Bart lying to them wasn't a good move either."

Connor nodded, "Yes, I know them. They are good men and I trust them too. What did Bart lie about?"

McGuire shook his head, "He told them that he was at his cabin when the murder occurred. There was a group of teenagers partying at the cabin. Pretty hard for him to have been there and not to have known that. Later, when I asked him where he was, he said he couldn't remember."

Connor nodded, "I have an idea what may have happened. I will need the report on the kids too. I don't think it is a coincidence they were there. In fact, I doubt any of this is a coincidence. I think this whole thing is planned out to the last detail. Trust me gentlemen, I will get to the bottom of it. Bart will not go down for this murder." He paused again for a moment before looking to McGuire, "I need to see him. I don't just want to read the answers to the questions, I want to see his face and listen to his voice. Can you make that happen, Nolan?"

McGuire nodded without hesitation, "Of course. I will be seeing him in the morning, you can meet me there. I don't think there will be a problem. I will just call you one of my staff."

Connor smiled, "Thanks Nolan. And thank you Simon for arranging this. Bart is a good man and I won't sit by and watch him get railroaded."

Connor finished the rest of his drink before rising from the table. He extended his hand to McGuire, "Thank you for coming, Nolan. I need to get back to my family. I will see you in the morning."

McGuire took Connor's hand firmly, "Nice to meet you Connor. It is good to see Bart has such good friends. I look forward to working with you."

Connor released his grip and walked to the cash register to settle his bill. Simon said his goodbyes to Nolan and joined Connor, "Do you think there is anything you will be able to do, Connor. I mean more than the police are already doing?"

Connor shook his head, "I am not really sure. I am going to attack this from the angle that he is innocent and being set up. I'm hoping the bias of that approach will shed a different light on the evidence. Time will tell, I guess."

Simon chuckled unpleasantly, "That certainly doesn't sound very promising."

Connor spoke soberly, "I know. I will do my best, but I'm not sure that'll be enough. It has been a busy day and I'm tired. I'm sure Angela and Janet Elaine would like to get to bed too."

Simon nodded, "Yes, tomorrow is a new day."

***

It was early when Connor rolled out of bed and went into the kitchen for coffee. Angela was already up and reading one of the several online papers they subscribe to. Since Connor was going to be seeing Bart this morning, they decided to spend the night at the condo.

Angela wanted to meet Leigh Ann's flight and be there for her. She wanted to offer Leigh Ann the opportunity to stay at their house with them.

Connor had argued that she would probably want to be in her own home. It was closer to the courthouse, lawyers and her family. Angela was determined to at least give her the option and to ensure Leigh Ann knew that she was there for her if needed.

Connor accepted that reasoning. He knew how strong-willed Angela could be when she set her mind to something. He also knew how fragile she still was. There have been many nightmares, sleepless nights, and many episodes of anxiety attacks. There have also been many occasions where she was obsessively consumed by staying close to Janet Elaine.

As time passed, the number of these incidents had diminished significantly, but they were not gone. Necessity had made Connor a keen observer of Angela and her fluctuating state of mind. He knew instantly when she had crossed into the realm of the irrational. It was equally clear to all that knew them that Connor would always be there for her and would always protect her, no matter what.

With coffee in hand, Connor sat next to Angela at the counter and gave her a loving kiss. Angela smiled warmly, "Did you have a good sleep, Connor?"

"Yes, thank you. How about you? Did you sleep?"

Angela nodded half heartedly, "A bit. I am worried for them, Connor, I really am. Leigh Ann would be devastated if anything were to happen to Bart."

"I know, Angela. I'm pretty sure Bart wouldn't be too pleased either. I will figure this out, Angela. I don't care who did it, if they can orchestrate something like this, they will have left a trail of some kind. It is inevitable and I will find it."

Angela smiled as she took a sip from her cup, "I know you will, Connor. All that I ask is you be careful. You have a family now. The stakes are high for you too."

Connor nodded reassuringly, "I will be careful, my dear. Of that you can be sure."

Connor looked to the clock on the wall and grunted, "I had better get dressed. I will be meeting McGuire soon and I don't want to be late."

Angela smiled and gave him a kiss, "I love you, Connor."

"I love you too." He rose from the chair with cup in hand, and headed for the shower.

***

McGuire was just arriving as Connor walked up the front steps, "Good morning, Connor. I hope you had a good evening."

Connor reached his hand out to McGuire, "Very nice, thank you. It looks like it is going to be a nice day."

McGuire reached out and shook Connor's hand, "Have you given Bart's situation any more thought?"

Connor chuckled, "I haven't really thought about much else. I have a working theory. I want to see how Bart looks when I ask him a few questions. I just hope I can prove my theory."

McGuire released his grip and smiled, "I don't suppose you would like to share your theories?"

Connor and McGuire continued up the stairs, "Not at this time. I don't want to get anyone's hopes up."

McGuire nodded, "I understand. Probably best I don't know too much anyway."

Connor smiled, "That I can guarantee. There are a few fuzzy lines that may have to be crossed."

McGuire belly laughed, "Yeah okay, enough said."

Connor smiled and continued, "Angela is going to meet Leigh Ann at the airport and give her a ride into town. I am hoping their girl talk may give up a clue or two as well. Wives often know more than they think they know about their husband's activities."

McGuire smiled, "Are you thinking that Bart was targeted specifically?"

Connor simply smiled as he continued walking, "At this point, that is the only thing I am sure of."

***

Leigh Ann's flight arrived on time and Angela was standing at the baggage carousel when she came in. Tears filled Leigh Ann's brown eyes the moment she saw Angela and she rushed to her waiting arms.

They stood together in an embrace for several moments before Leigh Ann pulled away. Angela immediately reached her thumb up to clear the tears from Leigh Ann's eyes and brushed her long brunette hair from her face.

Leigh Ann sniffled, "How could this have happened? Bart wouldn't hurt a fly. How could they think he killed someone?"

Angela just shook her head, "Connor is looking into it. He will figure out what is going on, Leigh Ann. That I promise you."

Leigh Ann half smiled as she turned to the carousel. Angela was close beside her, "I know you have other family close, but I just want you to know that you are more than welcome to stay at the house. I would love to have you there."

Leigh Ann nodded as she smiled, "Thank you, Angela. That is very generous of you, but I think I would just like to go home and get cleaned up. I want to see Bart as soon as possible. I still don't have many details and I have a lot of questions."

Angela smiled warmly, "Of course, Leigh Ann. I can drive you home and we can talk. I can tell you what I know. At least you will have some idea what is going on before you see Bart."

Leigh Ann grabbed the last of her bags off the carousel, "Thanks Angela, I appreciate that. I asked my girlfriends to take a later flight. They had nothing but questions and were talking a mile a minute. I just couldn't face flying back with that in my ear the whole way. No offence, but I was just going to hire a car so I could have a little peace on the drive."

Angela took one of Leigh Ann's two bags and pointed to the arrivals exit, "I won't hear of that. I'm just out here. I won't bother you. You don't have to talk if you don't want. I'm here either way. I'll get you home as fast as I can."

***

After Connor and Nolan finished talking with Bart, the two went to a small cafe for breakfast and further discussion. Connor was satisfied with the conversation he had with Bart and had formulated a course of action.

As promised, Nolan brought a copy of all the files with all the information that he had compiled to this point. Over breakfast Connor reviewed the materials and discussed some of the details with Nolan. Satisfied he had a clear picture of all the evidence against Bart, the two men split up. Connor gave McGuire a business card which contained the phone number he should use to call Connor.

Connor still owned a small holding company named Xavier Holdings, LLC. Its function was to manage Connor's real properties around the world.

The building that housed Xavier Holdings was one of his own holdings. It was his only commercial property in town, and it was always full. His pub, Too Shea, was also under the Xavier umbrella. He owned several other office buildings, houses and lease properties around the world and all were managed through this one office. The cash flow of the company was modest in terms of what he had once been used to, but it was the one asset he didn't want to liquidate when he and Angela made their retirement decision.

The managing of the company rarely involved him as it was primarily a paper moving business and he didn't need to be hands on very often. He was usually only needed a few days a month to make some larger maintenance decisions and sign checks. Aside from that, it was easily managed by the few employees.

Connor did maintain a large office for himself on Xavier's floor, but rarely used it. On occasion when he needed to stay in town overnight, he would stay in his office. Those occasions have diminished over the years. However, now he was grateful for still owning this space. It would serve as his base of operations. It should effectively isolate what he was doing and the accompanying inherent risks from his family.

Connor smiled as he walked off the elevator and through the glass door of Xavier Holdings. It had been almost three weeks since he was last in these offices. He did like the look and smell of the place.

At the front counter was Emily, the main receptionist. Connor was not exactly sure what she did all day. There was very little foot traffic to the office. When she was hired he simply wanted someone at the front desk as a buffer between the elevator and the offices, but beyond that he wasn't sure what she did to fill her days. He didn't really care either.

"Hi Emily, it is nice to see you again."

Emily rose from her chair and smiled nervously, "Hello Mr. Shea, I wasn't expecting you today. Was there something I needed to do for you?"

Connor smiled pleasantly, "No Emily, everything is fine. I will be in my office for the next few days. I have a special project that I am working on. I may need to call on your services from time to time, if you don't mind."

Emily smiled sincerely, "Anytime Mr. Shea, I am available for anything you need."

Connor nodded politely and continued on towards his office at the back. As he walked past the few workstations he noticed every set of eyes looking at him. He chuckled to himself, 'Perhaps I should have given them a heads up that I would be coming. Emily will have them all filled in shortly I'm sure.'

Connor's office was the only one on the floor without windows facing into the office space. Even the door to the office was solid. Unlike the rest of the office area, his office walls were paneled in mahogany and his carpeting was a deep red and very plush. There was a shelving unit along one wall that housed books, a television and stereo equipment. A seating area was arranged facing that space.

On the other wall was a small bar and beside that a door leading into a small bedchamber and another leading into a bathroom. The bar had a small fridge, and microwave. He would be able to stay here for short periods and have all the amenities he needed.

Sitting behind his desk he took a few moments to look around and take in the view of his office. He had designed it for a time when he spent more time here. His main office in those days was far more ornate, but this one was functionally tasteful and suited his more modest present lifestyle.

After a few moments of self-indulgence he turned to his computers and booted them up. While they were loading he picked up the phone and called Angela. He had not as yet mentioned to her his intention of staying here for the next few days.

He knew she wouldn't mind. It was also an opportunity to let her know that his regular cell phone would be off. He had acquired a disposable cell phone and that was what he intended to use primarily until this was over.

Angela answered quickly, "Hello?"

"Hello, Angela, I just wanted to let know that I have finished talking with Bart and am getting things rolling. I am in my office downtown and I think I will be staying here for the next few days, if that is okay with you?"

Angela had been expecting this call, "Of course, Connor. I know how totally engrossed you get when you sink your teeth into something. We will be fine."

Connor smiled and it could be heard in his voice, "Thank you, dear. My regular cell will be off and I don't want you to call me here. I'll give you my disposable number for emergencies, okay?"

Angela chuckled cautiously, "I understand, Connor. I take it you are a little concerned about who you may be dealing with?"

Connor was cautious, "Not really, I am just being careful. Anyone that is prepared to kill and frame someone else may be capable of other things as well. I want you and Janet Elaine safe. That is all. I doubt there is any real threat, though."

Angela was silent for a few moments, "I'm scared, Connor. I'm worried about you."

Connor kept his voice positive, "I'm sure we have nothing to worry about. I just like to cover all the angles. You know that, Angela. You have nothing to worry about."

Angela was quiet again for a few more moments and when she spoke she was unconvincing, "Alright, Connor, if you say so. Try to wrap this up quickly. I want you back home as soon as possible."

Connor understood the tone in her voice, "I will be fine, dear. Just stay with your mom and Simon and try to have some fun."

Angela spoke softly, "Bye, Connor. I love you." The phone went dead.

Satisfied everything was taken care of Connor opened The Onion Router browser on his dedicated computer. Most of his communications would be through TOR. He had used TOR many times in the past as it provided contact throughout the world that was virtually untraceable. This machine had its own IP and dedicated line so there was little risk of material on this machine finding its way on to the office network and vice versa.

The first email he sent was to an old contact from years past. He had never actually met this individual and only knew him as Chameleon. He was more than satisfied with the work Chameleon had done over the years. Connor knew it could be several hours before his contact got back to him. For the purposes of their communications he referred to himself as Eagle. He didn't have a lot of imagination when it came to names so this would have to do. It was important to maintain security so real names were never used.

Connor switched to his other computer and opened a satellite map of the area. His primary interest was the ground between Bart's house, the rest area he stopped at, and his cabin. Connor was certain that Bart had been drugged and abducted. That was the only scenario that fit the evidence for the frame up.

He would have been held before being returned to his own bed with his car in his driveway. Connor was certain this was what really happened. All he needed to do now was prove it.

When the area was open on the screen, Connor reviewed the entire region looking for areas that would have suited him if he had been an abductor working this plan.

Every area he found of interest he enlarged, printed, and then taped to his white board. He worked methodically over the entire map. He knew he would have to make certain assumptions that may or may not be true, but it was a start at least.

***

When Angela and Leigh Ann pulled through the gates and up to the front of the Prentice house, Janet was there waiting in her car. Seeing

Angela's car, Janet exited her vehicle and stood beside it until Angela came to a stop.

Her blonde hair blew lightly in the breeze and she was as stunningly dressed as usual. If life had dealt different cards, she could well have been a model. Her beauty was timeless. Her tongue, at times, left much to be desired. All these traits made Janet someone a person could admire, love and be embarrassed by, all at the same time.

Janet and Angela had been friends for most of their lives. Of all the people outside of her immediate family, Janet was one of the few people she could always count on and could always trust.

The friendship between Leigh Ann and Janet didn't exist before Angela's anniversary. In the few years since then, Janet and Leigh Ann had become fairly close. The three spent considerable time together, often engaged in activities that the more plastic women in their acquaintance wouldn't consider appropriate. They were each as equally comfortable on either side of the proverbial tracks.

As Leigh Ann exited Angela's car, Janet took her into a warm hug and offered a sympathetic greeting. Janet felt empathy but rarely showed it. After all that she and Angela have been through over the past ten years she tended to be more detached, but today was different.

Janet spoke solemnly, "I am so sorry Leigh Ann. I am here if you should need anything. Both of us are. You know that, right?"

Leigh Ann smiled as she pulled away from Janet, "Thank you, Janet. Yes, I do know that. But, Janet, no one died. Bart has been arrested and that is all. He hasn't been convicted of anything either. I think we are all pretty confident that he is an innocent man that has been wrongly accused. This is disheartening, but it will all be straightened out soon."

Janet shuddered, "Ah, well, yes, someone did die. The chick your husband is accused of killing?"

Leigh Ann blushed lightly, "Of course, how insensitive of me. I just meant that I didn't need sympathy. I feel bad for that poor young woman and her family, of course."

Janet slapped Leigh Ann on the shoulder, "That's it girl friend. That's what I'm talking about. But you rest assured we are going to help you get through this." Janet smiled.

Angela shook her head. It was nice to see Janet take a civil approach, but knew it wouldn't last. And sure enough, Janet reverted to her usual self.

Leigh Ann smiled as she headed up the stairs to the main door. As she reached for the handle it opened and their maid was standing there, "Hello Mrs. Prentice. I heard what happened. I am so sorry."

Leigh Ann was touched, "Thank you so much, Martha. I am sure everything will be fine."

Martha smiled, "Of course it will, ma'am."

Leigh Ann nodded as she entered the house and left her bags just inside the door. She looked to Martha reluctantly before she spoke, "If you don't mind, the girls and I would love a cup of tea."

Martha smiled, "Yes ma'am, right away."

Leigh Ann knew that Martha wouldn't join them or she would have invited her. For as long as Martha has worked for the Prentices she has always maintained a professional distance from Leigh Ann and her husband.

The women moved into the sitting room. Janet, of course, wanted to hear all about the vacation. The more sordid the details the more she liked it. However, Leigh Ann wouldn't oblige. She reluctantly said she wasn't in the mood to be talking about her trip.

The tea arrived and on the tray was a selection of finger sandwiches. The women ate and drank and talked. Angela shared stories of her recent vacation with Connor. Janet, of course, enjoyed the more graphic parts and Angela made sure she relayed plenty of them. Leigh Ann just laughed, knowing that those details were specifically and exclusively for Janet's entertainment.

When Janet's turn came, she talked about her business and how well it was doing. She talked about her father finally supporting her decision to work and actually being there to help out when needed. And most importantly she talked about Mike.

That relationship has been rocky since day one, but they had stuck together and had turned it into something they both cherished. Of course, Janet included as much foul language and juicy details as she could. She is Janet after all.

Angela knew that at some point she would have to talk about Connor, Bart and the information Connor had asked her to get. Angela cleared her throat carefully, "I'm sorry, Leigh Ann, but Connor did ask me to ask you a few questions. I hope you don't mind. He is staying in the city for the next few days trying to figure all this out. He was hoping you may have some information that would help him."

Leigh Ann smiled pleasantly, "Why would I mind, Angela? Bart and I are very lucky to have friends and family like you. I will do whatever I can to help."

Angela nodded thankfully, "Do you have any idea what business dealings Bart has been engaged in over the last little while? Is there anything new or out of the ordinary?"

Leigh Ann thought quietly for a moment, "To be honest, Angela, Bart doesn't talk about business when he is at home. That is unless something is bothering him, then he vents like a gossiping schoolgirl." All three giggled at that.

After a little more thought Leigh Ann continued, "Actually, come to think of it, he had been a little distant. I thought it was just him pouting because I was going away with the girls, but now I'm thinking that maybe it was something else."

Leigh Ann pressed her memory, "For about a week before I left, Bart barely slept. He was in his study from very early in the morning until very late at night. I didn't know what he was doing though. Again, I just thought he was being a jerk and punishing me. I haven't gone anywhere without him since we got married. I attributed all his behavior to that. I guess that just shows how self-indulgent I was." She shook her head, "My God, something was bothering him. Something he didn't share with me. Something I didn't press him about. The whole time I thought it was all about me. How selfish is that."

Angela spoke immediately, "Whoa there Leigh Ann. None of this is your fault. You had no way of knowing what was going to happen. I doubt Bart did either. You did nothing wrong. Bart is a big boy and if he needed or wanted to talk to you about something, I am pretty sure he would have. You need to drop that self-blame this instant. That can't possibly help."

Of course, Janet had to add her opinion to the mix, "Dammit girl, men love their games. We can't be responsible for the way they play them. You are here, and you have been here for a few years now. Like Ange says, he has a mouth, he could have used it. Not your problem, girl friend."

Leigh Ann laughed openly at Janet and shook her head, "That is what I love about you Janet. You cut right through the bull shit and get right to the point."

All three of them laughed at that. Angela cleared her throat again,

"So you have no idea what he was working on then?"

Leigh Ann was a little short, "I said I didn't." She shook her head lightly, "Sorry, Angela, I don't mean to snap at you. Bart said nothing to me. There may be something in his office. I can have a look if you like."

Angela smiled knowingly, "I can look Leigh Ann, if you prefer. I know you want to get cleaned up and go see Bart."

Leigh Ann thought for a moment before responding, "Actually, Angela, I would prefer if Connor came and did it. Nothing personal, but he probably has a better understanding of what he is looking at."

Angela did take a little offense, "I can do that, Leigh Ann, if you wish. You do recall that I owned and managed our family business and my late husband's businesses too?"

Leigh Ann rolled her eyes, "I am so sorry, Angela. I did forget. I guess I just assumed a male would be better at finding answers. I know how silly that is. Please, do have a look around. I trust your discretion."

Angela nodded confidently, "Thank you, Leigh Ann. Now go and freshen up. If need be, Janet can run you into town."

Leigh Ann didn't answer as she rose and headed up the stairs to the private rooms of the house. Angela watched her leave before rising herself and going into Bart's office. Janet remained seated sipping her tea and eating a sandwich before she suddenly realized she was alone. She looked around hastily then got up and followed Angela.

5

Connor was putting images of the area and notes of the information he had received on his whiteboard when the TOR machine notified him that an email had arrived. The email was from Chameleon and it contained a greeting expressing his pleasure in talking to Connor after all this time. That was followed by an estimate of the costs that would be involved based on the information Connor had already provided.

Connor replied with the list of preferred communication methods and the number of his burn phone. Privacy, security and anonymity were always of prime concern, this time was no different. These issues were discussed and agreed upon before Chameleon or Connor would move forward.

The first on his list was a need for information on the teens that had been partying at Bart's cabin. The fact they had been there was too much of a coincidence for Connor and he wanted Chameleon to look into the possibility of their presence being more than a coincidence. For the time being that was all Connor wanted from him. However, he did assure Chameleon he would be needing more.

With the email communication now complete Connor reviewed the whiteboards. He had all the crime scene photos posted, a list of known associates of Bart, a list of Bart's business interests as Connor knew them, and a map outlining the areas of interest. He now took more time to review all the material over again. Nothing became obviously apparent to him. He was hoping when he heard from Angela, she would have some more information that would be of use.

In the interim, Connor decided a drive out to the cabin and take a look at all the key places of interest along that route. He could have had Chameleon do that as well, but Connor wanted to be more of a participant in the investigation than he normally would be.

Sitting around waiting for answers and information wasn't something he was prepared to do with this investigation. Besides he really didn't have any idea where Chameleon was physically located. Connor had never given that a second thought. He would hire Chameleon do work all around the world, and no matter the task, Chameleon always managed to get it done.

Several miles out of town was the rest area and Connor's first stop. Bart said it was the last thing he remembered. Connor parked his car close to the restrooms. He would expect that Bart would have done the same. Bart said there were no witnesses, so it is safe to assume the parking lot had been empty.

Connor got out of the car and looked around. It was a nice spot. There was lots of parking and the area overlooked a river. The restroom building was halfway down the row of parking stalls. On the opposite side of the restroom building was a large area of manicured grass. This area was populated with picnic tables spaced sufficiently to offer a degree of privacy to each. The grass ran all the way down to the stony bank of the river.

Bart said he recalled parking, getting out of the car and going into the restrooms. Connor did the same. Bart also said he took the farthest bathroom stall in the line, so that was where Connor headed.

He looked around the outside area of the stall before opening the door. He carefully stepped into the stall and surveyed that space from the floor to the ceiling and all the walls that surrounded it. There were no signs of anything out of the ordinary.

One thing he did notice though, was that the walls of the stalls went almost to the floor. The bottom was only open about six inches. He nodded his head when he saw that. He knew there had been no marks on Bart from needles, so injection was unlikely, but Connor did know that there were some odorless and colorless gases that could incapacitate an individual quickly.

He would have to look more closely at that when he got back to the office. Right now, he pulled some small swabs and a small sterile container from his pocket. He wiped various places on the walls inside the stall. If a gas had been used, perhaps there were still traces on the walls. Next he pulled out his cell phone and called McGuire.

Nolan answered on the second ring, "Hello?"

Connor smiled into the phone, "Hello Nolan, Connor Shea here. I am at the rest area Bart was talking about. I was wondering if you could get a blood sample from Bart and have it checked for toxins. Specifically something that could incapacitate him quickly, or disrupt his memory, or knock him out without him knowing it. I have some samples of the walls too that I would like analyzed."

There was silence on the phone for a few moments, "Sure, Connor, I think I can arrange that. I will have to find a lab that will play ball, but it shouldn't be a problem."

Connor nodded his head, "Great, thanks, and Nolan, the sooner the better. Some drugs can leave the system rather quickly."

Nolan's voice was calm, "Not to worry, Connor. I am on it now. I'll call you when I get the results."

Connor nodded again, "Thanks. This is my burn phone, so please only call me on this. Bye for now."

Connor took a last look around the restroom before going back outside. As he walked he noticed a man going through a garbage can not too far away. The man's long grey hair, beard, and unkempt clothes suggested he was a homeless person.

Connor changed his course and walked towards him. As he approached, the man stood up to face him. He put down the plastic bag in his hands and waited. When Connor was almost beside him the man spoke, "Go away. This is mine. I don't share."

Connor put on his best smile, "That's fine. I don't want your things, sir. Honest."

The man's tension eased as Connor reached his hand out to him, "My name is Connor Shea."

The man looked at his outstretched hand for a moment before taking it, "Hi. My name is John. That is all you need to know. What do you want?"

Connor smiled, "I was hoping you could help me. Were you here last night?"

John looked suspicious, "Why?"

Connor maintained his smile, "Nothing really, a friend of mine was here and I was wondering if you saw him."

John eyed Connor closely, "What's it worth to you?"

Connor chuckled and reached into his pocket. He pulled out a wad of bills and peeled a hundred dollars from the roll and handed it towards John. As John reached for it, Connor pulled it back, "Ah ah, information first."

John pulled his hand back and looked to Connor's eyes, "Okay. Yes, I saw your friend. He was here last night. Now give me my money."

Connor snickered, "Not so fast John. I didn't tell you anything about him. How do you know you saw the man I am talking about?"

"Because I'm not too bright, that's how. This is one of the spots I work and it has to be one of the most unused spots on this stretch of road. I am here most days and I have to tell you, the pickings are slim. You said last night. There were a few families through during the day. Picnicking and those kids were making all kinds of noise. But last night no one came here, other than one man. I assume that was your friend."

Connor nodded, "Did he see you?"

John shook his head, "No one sees me at night. Hell, most don't see me during the day, or at least they pretend they don't."

Connor nodded knowingly and thought briefly that he would enjoy sitting with this man and listening to his story. His tone, body language and attitude indicated a man that had seen or done a great many things in life. Connor was certain there was far more to him than his tattered clothes and the dirt. There was a reason why he lived like this and he undoubtedly had a far different life at some point in the past. Connor was certain it would be an interesting story. He believed that it was probably a story that didn't warrant pity, but rather understanding and respect.

John shook his head again, "Like I said, no one else was parked here last night."

Connor nodded with appreciation, "Do you recall what kind of car he was driving? What did he do when he got here? How long was he here before he left? Did you see anyone else around here during that time, or a little before or a little after? How old did he look to be?"

It was John's turn to chuckle, "Hold up there big fella. You already got your hundred dollars worth. You want more, pay more."

Connor laughed out loud. John's expression remained unchanged.

Connor hesitated a moment and then pulled out his money and handed another hundred towards John. John took it immediately and reached his hand back out for more. Connor shook his head as he handed him another hundred. John took it immediately and put the money in his pocket before he cleared his throat.

"Your friend was driving a brand new Audi A4. That is one sweet ride. It is way nicer than that Porsche you wrap your ass in."

He hesitated, but Connor didn't bite. He simply smiled at John.

John nodded approvingly, "He was about your age, give or take. His hair was salt and pepper and well groomed. He wore a ball cap, a red plaid shirt, jeans and boots." John chuckled again, "Not real clothes. Rich dude clothes designed to make 'em look rugged and worldly but are pretty much useless in the real world. I'm sure you know what I mean."

Connor didn't bite at that inference either. John was clearly testing him and Connor knew it.

John nodded again, "Anyway, as soon as he went inside I went over to the car. I love Audi. I checked it out pretty thoroughly. I would have got in too if it hadn't been locked. There was nothing visible in the cabin, so I assumed whatever gear he had must be in the trunk. Anyway, I heard a bit of commotion in the restroom so I took off and hid behind a tree. I'm pretty sure no one saw me. A few moments later he came out and got back in the car. Only it wasn't him."

That did provoke a response from Connor, "What do you mean it wasn't him?"

John smiled proudly, "The man that came out was dressed in all the same clothes as the man that had gone in, but the man that came out had a completely different way about him. Physically he looked similar, but he carried himself completely different. I swear it was a different person. The size, build and the rest I could see was pretty much identical. It was mostly the walk that gave him away."

Connor smiled, "I thought you said you didn't see anyone else last night?"

John returned the smile, "I said I didn't see anyone else parked here. I am pretty sure the man that came out was not the same man that went in, but I can't be one hundred percent positive."

Connor stood silently for a few moments weighing the validity and implications of what he was hearing. Finally he smiled, "Is there anything else you can remember? Did you see anyone go in before my friend arrived? Did you see my friend come out after the car left?"

John just shook his head, "No, that was all I saw. I was going to go into the can and have a look, but decided I really didn't want to see what I might see, so I just got out of here as fast as I could. I haven't been back until a little while ago."

Connor nodded, "Thank you, John. You have been very helpful. Are you usually around here if I need to come back and ask you any more questions?"

John thought carefully before answering. In this short period of time he decided Connor was someone he believed to be trustworthy, "Yes, usually. Not tonight though." John tapped the pocket where he had placed the money and smiled broadly. "I have plans for tonight."

Connor's expression changed and John saw it, "Oh, so that is how it is, is it? I am not all pretty and suburban, so naturally you assume I am taking my money and going on a bender. Is that it?"

Connor half smiled, "It's really none of my business."

John nodded insistently, "Damn right it's none of your business, but let's get one thing very clear. Do not judge any man on appearance. You have no idea what his story is. My real intention for tonight is to go up the road a bit. There is a fully equipped truck stop there. I am going to have a feast of steak and eggs and bacon and pancakes and coffee and whatever the hell else I feel like. I am going to get a room. I am going to wash my clothes in the tub. Then I am going to have a long, long, long hot shower. Tonight I am going to slide my lily white ass into some fresh clean sheets and have a sleep like I haven't had in a very long time. And yes, dammit, I am probably going to have a few beers. Hell, I might even have a lot of beers. Is that alright with you, Mister Shea?"

There was notable sarcasm in John's last sentence and Connor felt embarrassed and a little ashamed of his presumption.

Connor shook his head lightly, "You are quite right, John. I am sorry." He reached into his pocket and handed another hundred towards John.

John stepped back, "I don't do charity. I sold you information for a price. You paid the price and you received the information. Our business here is done. Good day, sir."

Connor was humbled, "Listen John, I am sorry. I'm feeling a bit hungry myself. I hear truck stop food is pretty good. I really hate to eat alone. If it isn't too much of an imposition, can I give you a ride and can I ask that you join me for dinner. I'll even pay if you do me this favor."

John looked at Connor analytically and understood what Connor was really doing. He softened, "Sorry, Mister Shea. I tend to be a little defensive. Yes, I will bless you with my company and you may buy me dinner."

Connor chuckled, "Love it. We are going to have some laughs you and me."

John's expression didn't change as he walked to the Porsche. He tossed the bag of stuff he was carrying into the back seat. Then he looked Connor squarely in the eye. Connor didn't react at all as he opened his door and brought the car to life. When the engine was running he looked over at John, "Don't judge a man by his car."

John was a little surprised but then he smiled and nodded. He got out of the car and grabbed the bag from the backseat, "Pop the boot will you?"

Connor smiled as he complied. John placed his bag inside and closed the lid. He returned to his seat and looked to Connor, "Let's eat."

***

Emily was standing as Connor stepped off the elevator. She smiled warmly, "Hello, Mr. Connor. Sorry, I didn't realize you would be coming back. I have shut everything down for the evening."

Connor returned the smile, "That is fine, Emily. You have a good evening. I will just be in my office. I can turn on whatever I need. See you tomorrow."

Emily nodded politely, "Alright, sir. Have a good night."

Connor nodded politely and walked down to his office. Once he was seated at his desk he picked up the phone and dialed Detective Davidson. He was certain this new information would be of value to him.

After his call went through the receptionist, Davidson answered on the first ring, "Davidson, what is it?"

Connor chuckled, "Good evening, Detective. This is Connor Shea."

Davidson smiled into the phone, "Connor Shea as I live and breathe. How are you and your pretty wife doing? It has been a long time."

Connor smiled into the phone, "Yes it has detective, about three years I believe."

Davidson nodded, "You two were expecting as I recall?"

Connor's voice turned proud, "Yes. We had a girl. Janet Elaine is her name."

"Janet Elaine, a fine name, Shea. You must be very proud."

"We certainly are. Excuse my bluntness detective, but I believe you have Bart Prentice in your custody?"

Davidson nodded and his voice changed to a much less pleasant timbre, "Prentice? Yes, I have him on murder. What is this about, Shea?"

Connor cleared his throat, "Detective, I have known Bart for a great many years. I don't believe him capable of murder. I was talking to a gentleman earlier that witnessed Bart arriving at that rest area, but not leaving. He said someone else left in Bart's car."

Davidson was silent for a few moments, "A witness, eh. How come we haven't heard from him before?"

"I met him today at the rest area. He lives there or near there. He keeps to himself, but he distinctly remembers Bart arriving, going into the restroom building, but the man that came back and drove off in Bart's car wasn't Bart."

Davidson mulled over the words for a moment, "A homeless guy says he saw my killer go into a restroom and not come out? Is that what you are saying, Shea? Would you like me to release Bart on that person's testimony? Is that it?"

Connor took a moment to compose himself before he spoke again, "Of course not, detective. I would hope you would take a few moments and talk to him for yourself and hear what he has to say."

Davidson nodded, "I see. So I can assume from this that you are sticking your nose into my murder? You know how much I enjoy working with you, Shea?" The sarcasm in Davidson's voice was unmistakable.

Connor smiled into the phone, "Will you just talk to the man, detective?"

Davidson snickered, "Yes, Shea, I will. I follow up all possible leads. That is what I do. Is he still at the rest stop?"

Connor was silent a moment, "He isn't at the rest stop at the moment. He is at the truck stop just up the road. I had dinner with him and gave him a few bucks to get a room and a shower."

Davidson sighed, "So this witness has come forward to you with this information and you have paid him for it? Is that what you are telling me, Shea? Not exactly reliable information now is it?"

Connor understood what the detective meant, "I assure you detective I have not corrupted or manipulated the man's story. He is an honest man with integrity. He will tell you precisely what he told me. All I ask is that you talk to him. Oh, and detective. You may want to take a little cash with you. He is a bit of an entrepreneur."

Davidson nodded, "I will talk to him, Shea. I will do that of course, but I will ask that you stay out of this ongoing police investigation. I will ask that knowing full well you will ignore it, so let me add this. If you get in the way of this investigation in any way, I will have you arrested for obstruction, is that understood?

"If you find any information pertinent to this investigation, I expect you to report it to me immediately, is that understood? Tread very carefully, Shea. I am only interested in the facts and will follow wherever those facts take me. If I believe for one minute you are disrupting this investigation, your daughter will be looking at Daddy through prison bars. Is that understood, Mister Shea?"

Connor chuckled, "Always a pleasure talking to you, detective. I promise you, all I am interested in is the facts, too. I will get to the bottom of this if there is any way possible, but I will not do anything that would jeopardize Bart, me, or my family. As always, detective, you have my word on that."

Davidson nodded, "Very well, Shea. Thank you for the information.

Oh, and by the way, we have the gun."

Davidson paused for effect. Connor didn't bite, "Yeah, and?"

Davidson continued with pride, "Apparently he thought tossing the weapon in the river would make it disappear. Unfortunately for him it landed on a sand bar. With the low water we are having this year, a fisherman found it just below the surface and contacted us. Ballistics has matched the weapon to the slugs pulled from Ms. Harrison. The weapon is registered to Prentice. That pretty much seals this up."

Davidson hesitated a moment before continuing, "You and your wife should really start looking at finding a different crowd to hang with."

Connor knew what Davidson was inferring. Angela has been around far too many murders over the last ten years. Some directly related to her, some not. "Thanks, Detective, for those inspired words of wisdom. You are a man amongst men. I will make a note of that."

Davidson hung up the phone and turned to Williams, "Let's go for a little ride. There is someone I would like to talk to."

Williams stood and followed Davidson out of the squad room.

Connor replaced his handset in the cradle and stared at it for a few moments. Doubt was creeping into his mind. He was beginning to think that perhaps Bart had done this. He reflected on that possibility for a few moments before he shook his head, "No way. Not Bart. This is a frame up. It is a damn good frame up, but a frame up just the same. He didn't do this, I just know it."

Connor turned to his TOR computer and booted it up. While he waited for it to come to life, he called Angela.

Angela answered after a few rings, "Hello?"

Connor smiled at her voice, "Hi Angela. How are you? I miss you."

Angela cooed, "Hi darling. I miss you too. How is it going?"

Connor noticed the envelope on his desk for the first time, "I see you were by today?"

Angela's voice remained warm, "Yes, I missed you apparently. I left an envelope on your desk. It is a few things I found in Bart's office at the house. The police have taken everything else. His laptop and most of his files are gone."

Connor nodded as he opened the envelope and removed the contents, "Thanks, Ange. I was just talking to Davidson. They found Bart's gun. It is definitely the murder weapon."

Angela sighed, "Oh, that is not good."

Connor chuckled, "No, that is not good. I did meet with a man today that witnessed Bart at the rest area. It does give me enough doubt to keep looking, but frankly, it is going to be an uphill battle. They have more than enough to convict him."

Angela shook her head, "No way, Connor. There is no way he did this."

Connor's voice became more compassionate, "I know, Ange, I know. There is an explanation for all of this. I will find it. Kiss Janet Elaine for me. I love you both. I will talk to you again tomorrow."

Angela nodded, "I love you too, Connor. Please be careful."

Connor nodded, "Always, my dear, always."

Connor hung up the phone and focused on the papers Angela had delivered. There was a list of businesses that Bart owned, was a part of, or was considering purchasing. The list was shorter than one would expect, and Connor was thankful for that.

Another sheet contained a list of banks that Bart dealt with, some local, some offshore. Connor smiled without giving it a second thought. The last was a list of associates Bart dealt with on a regular basis.

It was clear that none of this information came from Bart's office in this form. The lists had been compiled from the records or information Angela had found in his office. Nonetheless, it was exactly the information he needed to press forward.

Connor turned to his TOR machine and opened a word processor and typed all the information in. He saved a copy for himself and planned on attaching a copy to his next email to Chameleon. When he was finished he opened the browser and went to his webmail account.

A message from Chameleon had arrived and he opened it. Connor had hoped there was a connection to someone orchestrating this murder. Unfortunately, Chameleon had been unable to make any covert connections to anyone. As best as he could determine, it was a simple coincidence. One of the kids knows the son of the caretaker. They knew when the caretaker would be away and that was when they planned the party at the cabin.

None of it had anything to do with Bart or this murder. Connor was disappointed naturally, but it was good to have that angle at least dealt with. Still he felt that it was just too much of a coincidence that they would be there on that night. Connor trusted Chameleon and accepted the conclusion no matter how uncomfortable it made him.

He opened a fresh email and attached the information Angela had gathered. In the body of the email Connor wrote, "Attached are known facts about Bart's business activities. Look into these and see what you can find out. I am not sure how you can do this, but the name of the victim is Leslie Harrison according to the police. Bart only knew her as Valerie. See what you can find about her. Report whatever you find as you find it. Thanks. Eagle."

The message was short, and to the point. Connor read it over a few times before hitting send. Once it had left his outbox, Connor leaned back in his chair. He realized it could be quite some time before he heard anything back. Waiting is always the hardest part.

He stood and walked over to his whiteboard. He placed the new information with the other details he had already gathered. He stepped back and stared at it for a moment, before turning towards his saxophone. He was glad he had remembered to bring it. Sitting in a chair facing his desk he began to play. While he played he remained focused on the whiteboard.

The notes he played were from memory. They were tunes he has played so many times that he didn't have to think about them. He simply played. The music relaxed him and allowed his mind to wander. 'Bart didn't do this. That is the first important fact. So if he didn't do it, then someone else must have. That is also an obvious fact. The intended end game to this plan was to have Leslie or Valerie or whatever her name was, eliminated, and in doing so implicate Bart in the murder to divert attention from the real actor and motive.'

Connor pulled the horn from his mouth and made a slight adjustment to the mouthpiece before resuming his play. 'So that being the case, Bart and the girl knew each other and must have some common knowledge between them.

'Wait, if they shared a common knowledge and she needed to be silenced, then he would have needed to be silenced as well. So no, she had knowledge of something that would be of interest to Bart and dangerous to someone else, except Bart never actually received the information.'

Connor nodded, 'That has to be it. So whomever the information concerned silenced the girl and implicated Bart. Whoever it is seems to be attempting to use or at least create an association between the girl and Bart. The pictures are an attempt to suggest adulterous blackmail. That is certainly not a very imaginative motive for murder, but it is a common one and an easy one to sell.

'The problem with that is Bart isn't that kind of man. Only people close to him would know that, so whoever the killer is, isn't close to him and doesn't have a lot of personal information about him.'

Connor put his saxophone in its stand and walked closer to the whiteboard. "What is the connection? Who is this woman? What could be so valuable that someone would kill to protect it and more importantly, kill to keep it away from Bart? Or was Bart just a convenient patsy and not involved in any way?"

Connor picked up a dry erase marker and stood in front of a clean section of the board. As far down on the board as he could he wrote down Bart's name and a few inches above it he wrote "girl". He drew an arrow with a question mark between them.

Two thirds the way down from the top he wrote, "phone call from Bart's home to girl", below that he wrote, "girl murdered". He looked at those two notations for a moment then drew a line from the first to the second. Below that he wrote, "911 call", below that he wrote, "Bart arrested".

Below the last line he wrote the notation, "Bart exonerated." Connor smiled as he looked at the board.

Next he moved to the second board and wrote down all the questions he had just been asking himself. A visual reference had the potential to make the answer to the questions easier. When he had completed that he stood back and tried to think of any other questions he should be asking. None came to mind.

The familiar sound of email arriving was audible from his TOR computer. Connor took a last look at the board before putting the marker down and casually walking to the computer. He expected that it was too early for it to be a message of importance. However, the email was indeed from Chameleon. Connor was surprised to hear from him so soon.

He opened the email quickly, "There was no evidence that Leslie Harrison existed prior to three months ago. Valerie is also an alias. The police ran the victims prints and dentals. Her real name was Jill Starling, 25, local girl. Police are notifying next of kin. Our interview will follow after the police have left. I will get back to you."

Connor nodded and returned to the boards. He erased "girl" and replaced it with her real name. He thought quickly that perhaps Bart knew her but quickly dismissed that as a possibility. He stared at the board for a few moments before adding new questions. "What happened three months ago that required Jill Starling to change her name? What exactly did she want with Bart?"

Connor put the marker back down and returned to his chair in front of the computer. He hit reply on the message and simply typed, "Thank you. Keep me apprised." And hit send.

Then he picked up his saxophone and began playing again.

6

With Janet Elaine safely tucked into bed, Angela turned in herself. She was tired from all the emotions brought on by the day and she needed sleep. The first part of the night had been kind to her and she slept deeply and comfortably.

As the night progressed, however, the dream came to her again. It always started the same way. She was happy and in the early stages of a new relationship. Then things get dark. She sees herself helplessly tied in that room in the cabin for days on end.

She remembers the crazy lady and her daughter that had held her captive. She remembered how insane they were and how much they enjoyed making her suffer. She remembered soiling herself and having to remain that way for hours before being able to get clean. She remembered the scarcity of food. The not knowing was the worst. Hour after hour passed, completely unsure if each would be her last.

Then she remembered the silence of the cabin. It usually only lasted a few hours. But then one day it was quiet, and that one day turned into another day, which turned to another day with no one coming to the cabin.

She recalled the terror as she accepted that no one would ever come again. She remembered the hunger and the thirst and the smells and the fear. She recalled thinking how she would remain tied in the room alone until she finally died of thirst and hunger. No one would know where she was and no one would ever know what happened to her.

She thought about how one day she would be found, dead, half dressed, decaying and soiled. She could imagine herself and how she would look on that day. As she thought about it she thrashed violently under the sheets as if she was still fighting against the ropes that bound her.

Then she pictured herself huddled in a ball below the window, all hope gone. She felt herself slipping away as time forced her to accept her own demise. It was always at this point that Angela snapped awake and sat straight up in bed.

Her eyes wide as she scanned the room before realizing it had indeed just been the nightmare. It was the same nightmare that has plagued her sleep on and off for the last several years. As she caught her breath she began to sob.

She flopped back onto her pillow unceremoniously as she wept. She really didn't care at this point if she went back to sleep or not. She knew that this time, just as every other time, morning would come and she would carry on as if nothing had happened.

No one would know the terror she lived in her sleep. There was nothing else she could do. It was times like this she wished Connor was here. He would wrap his arms around her and hold her until calm returned.

But he wasn't there. He was at his office working on the Bart Prentice issue instead of in bed with her. She wanted to resent him. She wanted to resent Bart, but she couldn't. She understood and respected Connor for what he was doing. She wrapped her arms tightly around her pillow and eventually fell back to sleep.

***

Connor woke to the sound of the phone ringing. He reached across the bed to the nightstand and answered, "Yes, Connor Shea."

It was Angela, "Hello, darling. How are you this morning? Did you sleep well?"

"Good morning, my dear. Yes, considering. I was up a bit late going over things. We have a real name now. The victim was Jill Starling."

Angela was quiet. Connor waited a moment before speaking, "Angela, are you there?"

Angela spoke up quickly, "Yes, sorry Connor. Janet Elaine is being a bit of a brat this morning. Jill Starling you say? I don't think I know that name."

Connor smiled, "I wasn't suggesting you did. I was just letting you know we are making progress; slowly, but progress. How is my little angel today?"

Angela giggled, "She is doing great. She slept well, but she is in a bit of a mischievous mood."

Connor laughed, "Don't know where she would be getting that from."

Angela giggled, "Must be from her father. It certainly couldn't be from my side of the family."

Connor laughed, "Of course, what was I thinking. What do you gals have on your agenda for the day?"

Angela spoke sharply, "Janet Elaine Shea, put that down. You know better than that. Go see Grandma. I think she has something for you. I will be there in a minute." She paused a moment, "Sorry, Connor, ah, Janet, Mom and I are going to take Janet Elaine for a little shopping. It should be a bit of fun girl time. That is if your little angel makes it through the morning."

Connor laughed, "Okay Angela, take a breath. Have a great day and I'll talk to you later."

Angela's tone softened, "Thank you darling, you too. I miss you."

Connor smiled into the phone, "I miss you too. Kiss my girl for me. Love you. Bye."

Connor had a warm smile on his face as he hung up the phone. He looked at it for a moment before turning his attention to his TOR computer. Connor was disappointed that there were no new messages. He left the TOR machine open and swung his chair to face his desk and his regular office computer.

He pushed the power button and when he was sure it was starting, he headed for the shower. The day was in full swing now and anything could happen.

After his shower, Connor returned to his desk to check his stocks and the daily online newspapers. As he read there was a knock at his door. Without lifting his head he spoke, "Come in?"

Emily walked in apprehensively, "Sorry to bother you Mr. Shea but I was just wondering if you were planning on being here all day?"

Connor was surprised by the question, "I am not sure yet, Emily. Why?"

Emily quickly realized how her question may have sounded, "Oh, no sir, nothing like that. No I was just wondering if you would need me throughout the day and if I should be sure to be accessible. That was all."

Connor chuckled, "Of course, Emily, I understand. No one is used to me being here like this." He chuckled again, "I know what this office does, and I'm not concerned. I will be here most of the time for the next several days. You can let the water cooler know that I am occupied with a project that is beyond the scope of this office. I am not here to spy on you all. This project will not require people from this office. Okay. It is a personal matter concerning a friend of mine. I may call on you from time to time, but it is not something I am planning." Connor smiled reassuringly, "This isn't a crack down on this office."

Emily smiled. Her anxiety waned, "Thank you Mr. Shea. People do love to talk. We don't see you very often so there were some concerns."

Connor laughed, then thought for a moment, "Listen, Emily, I will get you to do one thing for me. Take some money out of petty cash and grab a bunch of donuts and sandwiches for the gang, my treat."

Emily smiled, "Yes, sir. Thank you, sir." Emily turned and left the office, closing the door behind her.

Connor snickered and shook his head. He had forgotten how threatened people were when he was around. He knew it wasn't personal. It is just a reflection of his position and his power. As much as he missed the game of business, this aspect of status he didn't miss.

He was just an ordinary man, and not much different than most of the people that worked for him. The only difference in his mind between he and them were a few lucky decisions he had made in the past.

He did believe himself more a lucky man than a power broker or an inspired genius at business. He chuckled again and returned his attention to his online reading.

Connor had finished and felt caught up with the world when a knock came to his door. "Come in?"

It was Emily again, "Sorry to bother you, sir. I brought you a bagel and a coffee. I assumed you probably haven't eaten yet today."

Connor offered a genuine smile, "That is very thoughtful of you, Emily. Thank you very much. No, I have not eaten, nor have I had a cup of coffee yet."

Emily smiled broadly and proceeded further into the office and placed the coffee and bagel on the desk in front of Connor. She looked over to the bar area for a moment, "If you would like sir, I can put on a pot of coffee for you?"

Connor smiled, "Thank you, Emily. That won't be necessary. I'll come and grab a cup from the kitchen if I need. And please, can you call me Connor. Sir just feels wrong these days. Mr. Shea is even better than sir, but I would prefer Connor. Would that be alright with you?"

Emily smiled, "Yes sir. Er, Connor. I will do that. Thank you."

Connor nodded as Emily left the office. He picked up the coffee and took a sip. It was hot and delicious and just the way he liked it; black, no sugar. He wondered quickly if she had researched him or if it was simply brought that way with the assumption that he had sugar and cream in his office. He chuckled to himself, "Who cares, Connor?"

He leaned back in his chair and slowly consumed the bagel and coffee. He was just finishing up when his desk phone rang. He was so inside his own head that the sound of the phone startled him and he sat up abruptly.

He snickered as he picked up the receiver, "Hello?"

Davidson sounded almost chipper, "Good morning, Mr. Shea. How are you today?"

Connor was immediately curious, "I'm fine, detective. Ah, to what do I owe this pleasure?"

Davidson continued, "This is more of a courtesy call. I wanted to let you know that we have discovered that Leslie Harrison's real name was Jill Starling."

Connor smiled. It was obvious that Davidson was on a fishing trip. Clearly, he wanted to know what Connor knew and more importantly if Connor knew more than him.

"Jill Starling, you say? Can't say that name rings any bells. How did you find that out and what do you know of her?"

Davidson was cautious, "At this point we don't have much information on her other than she worked locally. At this point there doesn't seem to be anything particularly interesting about her. I take it you haven't come across anything that I should know?"

Connor smiled, "I'm sorry, detective, nothing. Now that I have a name, perhaps I will have a little more luck. Thank you for that."

Davidson wasn't pleased, "You are welcome, Mr. Shea. I do expect you to share your findings with me. It was not my intention to provide you with information. Ms. Starling's parents contacted me to ask why someone else had come around asking questions about her. Naturally I assumed it was your people."

Connor nodded, "I'm afraid I don't know anything about that, detective. Like I said, I have not heard anything about Ms. Starling."

Davidson's voice was guarded, "Thank you, Mr. Shea. It would be useful if you can find the time to please let me know what you find sooner rather than later, if you know what I mean."

Connor chuckled quietly, "I will do what I can detective. Thank you again for the call, and believe me, I haven't heard anything of any value as of yet."

Davidson hung up without saying another word. Connor hung up and shook his head. He didn't think Davidson would be calling again, or at least if he did, he would be looking for information first before sharing any.

A sound from the TOR computer signified the arrival of a new email. Connor turned casually to face that computer and opened the email from Chameleon. It read, "Eagle. Jill Starling, age 25, addendum." Below that were the names and address of her parents, plus it stated that she had been an only child. She had been living at home, presumably to help facilitate a speedy repayment of her student loan.

Connor picked up his coffee and took another sip before returning to the email. Next it read,

"Jill Starling had been working for Genstar, LLC.

The company is engaged exclusively in genetic research.

Jill Starling worked in the accounting department.

A month ago she stopped showing up for work. No notice and no forwarding address.

She hasn't been back to her parent's home since then. She had told them that she needed to get away for a bit.

Her parents had no information about what their daughter had been doing. All indications were that she was happy and working and there was nothing suspicious in her behavior.

Genstar, LLC is a wholly owned subsidiary of BP Holdings which is, as you know, Bartholomew Prentice's company.

I await further instructions."

Connor read the email over again several times before he sat back in his chair and stared at the whiteboards, "Could he really have done this? Did she move and change her identity to hide from him?"

Then Connor remembered the photos, "Was she blackmailing him? I have to see him."

Connor picked up the phone and dialed Nolan McGuire. After going through the receptionist, Nolan answered the phone, "Morning, Connor, how are you?"

Connor chuckled, "Early bird gets the worm and all that. I need to talk to Bart, can you arrange it?"

"Of course, Connor, I have an appointment to see him in an hour."

"That's great, Nolan. Would you mind if I joined you?"

"No, not at all. Can I ask what this is about?"

"I have a few more questions for Bart. My team has uncovered information that I would like to discuss with him."

"Okay, I'll see you there then. I would like a bit of a briefing before we go in though. I don't like surprises."

"I am leaving the office now, so I will wait for you and we can go over things."

"Very good, I will see you shortly." Nolan hung up his phone and Connor did the same.

Connor turned again to his TOR computer and hit reply.

"Find out everything about Genstar.

I want to know where their money comes from.

I want to know who manages it.

Everything you can find.

What other information have you uncovered about Bart's other holdings?"

Connor read it over again quickly before hitting send. Once it was out of his outbox he shut down his TOR computer and his regular computer, pulled on his suit jacket and left the office.

***

Connor and Nolan sat across the interview table from Bart. Connor stared into Bart's face for a few moments as he decided the best way to broach the subject. He decided the direct method was the best,

"Bart, tell me about Genstar, LLC."

Bart was surprised by the question, "Genstar? What about it? What do you want to know?"

Connor didn't answer. Bart shook his head, "I bought Genstar a few years ago. Actually it was shortly after Leigh Ann and I were married. They were and are involved in Genetic Research. They have made some fabulous progress in gene therapies and early detection of many genetic disorders. It makes money by licensing its patents. It is not a huge moneymaker by any stretch, but it pays for itself and that is all I really care about. The work they have been doing is really quite inspiring. What about them, Connor? What is this about?"

Connor remained expressionless, "Do you know a Jill Starling?"

Bart cast his eyes to the right for a quick moment before returning his gaze to Connor, "No, I don't think so. Who is she?"

Connor nodded, "That is the real name of the woman that was killed. She worked at Genstar. She worked in the accounting department."

Bart shook his head and looked to the right again, "No, sorry, I really don't know her. I mean other than that day that I saw her as Valerie."

Connor was silent for a few moments as he thought about the answers, "What exactly did you two talk about?"

Bart shook his head again as he recalled the conversation, "I received a phone call from her requesting a meeting. She said it was a matter of some urgency and she wanted to meet away from the office.

"I thought it was bit strange; very clandestine to be sure. Anyway, I agreed to meet her for lunch later that day. I arrived at the restaurant at the same time as her. We met up on the sidewalk, exchanged pleasantries and went inside.

"We were shown to my usual table and we sat. Initially we discussed the weather and other trivial conversation topics as we looked over the menu. We ordered and talked about business and the economy and speculative trends of the future.

"She struck me as an intelligent and quite astute young woman. I was impressed with her. The food arrived and we ate, still not talking about anything that I would have assumed was the reason for the call."

Bart shook his head and half smiled, "In hindsight, I think she was actually getting a feel for me and my mindset. I think she was trying to determine what kind of person I was and perhaps how I would react to whatever it was she wanted to talk about.

"I did lose patience with her after a bit and asked her what exactly it was that she wanted to talk to me about. It did take me awhile, I mean after all it is not every day I get to lunch with an attractive and intelligent young woman."

He chuckled quietly to himself before continuing, "She stopped eating, put her fork down and rested her chin on her hands. She looked me in the eye and asked me, 'What would you say if I told you I had information that strongly suggested some wrong doings in one of your companies. What would that be worth to you?'"

Bart frowned and looked a little angry, "I realized at that point that this was some kind of shake down. I was pretty sure she was bent on extorting me. I looked her in the eye and asked her what she was talking about.

"She smiled and said, 'I know some things. I also know that if what I know was to get into the wrong hands it could destroy you.'"

Bart shook his head in anger, "I asked her what it was she wanted. She told me she wanted three million dollars and the information she had would disappear. I do not tolerate blackmail from anyone, but I wanted to be sure of what I was dealing with."

Bart started fidgeting in his chair. He was clearly become agitated, "I didn't say another word. I summoned the server, and gave him money for the meal. I told Valerie that she should be ashamed of herself, I got up and left. I never saw her again."

Connor was silent for a moment before he spoke again, "Why didn't you tell us that in the beginning? Why did you just skip over such an important little detail?"

Bart was surprised at Connor's sarcastic tone, "Really, Connor, really? I'm not a fool. I know how it looks and it looks really bad. The obvious conclusion here is that I killed her to silence her. Nothing could be further from the truth."

Connor's elbows were on the table and he bowed his head into his hands for a moment. "Bart, we have known each other for a very long time. What makes you think that I wouldn't believe you?"

Bart looked him square in the eye, "Do you believe me?"

Connor shook his head, "I am having a few doubts here, Bart. I have to be honest with you. I don't think any of these doubts would exist if you had been honest and upfront with me in the beginning." Connor took a moment to think, "I don't believe you did this, Bart. But I can't help thinking Jill's murder has something to do with what she was talking to you about. I wish she had provided a little more detail. Nonetheless, it is pretty clear that someone has silenced her because of that information." Connor thought again for a few moments before standing, "I think I have all I need for now Bart. I have a little more to work with now. I'm confident we'll get to the bottom of this, one way or the other."

Bart was going to speak again, but thought better of it. He nodded to Connor and simply said, "Thank you."

Connor nodded and walked to the door. Nolan remained seated. Connor was sure he would be spending considerably more time with

Bart.

Once outside, Connor sent a text to Angela to see if they would be interested in meeting for lunch. Angela responded quickly with a location. Connor smiled as he headed to meet them.

***

The bistro was small but quite tastefully decorated. Angela had been here before with some girlfriends, but it was Connor's first time. The place was packed as Connor made his way to their table. He bent down and gave Angela a warm kiss before kissing Janet Elaine on the head and taking his own seat. This restaurant was close to Connor's office and he was a little surprised that he didn't know of the place.

Connor smiled as he looked to Angela, "So how has your morning been? Are you having a good hunting trip or is it more of a gathering trip?"

Janet spoke up first, "Oh Connor, most definitely a gathering trip. Wait until you see all the stuff Angela bought. You are just going to piss yourself."

Her smile was broad and almost sinister. Angela reached across the table and slapped Janet's hand lightly, "Janet! Don't listen to her Connor, she lies. We are having a fun morning and no, we haven't bought anything yet." Angela glared playfully at Janet.

Connor laughed, "No worries, Angela. I learned a long time ago of Janet's mischievous side. I think she may even be having an influence on poor Janet Elaine."

Janet laughed, "Lucky girl."

Elaine smiled, "How is your day going, Connor? Are you making any progress?"

Connor remained polite, "Yes, Elaine. Things are going well. I have just come from a meeting with Bart. I really can't discuss much at the moment as I don't have any hard facts, but I am making progress. Bart seems to be in good spirits."

Elaine nodded, "That is good. He is lucky to have a friend like you in his corner."

Connor noted the unmistakable tone in Elaine's voice, "Thank you Elaine. I know I should be home with my family. I get it. Angela is very aware of my friendship with Bart and she is supporting me fully on this." Connor looked to Angela, "Isn't that right, dear."

Angela didn't hesitate to respond, "Absolutely. Bart is a good man. Leigh Ann has been through a lot as well. This is grief neither of them deserves. I just hope you can get to the bottom of this quickly and return home. We all miss you."

Connor smile held a hint of guilt, "I know. I miss you too. I do. I will make it up to you when all of this is over. I promise."

Janet injected her comments in her usual manner, "Blah, blah, blah, all this sentimental crap is making me hungry. Can we order already? I have so much more shopping to do and I can only afford to take this one day off."

Elaine chuckled, "Sorry, Janet, I forgot it was all about you."

Janet nodded and smiled, "Damn straight, girlfriend. We need some serious calories for this afternoon."

Everyone chuckled lightly as they picked up their respective menus. Connor looked to Elaine, "I love Angela, and Janet Elaine and you too. But seriously, would you do any different if this was happening to one of your dear friends."

Elaine just smiled without looking up from her menu. Connor shook his head lightly and returned his focus to the menu.

Angela noticed the look on the face of both Connor and her mother and her heart felt heavy. She hoped that this whole thing wouldn't drive a wedge between the two of them. Their relationship has been strong, but they are clearly on opposite sides on this situation.

7

As Connor made his way back to his office he thought about how much he enjoyed seeing the girls. He hoped that this whole thing would be behind them soon.

Once at his desk he booted up both his regular computer and his dedicated TOR machine. Satisfied both were loading he went to the lunchroom and poured a cup of coffee.

By the time he was back both machines were up and waiting. Placing his cup on the desk he turned to the TOR computer first and opened his web mail.

There were a couple emails waiting for him from Chameleon. He opened the oldest one first.

"All BP Holdings divisions and holdings appear to be clean. None appear to be suspicious in their activities or financials. We have finished checking out the names of the individuals that you submitted and they all appear to be clean. All are legitimate key persons in BP Holdings' various operations."

Connor read the email over again a few times before closing it. He leaned back in his chair and stared at the boards and realized he hadn't updated them.

He added the most recent information and updates. The model still wasn't complete. There were still questions that needed to be answered. The problem Connor saw was that everything that had come to light so far still pointed directly at Bart. Connor shook his head as he returned to his desk and opened the second email.

This one read, "Addendum: Jill Starling, 25.

When she left Genstar and her parents, she stopped using her bank account and her credit cards.

Leslie Harrison had come into existence four weeks earlier. A bank account for Leslie Harrison had begun seeing increased activity. There appeared to be withdrawals from Jill Starling's bank account with corresponding deposits in the account of Leslie Harrison, and then all activity on Jill's account and credit cards ceased.

Digging a little deeper it appears Leslie Harrison had been in communication with an address in the Caymans. We have not as yet determined who the individual is, but it is pretty safe to assume that a bank account had been set up.

Jill's parents weren't much help. They seemed genuinely surprised that she could have been involved in anything like this.

We were in touch with some of Jill's friends and it was the same there. Nothing that indicated there was any knowledge of what Jill was up to.

My techs have reviewed the photos that you sent. Jill's face was artificially introduced to the images. They were not able to determine what face was there originally, but they are certain Jill was not the person that was originally in the bedroom photos. The outside photos were real.

Awaiting further instructions."

Connor read the information over again carefully then added the details to the boards. Once satisfied, he hit reply in the email client, "Dig deeper into Genstar. That has to be the connection. I don't care what you have to do. Your budget is now increased by an additional $100,000 – make it happen."

Connor read the email over again and when he was satisfied, he hit send. He thought to himself, "I have spent three hundred thousand dollars so far and all I have managed to do is provide more information that almost exclusively suggests Bart did this. The photos are the only things they have to suggest otherwise." Connor picked up his saxophone and began playing. His mood needed a little help to improve.

***

The girls had spent the morning shopping at some of the boutique stores downtown, but now they wandered through a major shopping mall. Not being a weekend, the mall wasn't as busy as it could be.

This mall was one of the finest in town. The architectural style suggested Victorian, but it was most definitely a modern twist on that traditional style. There were ornate elements throughout, all painted white. The entire ceiling, four stories above the ground floor, were vaulted and interlaced with stained glass which gave the mall a bright, cheery atmosphere with subtle shimmers of color across the walls and floor. In the evening the subtle lighting made the entire space almost glow.

This was one of Angela's favorite places to shop, not just for the ambiance, but also for the selection of stores it housed.

Some of the shops were major national chains, but there was a good mix of boutique type shops as well. A location within this mall ensured a steady flow of customers year round and it appeared that any business that opened here prospered.

The women walked and talked their way around the mall. Angela was pushing Janet Elaine's stroller, and each of the women had several packages in their hands. There was no doubt they were enjoying themselves and each other.

They approached a woman's store that catered specifically to a more mature clientele. It was not one of Angela's favorite shops, but Elaine enjoyed it. Directly across from the main door of the store was a bench. Noticing Elaine's intent to go into the store, Angela made her way to the bench and sat down.

Elaine saw it and smiled, "Are you afraid to go in there my dear?"

Angela laughed, "Afraid? No, don't be silly, Mom. I'll sit out here with Janet Elaine. You go ahead on in. Take your time. I'm in no hurry. I'm sure Janet would love to help you."

Angela smirked deliberately at Janet. Janet couldn't care less, "Sure thing, Elaine. Let's leave the princess out here and you and I can go have us some fun."

Elaine laughed, "Yes, Janet, let's have some fun. We'll be back in a few minutes, dear."

Angela waved sincerely, "Take your time, take your time. I could use a break."

Elaine and Janet didn't respond beyond a chuckle as they turned and entered the store. Angela sat back in the bench knowing full well it would be some time before those two returned.

Angela pulled her cell phone out of her purse and checked her messages. There weren't any. Then she leaned forward to check on Janet Elaine. She had fallen sound asleep some time ago and was still sleeping soundly. Angela smiled as she opened the eReader app on her phone and began reading the novel by SM Dougan she had started on the boat.

It wasn't long before she was completely engrossed in the story. She didn't notice the gentleman approaching until he stopped and looked down at her. Angela looked up with a start. He was finely dressed in custom-tailored garments. The man noticed the inquisitive look on her face.

When he smiled the subtle wrinkles around his eyes deepened as if to validate the salt and pepper of his hair. His voice was pleasant and warm with a heavy Australian accent, "She is adorable. Children are so precious."

Angela let her guard down slightly and smiled, "Thank you. Yes, she is a blessing."

The man's brow furrowed slightly, "You look familiar to me." He hesitated for a moment, "Angela, isn't it? Connor Shea's wife? I am an old friend of Connor. How is the old man doing these days? It has been a long time. Is he still blasting that horn of his?"

Angela's security was reinforced, "He is great. Busy. Working, of course, and yes, he still plays regularly at Too Shea"

The man nodded, "I'm not surprised, but I thought he retired."

Angela chuckled, "We are. Well, as retired as we will ever be I guess."

The man chuckled, "I know. It is hard to stop when you have given so much to a particular life."

He hesitated a moment, "Tell Connor I said hi, will you. I do have to get going. It was nice to meet you and your daughter, Angela. I will have to swing by Too Shea and check it out while I'm in town."

He hesitated before continuing, "Connor is a lucky man. I certainly hope he doesn't do anything to lose you." The man chuckled and started off down the mall.

Angela shook her head. She thought his last statement a little strange, but thought perhaps it was some form of joke where he came from and didn't give it another thought.

The man was well down the mall when Elaine and Janet emerged from the shop. Neither woman was carrying any new packages. Angela smiled and teased, "What? After all that you didn't buy anything?"

Elaine ignored her, "Who was that gentleman you were talking to Angela?"

Angela shook her head, "I didn't catch his name. He said he was a friend of Connor's."

Elaine looked down the mall in the direction the man had walked, "I see. There is something not right about him. I'm can't put my finger on it. I think I know him from somewhere, but I can't for the life of me remember where." She shook her head, "No matter, I guess. Are we ready to attack some more shops or call it a day."

Janet spoke up immediately, "It has been a slice as always, ladies, but I am done, done. There is only so much of this girlie stuff I can handle in one sitting."

Angela laughed, "Janet's right. I think it is a good time to head home. Janet Elaine is worn out and sound asleep."

Elaine smiled, "I'm glad you said that. It has been fun, but my feet are killing me."

***

After playing his saxophone for an hour or so, Connor returned the instrument to its stand. He stood with a dry erase marker in his hand staring at his whiteboard when there was a knock on the door, "Come in?"

Emily opened the door and smiled, "I just wanted to let you know that I was heading out for the evening. Was there anything you needed before I left?"

Connor looked at his watch quickly, "Wow, that was a fast afternoon."

The time had passed quickly. He looked to Emily with a smile, "Thank you, Emily, no. I am fine."

Emily nodded, "Well goodnight then. Your sax sounded great, by the way."

Connor nodded, "Thank you. It helps me think. Have a wonderful evening."

Emily closed the door behind her without saying anything further.

Connor returned to his chair with a smile on his face. He looked at the boards as he thought about how nice it was of Emily to come in to say goodnight and to comment on his music. He thought how little things could make all the difference in someone's life.

As Connor stared at the boards, the smile left his face and he spun back to his TOR machine and opened the email client. He addressed an email to Chameleon and began typing.

"Chameleon.

Genstar – what specific projects have they been working on for the last" Connor stopped there and thought about the timeline. Jill was killed a few days ago. She must have noticed something several months ago to cause her to start creating her alter persona. She would have needed some time before that to become curious and for time to elapse to notice a trend. He looked back at the email and finished the sentence.

"8 – 12 months. Check their financials, and follow the money on payables. If you find anything out of the ordinary, trace it back as far as it will go. I feel strongly that Genstar or more likely someone at Genstar is at the heart of this."

Connor knew he had already asked Chameleon to look closely at Genstar, but this email was intended to give him a particular area of focus. Connor read it over again before he hit send. As the email left his outbox he again recalled what Bart had said about Genstar. It was engaged in genetic research and made its money through the licensing of the processes they have developed. Their very existence was focused on comparatively small things that make huge differences in people's lives. There is nothing so small and so huge as genetics. The existence of everyone and their uniqueness is the direct result of genetics. There has to be a connection there.

Being in a field that had such impact might sway someone to the darker and more privatized aspects of the field. What specifically that could be, Connor could only guess, but he was certain that was where the answer lay. Whatever those specific aspects were, the practitioners felt that what they were doing was worth killing to protect.

Connor couldn't help wondering whether or not Bart was aware that something was going on. This was his business, and as such he should have been fully aware of all its involvements. If not, then at least he should have been aware of money changing hands. If he was aware, why wasn't he as suspicious as Jill had become.

There were only two things that Connor could think of. Either Bart was not at all aware of anything unusual taking place, which would suggest that he wasn't as hands on as he probably should have been. Or he was fully aware of what was going on and was trying to save his own skin.

Connor thought about both scenarios carefully and about the person he knew Bart to be. Finally he shook his head, there was no way he could be involved. If he was aware he would have taken actions on his own. The only logical explanation is that he was not overseeing that company's operations with any kind of regularity. The only way a scenario like that could exist was if someone he trusted was at the helm. Whoever that person was must have been aware that something was happening. It was too hard to believe that that person, too, was completely oblivious to anything amiss.

Connor's head was swimming with the analysis of the various possibilities. He needed a distraction. He picked up the phone and dialed the house. Angela answered, "Hello?"

Connor smiled into the phone, "Hello, my dear. How are you this evening?"

Angela's voice was warm, "I'm great. How are you doing?"

Connor could hear Janet Elaine speaking excitedly in the background, "Daddy?"

Angela chuckled, "I think there is a young lady here that would like to talk to you."

Connor's smile grew as he waited for Janet Elaine to come to the phone. It wasn't long before a young girl's giggle came through the handset.

Connor's heart sank, "Hello my little princess. I miss you so much. I will be home in a few days. You be a good girl for mommy."

That was followed by a little commotion before Angela was back on the phone. Her smile came through her voice, "She misses her Daddy."

Connor nodded, "I miss her too. I miss you both. It shouldn't be too much longer. I am making progress."

Angela giggled lightly, "By the way, we ran into a man in the mall today. I think he knows you."

Connor was curious, "Really, who was it?"

Angela's voice was calm, "I didn't catch his name. He was a nice gentleman, probably in his early fifties. He was very well dressed and had great manners. He had an accent too, English or Australian, I think. I'm not very good at those things.

"He said he was a friend of yours and asked me to say hi to you for him. He said that he hoped you didn't do anything that would cause you to lose me." Angela giggled.

Connor didn't laugh as he looked over his white board and searched his memory of the people he knew as friends and none matched the description Angela had given. Then he thought deeper of people he had met over the years. There were a great many of them from many parts of the world. With a chuckle he gave up trying, "I can't think who it might be. I'm sure if he wants to get in touch with me he will. He was probably in town on business and stopped in at the mall to pick up some gifts for family back home, or something like that. That was probably just some flattery or his sense of humor or something."

Angela chuckled, "Probably, because every man away on business thinks of bringing gifts home to the family. I thought you were the only one that did that, dear."

Connor knew she was teasing and ignored it, "I should probably get back to work. I just really needed to hear your voice and Janet Elaine's too."

Angela spoke with a hint of pride, "I am glad you called. Janet Elaine misses you. She hasn't seen much of you since we have been back."

Connor was hesitant, "I know, but security is everything at the moment. I have to stay away from all of you until this is done. I need to be able to work in quiet and focus on what I'm doing to try and clear this up as soon as I am able. Bart really doesn't have a lot of time. I know you understand."

Angela was still calm, "Of course I do, Connor. You are a good man and a good father and a good friend. I wouldn't have it any other way. I love you. Have a good evening."

Connor smiled, "Thank you Angela. It means a lot to hear that. I love you too. Good night."

Connor replaced the handset but kept his hand on it for a few moments as if it were the very hand of his family he was touching.

***

The phone ringing woke Connor. He glanced at the clock as he reached for the phone. He shook his head as he pulled the phone to his ear, "It is five AM, this had better be important."

Nolan dismissed Connor's tone and spoke anxiously, "Connor, Bart is dead."

Connor sat up quickly, "What are you talking about, Nolan? Bart is dead? What happened?"

Nolan took a moment before continuing, "The preliminary says he had a massive heart attack. They found him this morning. I am heading over to see Leigh Ann right now."

Connor was silent for a moment, "I am so sorry to hear that, Nolan. He was a very good man. His wife is going to be devastated. Thank you for the call Nolan, I appreciate it."

A slight twinge of emotion found its way out of Nolan's mouth, "You are welcome, Connor. I thought you would like to know as soon as possible. I will be in touch later."

Connor nodded into the phone, "Thank you."

He hung up and sat on the edge of bed with his hands in his face. His mind raced as his memories of Bart replayed, "I am going to miss you old man. You are gone way too young."

After a few more moments Connor headed for the shower. He needed a bit of time to think. He was not sure what he needed to do first, he just knew he needed to do something and a shower was a good place to start.

Once he was dressed his mind had a chance to calm down and he was able to think normally. He went to his desk and booted up both his computers. While he waited he went to the kitchen area and put on a pot of coffee. No one had arrived in the office yet as it was still well before normal business hours.

With a fresh coffee in hand he returned to his desk and picked up the phone. He glanced quickly at the clock on the display on the phone. Angela would be up now. He dialed the house and Angela answered after two rings, "Hello?"

Connor took a deep breath before he spoke, "Good morning my dear. I received a bit of bad news this morning. Are you sitting down?"

Angela's voice expressed her concern, "What is it Connor? What has happened?"

Connor took another deep breath, "Bart is dead. They found him in his cell this morning. Apparently it was a massive heart attack."

Angela was silent for a few moments, "He was so young, Connor. I can't believe it. Poor Leigh Ann. My God, Leigh Ann. I have to go Connor. I have to call her."

Connor didn't question it, "Yes, of course Ange. Give her my best. Is your Mom still there?"

Angela spoke quickly, "Yes, yes. She is. She'll watch Janet Elaine. I have to go."

Connor nodded, "Yes, Ange. Love you."

He hung up and turned towards his TOR machine. He opened his email client immediately and the first thing he saw was an email from Chameleon. Connor thought quickly that he probably wouldn't need to pursue this investigation any further. Without Bart there really didn't seem to be any point. That notion passed quickly. Connor knew he would continue if for no other reason than to clear Bart's name.

Chameleon's email was now open and Connor read it over quickly. The first part of the email discussed Genstar. As far as Chameleon was concerned it was a legitimate business whose balance sheet seemed to be in order. There appeared to be some investments in a few other companies and all but one appeared on the up and up. Chameleon's team was having difficulty finding information on the remaining one. It was a privately held company so the usual disclosures weren't available. A little more digging would be required.

One key point that Connor had not previously been aware of was that Leigh Ann was the CEO of Genstar. Bart was the principle and the major shareholder but exclusively Leigh Ann oversaw the operation.

Connor shook his head, "There is no way I can talk to Leigh Ann about Genstar, at least not for a few days. Her mind will naturally be elsewhere. I do have to give her a chance to mourn. I know she will want to clear his name, but the urgency just isn't there anymore."

Connor returned to the email and continued reading. It appeared that one of the Genstar people has a lifestyle above his pay grade. There is clearly a source of income beyond his Genstar salary. Chameleon was looking further into this person but didn't offer a name. Chameleon expected to have more information by end of business today.

Connor nodded as he finished the email, then he read the entire thing over one more time. Satisfied he had all the information straight in his mind he went to his boards to make a few more notes. As he completed and sat at his desk reviewing the boards he noticed the light coming under his door increased. The Xavier employees were arriving to begin their day.

8

The unavoidable noise of the office coming to life convinced Connor to go for a walk and perhaps have some breakfast. The park was near the office and it was a place he enjoyed going to when he needed fresh air and time to think. It had been some time since he was last in the park and he was enjoying the time. With several hours now passed, he returned to the Xavier offices.

As he exited the elevator Emily was there to greet him, "Hello, Mr. Shea."

In her outstretched hands were a number of envelopes. Connor looked at them for a moment before he smiled and took them from her, "Thank you, Emily. Sorry, my mind is somewhere else at the moment. Forgive me. Anything happening that I need to know about."

He was referring to Xavier and Emily knew it, "No sir, it is a pretty quiet day so far." Her smile was warm and sincere.

Connor nodded as he continued through the main office area and into the coffee room. Taking a cup of coffee he continued into his own office and closed the door behind him. He placed the coffee and the mail on the desk before turning to boot up his computers.

He had left the office before reading the news and thought now would be a good time. While the machines went through their process he gave his attention to the mail. There was nothing of any real significance. These were the things his team generally dealt with. Connor assumed that Emily giving it to him was her way of saying they were here and working and he should give them a little attention also.

He chuckled to himself at the thought of that, "Subtle. When this is done, I will have to do something for this office. It is long overdue."

He put the mail aside. He would return them to Emily later in the day. With the machines live, Connor turned to the regular machine first. He opened the first of his news sites. As it loaded the first headline was about Bart. This was one of the main reasons he preferred his online papers, they are far quicker at updating their stories and information.

Bart's death was very recent news, but the papers were already talking about it. Connor read that story first. There wasn't much information in it that he didn't already know. Obviously they wanted to run a story as soon as possible. He was certain there would be many more articles in the coming hours and days that would provide much more information. The one thing that did catch Connor by surprise was their opinion of Bart and his work.

Connor had known him as a friend for a long time, and had always thought of him from that perspective. It was interesting to read the opinions of strangers. Bart was more respected in the community for his philanthropy and good works than Connor had known.

He knew Bart was involved and supported many causes that were dear to his heart, but this was the first time Connor was aware of just how in-depth that support really was.

Connor wondered momentarily how the world would view him when he passed. He knew he had lived a far quieter life, especially over these last few years. He doubted anyone even remembered him from his glory days. He chuckled, "That really isn't what matters anyway. My family is what matters."

He thought for a few moments of the possibilities of picking up Bart's torch and continuing in his footsteps in his friend's honor. He dismissed the idea just as quickly. Leigh Ann will undoubtedly be doing that. Besides, if he hadn't been doing it all this time, why would he suddenly start doing those things now. He attributed these thoughts to the normal desire to respect a friend that has passed and nothing more.

Connor continued reading the papers until he had completed all the stories that were of interest to him. After closing those down he logged into his regular mail. It had been several days since he checked it and knew there would be things that needed attention.

As expected there was the usual collection of spam and junk mail, but there were also a few items of business and personal interest. He would spend the next several hours taking care of those. The TOR machine and the email client were open. He would know the minute anything new came in.

***

Angela's mind recalled the dark memories of her own life. As she drove to the Prentice estate she recalled all the people that had died, some of whom she barely knew and some that she loved. As she drove up the long drive that led to the front door she forced herself to focus and she pulled on her best supportive facade. Parking in front of the steps, Angela vacated the car and walked slowly to the door. Visits to friends under these circumstances were never pleasant, but she wanted and needed to be there to support Leigh Ann.

Martha opened the door as Angela approached. The sudden appearance of Martha startled Angela, but she didn't show it as she smiled, "Hi Martha, is Leigh Ann in? I would like to see her. How is she doing?"

Martha didn't smile. Her face wore the pain in her heart, "I'm sorry, Mrs. Shea, Mrs. Prentice gave strict instructions that she isn't to be disturbed."

Angela frowned, "It's me Martha, I need to see Mrs. Prentice. She really needs me right now."

The expression on Martha's face understood and agreed with Angela, but she had her instructions, "I am really sorry, Mrs. Shea. She was specific. She said no one and she did mention you personally. She is very tired and is sleeping. I really do not want to disturb her right now. I hope you understand."

Angela nodded sympathetically. She could see what Martha's words weren't saying, "I understand, Martha. Thank you. I love Leigh Ann and I know she needs me, but I understand. Please let my sister know that I was here. I will call her later. Thank you, Martha."

Martha feigned a smile, "Thank you, Mrs. Shea. I will let her know. I hope she calls you back. Good day." With that Martha slowly closed the door.

Angela stood facing the closed door for a few moments before turning and returning to her car. As she opened the door she hesitated and looked up at the windows on the second floor. She was certain she saw the curtains in the master suite flutter as if someone had been holding them open and suddenly released them.

Angela sighed quietly as she sat behind the wheel and brought her car to life. Sliding the shifter into drive, she slowly headed back down the drive. Her only thought now was to see Connor.

***

With the regular business out of the way, Connor turned his attention to his TOR machine. An email had arrived from Chameleon. He assumed that he had been so consumed with other matters that he had simply missed it.

He opened the email and began to read. The first thing Chameleon discussed was a company named "Xenium". He was not certain exactly what kind of business Xenium was engaged in, and now considered it an organization of interest.

The principle of the company was Leigh Ann Prentice. A paper trail showed Genstar provided the start up capital for Xenium to the tune of twenty-five million dollars. The financial records were maintained offshore and would take a little longer to acquire. The main operations center for the company appeared to be based locally with branch offices in Central and South America. Details remained limited. The investigation continues.

The other person of interest, one George Snyder, was a vice-president at Genstar but appeared to have received payments from Xenium monthly over the past four years. Leigh Ann Prentice also appeared to be receiving monies from Xenium going to an account offshore.

Next Chameleon stated that he didn't have any concrete details as yet, but was confident, from what he had uncovered so far, that Xenium was dealing in things that were less than legitimate. He also believed that Leigh Ann Prentice and George Snyder were the main persons behind the operation.

Connor sat back in his chair in shock. He was having some difficulty believing Leigh Ann could be involved in something that wasn't on the up and up. Bart was always upfront about his businesses and holdings. It was a matter of considerable pride to him, so either he was not aware of what Leigh Ann was involved in or he was hiding it.

Connor had only known Leigh Ann for a few years and had no idea what kind of person she was aside from what he had seen of her with Bart. Bart had met her at Connor and Angela's first anniversary party, so even Angela didn't really know much about her background.

The relationship between Bart and Leigh Ann evolved rapidly and they were married a little over a year after they had met. Connor knew Bart to be a very diligent individual and knew that no matter what his emotions told him he would have taken the time to run a check on Leigh Ann before he would ever consider marrying her.

Bart had never talked to Connor about that and if he had run a check he didn't share whatever information he had uncovered. Connor could only assume a check had been done and nothing had been found that concerned him.

Connor hadn't run any such checks on Angela prior to their marriage, and believed such a check of her was unnecessary. For as much as he knew about Angela he knew she had an extensive public background and he was not in the same position Bart was with Leigh Ann. Time of course tells all, and Angela had proven over and over just how lucky Connor was to have her in his life.

He hoped that the same had been true for Bart with Leigh Ann. Now he was wondering what Bart might have actually known about her sideline business, and more importantly, Connor was very curious about what exactly she was involved in.

Connor's concentration was broken by the sound of the phone ringing. He looked at it curiously for a second before picking up the handset, "Shea."

On the other end was a remorseful sounding Detective Davidson, "Hello Connor. I heard about Prentice. I just wanted to call and offer my sympathies. I know how close you two were. I am very sorry for your loss."

It was a couple moments before Connor could respond, "Thank you, Detective. Your call surprises me, but I do appreciate it."

Davidson chuckled, "Yeah, sorry about that. It is kind of out of the blue. We really haven't talked much over the last few days. I just wanted to say sorry and to let you know that we have officially closed our investigation."

Connor was a little confused and it came through his voice, "Thank you, Detective. Thank you for letting me know."

Davidson's pronunciation of his words was exaggerated, "Yes, Connor. We have closed the investigation. We are no longer looking into the death of Jill or Bart. I hope you understand."

Connor sat up and nodded. His voice returned to its usual confidence, "Yes, Sam. I understand. Thank you. Feel free to call anytime. Perhaps we can grab a coffee or something."

Davidson laughed, "My social calendar is a tad full at the moment, Shea, but thank you. I am available in the office if you want to talk. Sometimes it is good to have someone to just talk at, if you know what I mean." He hesitated a moment before continuing, "Good luck to you, Connor." With that he hung up the phone.

Connor replaced his handset and turned his attention to the boards. He knew the purpose of Davidson's call was to suggest there was more going on than he originally thought. Clearly Davidson couldn't vocalize his suspicions, but he wanted to be sure Connor continued the investigation. With the police now out of the picture, Connor wouldn't have to worry about stepping on any toes.

It was equally clear to Connor that Davidson had left an open invitation for Connor to contact him anytime if he needed assistance. That was a resource Connor knew he would avail himself of at some point.

It was then he realized he was not stopping his investigation. He had toyed with the idea of abandoning it since Bart was dead. Then he believed he would continue simply to clear his name. He was now certain he would see this through to whatever end there was. He believed in Bart and knew there was no way he had anything to do with the killing. It was clear to him now that Davidson felt the same way.

Connor was about to turn to his TOR machine when there was a knock at his door. As he turned, it opened and Angela came in carrying a large manila envelope. Her smile warmed up the whole room. Connor was surprised to see her, "Angela? I thought you were going over to see Leigh Ann?"

Angela tossed the envelope on his desk unceremoniously as she walked around to Connor and gave him a big kiss, "I did, but Martha is standing guard at the front door. Apparently, Leigh Ann is resting and does not want to be disturbed. Not even by me."

Connor could tell Angela was hurt, "I'm sorry, Ange. I know you want to be there for her, but I imagine the news came as a bit of a shock. Give her a little time. You can probably go back later to see her."

Angela nodded agreement, "Yeah that is what I thought too." She pointed to the envelope she had tossed to the desk, "Emily asked I bring that in for you. She said a courier dropped it off."

Connor took it in his hand and looked it over, but instead of opening it, he returned it to the desk, "Are you hungry? I could use a bite."

Angela smiled, "I thought you might. Mom is spoiling Janet Elaine as usual, so I don't need to rush home."

Connor chuckled, "Sounds good."

He turned to his TOR machine and shut it down, then turned to his regular machine and just logged out of it. The whiteboards caught Angela's eye, "Wow, you have really been getting into this."

Connor nodded, "Yeah, I am going to continue too. I am determined to clear Bart's name."

Angela nodded without hesitation, "Good. I'm sure Bart would appreciate that and I know Leigh Ann will for sure."

Connor was about to ask Angela what she knew about Leigh Ann's business interests, but decided not to. That could generate a lot of questions that Connor was not prepared to answer. He decided to wait for a later time. Connor took Angela by the arm and led her out of the office.

9

Connor returned to the office refreshed and ready to continue. A simple lunch and time with Angela rejuvenated his strength of purpose. Their relationship has done nothing but grow and improve over time and Connor was certain he loved Angela more today than he did when they were first married.

As he breezed by Emily he offered her a warm smile and nod. As he went through the main office space he could see everyone busily doing their jobs and none looked up as he passed. The novelty of Connor in the office was now gone. Connor was pleased that that uncomfortable distraction no longer existed.

He closed his office door and sat in front of his computers. He started up the TOR machine before turning and logging back into his regular machine. As he waited for them to finish their start-up, he walked to the bar area and poured himself a drink.

This particular brand of rum he had imported himself and kept the entire shipment here. It was only when he came to these offices did he drink it. It made both coming here and the rum itself extra special given the time between visits.

He took a sip of his drink before returning to his desk. He looked at his regular computer first. He reviewed his usual office programs, but there was nothing important that needed his attention, so he turned to the TOR machine. When the web mail client opened he saw another email from Chameleon and he opened it immediately.

The first line of the email read,

"CAUTION: Be advised, our investigations have been discovered.

One of our assets in Peru has been terminated.

I am uncertain of the extent of the breach.

You may be in imminent danger.

There is a high probability that Mr. Prentice was murdered. Test for succinylcholine.

Acknowledge this email immediately if you are safe."

Connor was in shock and thought out loud, "Someone has been killed because they were investigating this? What are these people in to? What was Bart into? What is Leigh Ann into?"

Out of the corner of his eye, Connor caught a glimpse of the manila envelope Angela had brought in earlier. He turned to it, picked it up, and in one motion, ripped it open.

Connor was shocked by the contents. The envelope contained a dozen photographs. The images were of him, Angela, Elaine, and Janet Elaine. There were shots of Janet Elaine's daycare, Connor's home, this office building, their cars and pictures of Angela, Elaine, and Janet Elaine in the mall.

Connor's hands shook as he looked through the photographs. Attached to them was a piece of paper and typed on the paper was simply, "He is dead. Drop it."

Connor tossed the envelope and images back on his desk and sat back in his chair, still shaking. Clearly whoever sent this knew he was investigating the murder and knew everything about his family. He needed to think. He needed to figure out what to do.

He downed the drink and rose from his chair to get another. This time he brought the bottle back to the desk with him. He poured another and downed it. Then he poured another and put it on his desk and stared at the phone. He knew he had to call, but what would he say. He had put his entire family in danger. He reached for the phone, but stopped before actually touching it and looked around his office suspiciously.

He turned to the TOR machine and hit reply.

"Received and understood.

Send someone to sweep my office for bugs.

I need a chopper to my home immediately to remove my family to a safe location. I do not want to know where they are, just get them somewhere safe. I will call them shortly to advise them to get ready. Acknowledge immediately."

Connor read it again and hit send. He sat silently tapping on the desk hoping for a quick reply. He grabbed his glass and took another drink. The minutes seemed like hours, but finally a new email came in and he opened it. "The chopper will arrive in twenty minutes. Have them ready to move as soon as it lands. As well as the pilot there will be two armed men on board. Their helicopter will be escorted by one gunship."

Connor hit reply and typed, "Thank you." Then he deleted the emails and walked out of the office and took the elevator to the top floor of the building. From there he went straight to the stairs and up to the roof. When he walked onto the roof he was surprised by the amount of wind there was. He adjusted quickly and scouted to ensure he was alone.

Satisfied, he pulled the burn phone from his pocket and dialed the house. Angela picked up on the second ring, "Hello?"

Connor hung up immediately and counted to ten slowly before he called the number of the burn phone he had given Angela for emergencies. She answered on the first ring, "Connor, what's wrong?"

Connor shook his head, "Are you outside?"

Angela answered trying unsuccessfully to control her anxiety, "Yes, yes. I am outside. What's wrong?"

Deadly Truth

Connor took a deep breath before he spoke, "Listen to me very carefully, Angela. Please don't say anything until I am finished, it is very important."

"Of course, sure, what is it?"

"A helicopter will be arriving in a few minutes and you, your Mom if she is still there, and Janet Elaine must get on it. When I hang up, go into my den. Pull the credenza away from the wall. Behind it there is a backpack. Take that backpack with you. It has everything you will need. This is very important; do not take anything else from the house. I know Janet Elaine will want her stuffy, but leave it behind. Is that understood?"

"Yes, Connor, I understand. What is happening?"

Connor paused for a moment, "There has been a development and I need to know you are safe. Keep this phone with you but do not contact me. I will contact you when it is safe. Is that understood, Angela?"

Angela's voice was distant, "Are you going to be okay, Connor?"

Connor tried to chuckle, "Yes, I am going to be just fine. Don't worry. I have some very skilled individuals here to help me, but I have to stay for a little while. I love you. Stay safe and remember security is everything. Lay low and don't attract any attention to yourselves. I will contact Simon and let him know what is going on too."

"Should we pick him up?"

Connor took another breath before he spoke, "Yes, you will be stopping at the condo. He will be on the roof waiting for you."

"I love you, Connor. Please stay safe."

"You know I will my dear. Give Janet Elaine a kiss for me."

Connor ended the call and immediately dialed Simon's cell. He answered quickly, "Hello?"

"Hi Simon, I'm sorry I can't give you many details, but please go to the roof. A chopper will be there in a few minutes to pick you up. Angela, Elaine and Janet Elaine will be on it. I need you to take care of them."

The shock in Simon's voice came through, "Connor? What the hell is going on, man? What are you talking about?"

Connor quickly realized Simon didn't know any of what has been happening. "Sorry that this is out of the blue. As you know, I have been looking into the murder that Bart was accused of. The trail is leading somewhere rather dangerous and there is a possibility that my family is in danger. I have gone too far to walk away. I need you all to go somewhere safe. A chopper is coming to pick you. I have no idea where you will be going. All I know is that it is somewhere safe. I will contact you when all of you can return."

Simon was silent for several moments, "Okay, Connor, I get what you are saying, but I think I would be of more use staying here and helping you."

"Thank you, Simon, normally I would agree, but under the circumstances, I have great help. What I really need is to know the family is safe and I know you are more than capable of taking care of them."

Simon was silent again. Then he spoke softly, "Alright, Connor. I will do as you ask. How much time do I have?"

"The chopper should be to your building in ten minutes. Please don't pack anything, just go to the roof and wait for it, okay?"

"Very well, Connor. I don't like the idea of abandoning you."

Connor's voice calmed, "Thank you, Simon. You aren't abandoning me, you are helping me protect those that matter most."

Connor ended the call and immediately dialed Detective Davidson to let him know what was going on and hopefully solicit some help. Connor's call was passed from the switchboard to Davidson's desk, "Davidson!"

Connor took a breath before he spoke, "Hello, Detective, Connor Shea here."

"Ah yes, Shea, what can I do for you?"

Connor forced composure on himself, "My investigation has come to an interesting bend in the road. I have it on good authority that Bart may not have died of natural causes. Can you get them to test for succinylcholine? It may already be too late, but I think it is the poison that was used to kill him."

Davidson was silent for a moment, "Okay, Connor, I will request the test. What is going on?"

Connor proceeded to inform Davidson of what he has learned and what he suspects. When he was finished there was a moment of silence before Davidson spoke, "Are you sure?"

Connor nodded into the phone, "As sure as I can be. Please order the test on Bart and bring Leigh Ann in for questioning. I would really like to talk to her."

Davidson spoke quietly, "I will order the test, that isn't a problem, but I can't have you in on an interview with a person of interest in a police investigation. You know better than that. Besides, this investigation is officially closed. Are you prepared for me to reopen it?"

Connor nodded into the phone, "Alright, alright, that is fine. I will go to her place and talk to her. I have questions that she needs to answer. Give me some time. Is that okay?"

Davidson spoke without hesitation, "Whoa there big fella. You can't go around banging on people's doors either. The law protects everyone equally and without prejudice."

Connor's snicker was louder than he wanted, "I understand, Detective. We are family friends, so I am going to visit a friend whose spouse just passed away unexpectedly. Is that alright, Detective?"

Davidson's smile could be heard in his voice, "Please give Mrs. Prentice the department's condolences. You have two hours, Connor, then I will be coming to talk to her myself."

Connor ended the call and put the phone back in his pocket and made his way back down to his office. He went directly to his TOR machine and opened the email client. There weren't any new messages so Connor opened a window to create one. "Chameleon:

My family was at the mall yesterday and they met a man that claimed to be a friend of mine. I am not certain of the time, but I am confident there must be a surveillance video of the meeting. We need to find that man.

Detective Davidson is ordering the test for the succinylcholine.

I am going to visit the Prentice widow.

Please contact me by phone if there are any emergencies. You have the number."

Connor read it over before hitting send. He turned his attention back to the boards and looked at everything from the perspective of Leigh Ann being the actual murderer. There was no question it was a real possibility, but could she have killed Bart? Connor couldn't answer that question confidently, either way. There was nothing else for him to do but to go to the Prentice estate and talk to Leigh Ann face to face.

Deadly Truth

***

Two modified black Bell 412 helicopters approached the Shea residence. They were coming in just above the treetops and moving very fast. The lead chopper dove and touched down as close to the house as it was able. The second helicopter circled the area.

As Angela, Elaine, and Janet Elaine rushed from the house, the large sliding door on the first helicopter slid open. Inside were two men dressed in black, wearing black balaclava and armed with assault rifles.

Angela looked skyward as she heard the sound of the second helicopter circling. The large doors on that 412 were open and the men in the back were dressed the same as these men and were clearly searching the area around the house.

There was a feeling of excitement in Angela, but it was overpowered by a sense of fear. All she could think of was, 'What has Connor gotten into that requires these kinds of measures.' She suddenly felt nauseous as she climbed aboard the helicopter and sat. She was able to hold back the vomit, but the thought of the danger Connor must be in terrified her.

No sooner were the three aboard when the chopper door slid shut and the chopper lifted off the ground, turned to the south-east, dipped its nose and climbed up to treetop level again. The second chopper pulled in formation beside and slightly behind the first chopper. The course they flew was the reciprocal direction to how they had arrived. Angela assumed that was intentional as they probably scouted this course on their way in to ensure it was a safe route back out again.

The noise inside the helicopter was loud and Angela reached behind her head to take the headset hanging there. As her hand reached up, it was gently intercepted by one of the men in black as he shook his head no.

Angela was surprised, but obliged quickly. Clearly she would have to put up with the noise for now. As they flew and began to approach town, the choppers both climbed for more altitude. Angela believed this was necessary if they had the intention of landing on the roof of Simon's building.

Moments later Angela's suspicions were confirmed. The helicopter they were in slowed and descended towards the roof of Simon's building. The second chopper hovered close by and turned slowly in a circle as if scanning the horizon.

The roof of Simon's building wasn't equipped with a helipad, so the 412 had to hover a foot off the roof top. The wind at this height was significant but the skill of this pilot was obvious as he managed to hold the bird stationery for Simon to climb aboard.

As soon as Simon was aboard, the large sliding door was closed and the chopper headed off due East. Simon tried to speak but quickly realized it was futile and just smiled instead as he lay a caring hand on Angela's knee.

***

Connor arrived at the Prentice house and drove to the steps at the front of the house. Exiting his car he walked casually to the door and rang the door chime. He carried himself as he would under any other circumstance. Casual was the manner he felt was the best approach. After waiting several moments the door remained unanswered. Connor rang again, it was not like Martha to not answer the door quickly. After a few more moments, Connor pulled out his cell phone and dialed the Prentice house number.

From outside he could hear the phone ringing both on his handset and inside the house. The phone continued to ring until the voice mail answered. Connor hung up immediately. He reached his hand out to the doorknob and gave it a twist. It wasn't locked.

Once inside he started calling out for Martha and Leigh Ann as he walked cautiously through the main floor of the house. When he didn't find anyone and no one answered, he made his way to the second floor. He recalled where the master bedroom was from a past tour of the house. The door to the master was closed and Connor tried the knob immediately.

This time, the door was locked. He knocked politely, "Leigh Ann, are you okay?"

Connor waited for a reply but there wasn't one, so he tried again, "Are you okay in there?"

Again his call was met with silence. He shook his head and took a breath before raising his right leg and kicking the door.

The door shuttered but did not yield. Connor grunted and stepped a couple feet away before he charged it with his shoulder. This time the door flew open and chunks of wood from the jam sprayed through the air. Connor fell to the floor just inside the room.

He cursed as he stood and focused on the room. In front of him was the bed and on the bed was Leigh Ann. Connor walked towards her and as he got close he could see the bullet hole in the center of her forehead.

Connor stared at her for a moment before shaking his head. He pulled out his cell phone and dialed the police. Davidson answered, "Davidson!"

"Hi Sam, this is Connor. I am at Bart's house. Leigh Ann won't be answering any questions. I'm afraid she is dead."

Connor could hear the sound of shuffling before Davidson answered, "Alright, Shea, a cruiser is on its way. I'll be there as fast as I can. Please wait for us outside. Oh, and by the way, thanks for the heads up on the succinylcholine. I got a call from the M.E. just as I was about to call him. Apparently this M.E. is no stranger to that particular drug. He found an injection site in the crack of Bart's ass. They almost missed it. Shocker, I know. Anyway, thought you would like to know. See you soon."

The line went silent and Connor ended the call on his phone and made his way to the outside stairs of the house and sat down.

His phone rang and it startled him. He answered it without thinking, "Hello?"

The voice was strong and precise, "Hello Mr. Shea. Your family is safe and secure. They are a little scared and anxious, but none the worse for wear. Chameleon has some more information for you about Mrs. Prentice. He will send you an email shortly."

"Thank you. I am at the Prentice's house now. Leigh Ann is dead. There is no sign of Martha. The police are on their way."

"Understood. I don't want to talk too long as this line is not secure. Check your mail. I am Lance Volcano and I will be waiting for you at your office. This will be my only phone call. Goodbye Mr. Shea."

The line went dead, and Connor pushed his phones end button anyway. He looked at the phone for a moment and then smiled. He was pleased to know everyone was safe. He had no idea where they were but that had been the whole idea. At the same time that knowledge created a particular loneliness within him that he had never experienced before.

Moments later two police cars with lights and sirens screaming for attention pulled through the gate and up to the front of the house. Connor remained seated as the officers exited their vehicles and approached him.

Connor smiled, "Hi guys. Mrs. Prentice is up stairs. I had a quick look around, but I didn't see anyone and there was nothing out of place."

Two of the officers walked past Connor and entered the house with their weapons drawn. The third stopped in front of Connor.

"Mr. Shea? Davidson said you would be here. I would like to get your statement."

Connor nodded, "Of course."

He took a deep breath and began telling how he had arrived, why he had come, and what he found inside. When he was finished, the officer looked up from his notepad. "Good thing you happened by. It could have been some time before the body was discovered."

Connor noticed the tone in the officer's voice, "Yes, it is. I have no doubt I was expected and the body was left where I could find it. I don't think I will go into it any further with you, officer. I think the details are a little above your pay grade. Davidson knows what is going on and I'm sure he'll give you whatever further details he feels you need."

There was no mistaking how annoyed the officer became. Connor smiled on the inside and remained seated. The officer was about to speak again, but stopped when he noticed Davidson's car approaching. Connor smiled openly.

10

Connor arrived at his office to find a rather large, broad man standing behind the desk. The size of him was intimidating and Connor smiled at the sight of him. The man was wearing a dark suit with an open shirt collar. Connor could see the headset with the earpiece in one ear and a small microphone was wrapped around to the side of his mouth. The man smiled as Connor approached the counter, "Good Afternoon Mr. Shea. Your offices are swept and secure. Your employees have been given a two week vacation with pay and a five thousand dollar bonus to stay away from the office. If you need anything I will be here."

Connor nodded politely and offered his right hand across the counter, "I certainly am generous to my staff. I wish I worked for me." Connor chuckled, "What did you say your name was?"

The man behind the counter took Connor's hand without showing emotion. Connor caught a glimpse of the butt end of a holstered 9mm inside the man's jacket, "I am Lance Volcano. You can call me Lance."

Connor nodded and chuckled, "Your parents must have a great sense of humor?"

Lance smiled, "Of course it isn't my real name, sir."

Connor returned the smile, "Of course it isn't. I'll be in my office. I am glad you are here Mr. Volcano."

Connor turned away and walked into the main area of offices. As he passed the privacy wall that separated the office space from the reception lobby, Connor saw two more men standing with automatic weapons in their hands.

Connor had not expected them and flinched with a start as he first caught sight of them. Both men nodded and smiled as Connor continued on to his office. He shook his head and smiled at the way he had reacted when seeing them.

He came to the realization that initially this investigation would cost him a few hundred thousand dollars, but now it was very clear the price tag was getting far larger. He quickly made a rough guesstimate and expected his costs were now well into seven figures. He sighed, but knew he wouldn't consider stopping.

He sat at his desk and started both computers. Certain they were starting up, he went to the coffee room with his mug in hand. When he walked into the room he saw a fresh pot already made. He nodded and smiled as he poured himself a cup. He looked in the direction of the other two men and raised his cup, "Thanks guys. Feel free to help yourself."

Both men responded by holding up a cup of their own.

Connor chuckled to himself, "Okay, the coffee was for them, they didn't make it for me. I guess that is just a little more of that self-important ego of yours Mr. Shea."

Connor closed his office door and sat in front of his regular machine. He went through his email and again there was nothing of any real importance needing his attention. He thought quickly of the number of times he normally goes through his mail these days and how rarely there was anything that needed his attention. He chuckled to himself. He also realized that just because he was in this office didn't mean he would be busy with business.

There were a couple of invitations to a couple of parties and some friendly emails from friends. He smiled at the emails and thought of how much and how quickly things in his life had changed. He glanced at his TOR machine for a second before deciding to deal with the seemingly frivolousness of his real life first.

He responded pleasantly to all the emails without making hard commitments to anything. He felt good addressing conversation with friends - even if it was only digital conversation. In his life, his family and his friends were the only things that truly mattered.

Giving up the major corporate ownership had proven to be the best decision of his life. However, the last couple of days had thrust him into a world that was so far removed from his real life that he was almost starting to lose sight of what his life now was all about. These few emails helped return him to ground and to reflect on the things he considered most important.

Once his family was threatened, all bets were off. There was nothing he wouldn't do to protect them. His resolve to ensure their safety was all that mattered to him now. He had often asked himself what exactly he would be prepared to do to protect them and what exactly he was capable of. He now knew beyond all doubt the answers to those questions.

He turned to his TOR machine and opened the email client. As Lance had promised, there was an email waiting for him.

"RE: Leigh Ann Prentice – Deceased.

I am not certain at this time the extent of Mrs. Prentice's involvement in Xenium. I do know she was the one that filed the papers that created the company. Her partner, George Snyder, came into the picture at a later date. However it would appear that George Snyder was the one running the business. It appears Mrs. Prentice's direct involvement has gradually been reduced.

George Snyder makes regular flights to and from Peru and Mexico. Most trips last no more than a day to two.

"My associate in Peru seems to have uncovered some kind of smuggling operation. The operation seems primarily centered around the smuggling of young females from Peru. Other indications suggest the same type of operation exists in Mexico.

"Both operations appear to be loosely connected to Xenium, loosely in the sense that the money trail takes a dirty path from Xenium to those foreign operations. Attempts to launder have been found.

"My associates have located a copy of the mall surveillance recording. The man in the video appears to be George Snyder. At this moment George Snyder is in the wind. We are trying to track him down, but so far he is at large. I don't believe he gets his hands dirty directly, and appears to have a skilled network of associates working for him. It is clear that his Peruvian connections have tipped him off to the investigation.

"My associates at your office are at your disposal. I do not recommend leaving your offices until we can get a better handle on what all is happening.

"I will get back to you as more information comes available."

The email ended there. Connor read it over a few times, before sitting back in his chair and clasped his fingers under his chin as he considered everything Chameleon discussed.

***

The helicopter flight lasted just over an hour. They flew at treetop level whenever they could and only climbed to higher altitudes if the terrain demanded it. When they finally landed, it was on a small island just off the coast.

The main compound was in the center of the island and surrounded by a tall chain linked fence. The main building in the center of the compound had a large array of antennas and dishes on its roof. It was the tallest building and the top floor windows were black and reflective.

There were a few buildings that were obviously some form of barracks and on the other side of the main building was a room of smaller cabins. It was the cabins that Angela, Elaine, Simon and Janet Elaine were escorted to.

Shortly after entering the cabin, a young uniformed woman knocked on the door and walked in. She was a pretty girl with stunningly blue eyes and her blonde hair was tied back in a ponytail. She was dressed in fatigues with a holstered sidearm clearly visible. As pretty as she appeared, there was no mistaking the air of danger that surrounded her.

She smiled warmly as she entered and reached her hand out to Angela, "Angela Shea, my name is Samantha. I will be your liaison while you are here. If there is anything you need, please don't hesitate to let me know. I have strict instructions to make your visit as comfortable as possible and I will be pleased to do so."

After shaking Angela's hand, Samantha turned to Elaine, then Simon in turn. When she looked towards Janet Elaine her smile broadened even further as she squatted down in front of her and stuck her hand out, "And you young lady must be Janet Elaine.

"I have heard many great things about you. You are strong and smart and now I can see you are cute as a button, too. You and I are going to have a lot of fun. I hope you will hang out with me from time to time."

Janet Elaine smiled broadly as she shook Samantha's hand and nodded jubilantly. Samantha chuckled pleasantly, "Great. I look forward to it."

As she rose she looked towards Angela, "Dinner will be at 18:00 in the main hall. We have quite an excellent cook here. I'm certain you will enjoy the food. Our compliment is light at the moment, so there won't be much of a crowd."

She hesitated a moment before continuing, "This cabin has two bedrooms and there is a selection of fresh clothes in the closets that should fit you. The bathroom has a shower and a tub. Feel free to freshen up before dinner. I will leave you for now. As I said, if you need anything let me know."

Samantha turned and left the cabin. Angela turned to Elaine and smiled pleasantly. Elaine returned a genuine smile. It was clear they all felt welcome and safe.

***

Lance Volcano sat in a position that allowed him a clear view out the glass doors to the hallway and the elevators. There had been no movement down the hall or out of the elevator since Connor's arrival. He thought to himself how much he would like it to stay that way.

The thought had no sooner gone through his mind than he noticed the elevator stopping on this floor.

As the elevator doors began to open Lance spoke into the mouthpiece, "We have visitors. Look alive."

He knew the men on the other side of the wall would receive the message and knew to prepare if a need for them should arise.

With the elevator doors full open, Lance could see a couple of men dressed in work clothes. One of the men was holding the handle of a two wheeled cart with several boxes stacked on it. The way the man moved suggested the load was heavy. The second man was behind the load and trying to look busy assisting the first man in moving the cart.

Lance maintained eye contact with the men and hoped they would carry on down the hallway. No such luck. They came straight to the doors to the office. The lead man backed into the locked door. He didn't look happy as he pushed the load away from the door and stood it upright on its own.

He turned towards the door and looked squarely at Lance and pointed to the door. Lance shook his head and pointed to the sign on the door that stated the office was closed. The man grew angrier as he slapped the stack of boxes and pointed inside the offices. The man that was assisting him remained quietly standing half behind the stack.

Lance rose from his chair and as he did, he casually pulled his MP5 a little closer to him. The lead man pounded on the door harder, then pounded on the stack before waving Lance to come and open the door. Lance shook his head and waved them away with his left hand.

The man behind the stack stepped into full view. He raised an assault rifle and fired a succession of three round bursts into the glass door. Lance dropped to his knees quickly, pulling his MP5 down with him. Once he was low he moved to the side of the counter, using it to shield his position.

The two men behind the privacy wall rushed into the lobby with their MP5's shouldered and ready. As soon as they identified the two targets they fired several rounds at each. The two delivery men clearly didn't expect them. Both delivery men went down quickly and lay on the floor motionless.

Lance came from behind the counter and shouldered his own weapon and moved towards the two fallen men. He checked each quickly for life. His two partners had also moved up and were checking the hallway for others.

When they were satisfied these two were the only ones, they dragged them into the lobby of the office, then pulled the stack of boxes into the office as well.

Connor came rushing from his office yelling, "What the hell is going on?"

When he saw the men on the ground and their weapons lying beside them, his jaw dropped.

"My God, seriously, they were sent to kill me?"

Lance spoke first, "It would appear so, Mr. Shea. You need to shut down your office and we need to leave now. These two will be missed and you can be sure someone will be coming to look for them."

Connor nodded as he returned to his office and shut down all his equipment. Satisfied everything was off, he returned to the lobby. When he arrived three more men were in the lobby. They were putting the two fallen men into body bags. Their primary concern was the removal of the bodies from the scene.

Connor looked at them stunned. Lance smiled, "Are you ready?"

Connor shook his head, "What are they doing?"

Lance stepped forward and took Connor by the elbow, "We have to go. They will manage the scene. The police will be here very soon and we would rather not be here when they arrive. We must leave now."

Connor nodded quickly and followed Lance to the elevator. They rode to the top floor and then ran to the roof. Within minutes a black helicopter arrived. He and Lance boarded and flew off. Connor saw another helicopter coming in behind them and hovering just above the roof. A few moments later the four men came onto the roof carrying the two body bags. They climbed onto the helicopter and it flew off in another direction. Connor looked at Lance, "Where are they going?"

Lance knew what Connor was talking about and remained emotionless, "That is not of your concern, Mr. Shea. They are doing what needs to be done."

Lance pulled a hood out from under his seat and handed it to

Connor. "I'm sorry Mr. Shea, but I must ask you put this on. It is for your own protection. We are heading somewhere we would prefer to remain secret."

Connor was going to argue, but the look on Lance's face convinced him that it was probably a good idea to do as he was told.

***

They had been in the air no more than twenty minutes when Connor could feel the chopper descending. Lance spoke casually, "You can remove the hood now, Mr. Shea. We are here."

Connor didn't hesitate to comply. Looking out the window he could see they were landing in a clearing amongst some dense trees. They had dropped below tree top level before he was able to get any kind of bearing.

Within a few seconds the chopper came to rest on the ground. A cabin was situated in the clearing that was just large enough for the building, a helicopter pad and a barn. Given the proximity of the barn to the helipad, Connor assumed it was where the helicopter was stored.

Within minutes of Connor and Lance exiting the chopper, a couple men with wheel dollies arrived, jacked the chopper onto the dollies and wheeled it into the barn. Connor shook his head, not really sure why such measures were being taken. It didn't make sense to him that they would need to be so clandestine.

As he and Lance made their way to the cabin, Connor could see traces of equipment and apparatus amongst the trees. He had seen such things in movies; it was part of an obstacle course used in training ground troops. He was starting to wonder what exactly he had gotten himself into.

When they entered the cabin, there was another man standing at the far end of the room looking towards them. This man was dressed in a dark suit. He smiled when they entered, "Hello Mr. Shea. It sounds as though you have had a bit of excitement today. I am glad you are okay. Can I get you something to drink?"

Connor nodded, "Sure that would be great, thanks. Who are you?"

The man's back was to Connor as he was opening a beer. His voice was matter of fact, "You can call me Bill."

Bill turned and walked towards Connor with the beer in his outstretched hand. Connor received it with a smile and took a quick drink before speaking again, "Bill is it? I don't imagine that is your real name?"

Bill smiled, "Correct, it's not."

Connor nodded, "Okay Bill, it would appear things have gotten a little out of control. I am trying to clear a friend's name of a murder he didn't commit. I am not sure how that investigation turned into some kind of paramilitary operation."

Bill nodded as he sat at a table. He thought for a moment before he spoke, "There is really nothing I can tell you Mr. Shea. Chameleon will bring you up to speed shortly. I'm sure he will answer all the questions he can."

Connor was surprised, "Chameleon is here? I have never met him. I would like to see him."

Bill shook his head, "No, he is not here. You will be talking to him shortly over a secure connection." Bill looked at his watch, "He'll be calling in five minutes." Bill pointed to a couch, "Have a seat Mr. Shea. Make yourself comfortable."

Connor chuckled, "I don't think comfortable is something I will be able to feel until this mess is cleared up."

"Very well, Mr. Shea, you may as well come into the CIC now then."

Bill opened a door to the far left of the cabin. There was very little light coming from the room, and Connor could hear voices that sounded clear and other voices that sounded like they were coming across some wireless connection.

Connor walked quickly to follow Bill into the room. The door was closed as soon as Connor entered. Bill pointed to a leather chair against the back wall. The chair faced a large screen mounted on the opposite wall.

As his eyes adjusted, Connor could see the room more clearly. Below the large screen were four men sitting behind computer screens and facing in Connor's direction. All four wore headsets and were talking at the same time, but Connor couldn't make out what any one of them was saying.

On the far wall opposite the door was a shelving stand that contained what appeared to be computer servers, some firearms, a few books and rolls of what Connor assumed were maps. Between the large screen and that wall was a large map of the world. A collection of red pins was stuck into the map indicating various places around the world. There were no identifiable logos or names anywhere that would give any indication of who these people were, but Connor was certain they were involved in things far beyond the work he routinely hired them for.

In Connor's business days, he had used the services of Chameleon for a great many business investigations. Some of which would be considered corporate espionage, but at no time did Connor even remotely think Chameleon's organization was anything like this.

One of the men at the computers pointed to Connor. Bill smiled and walked over to Connor. He reached down beside the chair and pulled up a headset and handed it to Connor. "Chameleon is online and would like to talk to you."

Connor took the headset and slipped it on. He adjusted the mouthpiece to better line up with his mouth, "Chameleon? Connor Shea. What the hell is going on?"

Chameleon sounded strong and sure, "Yes, Mr. Shea, I would imagine things are looking a little bizarre to you at the moment. I will do my best to explain." The voice had a heavy Australian accent. Connor didn't make the association to what Angela had said about the man in the mall.

Chameleon paused expecting Connor to say something. When he didn't Chameleon continued, "I think a little background may be in order. My organization has been around for many years now. Most of the people that work for me have an extensive background in shall we say, alternative measures. They are highly trained in a number of fields and are using their expertise to assist me."

There was another pause before he continued, "Many years ago I realized that the country I was serving was not actually being run by the government. The government was at best a pawn or employee of a nefarious group of self-serving individuals.

"People all over the world were being killed in the name of this noble cause or that noble cause none of which were any more than a smokescreen for a real and hidden agenda. When I realized that, I left and started this. It didn't take long for me to amass a large group of like minded individuals."

Connor was shocked, "Are you kidding me? I have been using mercenaries all these years to do my legwork? You are criminals. This has to end now. I won't be a party to this any longer."

Chameleon's voice didn't falter, "Please, Mr. Shea, we aren't really mercenaries. Hear me out. You don't fully understand what I am trying to tell you. We allied ourselves with chosen individuals around the globe.

"Those people were in a position to help improve things in some way within their own worlds. And yes, they all had deep pockets and yes, we used our abilities to help them to deepen those pockets even further. Frankly, operations like this are not cheap to run and we need significant cash flow to continue our work.

"You were just such an individual, Mr. Shea. As you recall, I contacted you that first time and offered information on a deal you were considering. You took my information and ran with it and it resulted in you making a lot of money. What you probably don't realize is that your actions actually saved lives.

"You kept the company profitable and you improved the lives of everyone that worked for you at the same time. I doubt you even knew what had been happening overseas, but because of you, things for them improved."

Connor shook his head, "What the hell has that got to do with this? I am two seconds from walking out of here."

Chameleon laughed, "We both know that can't happen, Mr. Shea. You have no idea where you are and you would probably not survive trying to find your way to civilization. I will take you anywhere you want to go, but wait until after I have finished. Please."

Connor went silent as Chameleon continued, "I investigated you back then. I determined that you were the kind of man that would be willing to walk away from all the power and money to stay with your wife and help her in her recovery and to build a life for the two of you and your child.

"Of course none of those influences existed in those days, but the indications were only that that was your nature. It was that kind of compassion, loyalty and values that underlined your business morals and ethics.

"Yes, you stepped on people, and yes, you even destroyed a few, but frankly, they were mostly one and two percenters. Not exactly people most would care about, but more importantly, they were usually people whose actions were harming others. So we helped you. You made a lot of money and as such you were able to afford to use us to help you make even more money, which in turn helped a lot of people you never knew."

Connor stood as he spoke sarcastically, "I have a lump in my throat and I'm feeling all warm and fuzzy, give me a break. The bottom line is you are hired guns and you kill people."

Chameleon remained calm, "That is correct, Mr. Shea, we have killed. But I can absolutely assure that has always been a last resort. We are not available to just anyone. It takes far more than cash to acquire our services."

Connor's voice softened, "You are a mad man. You are no better than the rest of them. I feel like I need a shower."

Chameleon fought to remain calm, "Really, Mr. Shea, really? You didn't seem to mind when you were making money and didn't know who we were. Now all of a sudden you have an issue with us? Believe me Mr. Shea, we weren't the bad guys."

Connor thought for a few moments before taking his seat again, "Okay, I'm listening. I am in this far, let's hear it, everything. What have I put my family at risk for?"

Chameleon sounded in control again, "Very well, Mr. Shea, and thank you."

Chameleon paused for a few moments to allow the air to clear before continuing, "As you are aware, Leigh Ann Prentice was a sperm donor child like your wife; same donor. They are, er, were, half-sisters."

Chameleon paused again for effect, "From what I have determined, Mrs. Prentice was a proponent of the sperm donor concept. She was a strong advocate for the practice to be available. However, she took the process a bit further.

"When she first started Xenium she actively sought out and solicited viable sperm and egg donors. Xenium used the facilities at Genstar to do the actual in vitro fertilization.

"Her program was different than the norm as she worked for people that wanted children but either didn't want or were unable to carry a child to term. She would find surrogates to actually carry the babies until they were born. The parents of the child paid Xenium handsomely for the service and in turn, Mrs. Prentice paid the other parties involved while maintaining a respectable profit for Xenium.

"In the beginning that was the full extent of Xenium operations. It was arguably performing a needed service to a niche market, and the business was doing well and growing. Mrs. Prentice had taken twenty five million dollars from Genstar to get the ball rolling and was in the process of starting to pay dividends to Genstar. Genstar was the primary investor in Xenium.

"As the business continued to grow George Snyder came into the picture. In a very short time George Snyder was working at Genstar and was a key figure in Xenium. As time progressed, Mrs. Prentice's involvement started to dwindle and Snyder's grew.

"Not long ago the business made a sudden change in its operations. It was still involved in the same basic business but the business model changed.

"The sperm and egg side of the business was conducted completely outside of Genstar. The rate they paid to the surrogates vanished and the price to the would-be parents increased."

Chameleon paused before continuing, "The operations were

maintained in offices locally. Everything outside the business looked to be on the up and up. A lead took us to Mexico and then Peru. We learned that Xenium became engaged in slavery of a sort.

"They were offering young women the opportunity to come up here for free. All they had to do was carry a baby to term. When these young women arrived, they were held captive and in most cases, kept for several pregnancies.

"Indications are that not one single woman has actually made it out of captivity. Naturally, the customers of Xenium know nothing of this aspect of the business and they are never introduced to the surrogate. The outward explanation given is that it is to ensure the anonymity of both parties.

"The demand for adoption of new born babies is high in this country, but it is also very high in other countries around the world. The waiting list through conventional methods is excruciatingly long and the standards for adoption can be very high. Xenium offers an alternative solution. As you can probably imagine, their profitability has gone through the roof.

"Naturally any enterprise that operates under the radar and makes a lot of money tends to attract interest from individuals that, shall we say, have a different set of standards than the civilized peoples of the world. These types of people don't like to have their boat rocked, and tend to deal with problems quite violently."

Connor chuckled at the irony of that statement. Chameleon didn't miss it, "Yes, Mr. Shea, I understand that at this point you think of us as no better than mobsters. I get it, but let me finish. There is much more to tell."

Connor chuckled again, "Yes, Chameleon, please do continue. This is quite the story. I am still unsure however, what any of this has to do with Bart, or me and my family."

Chameleon remained silent for a few moments before continuing. "This whole thing starts with Jill Starling. She worked in the accounting department at Genstar. She was an accounting student and was working there to pay her way through school. It would appear that she found information on Genstar and Xenium, and copied the data.

"In time, she established the alias persona of Leslie Harrison in an attempt to protect her true identity. The whole purpose for her to do so was to blackmail Snyder and anyone else she could find that was associated with the operation.

"Given the financials, I would say Leslie Harrison had been successful at least a few times. However, it would appear that Snyder didn't like being squeezed by her. It would also seem that he became worried about Mrs. Prentice getting the notion of trying something similar, or worse.

"Snyder decided to have Leslie killed and to recover the information. It was his full intent to make it appear as though Bart was the killer. They tried to create a scenario where Bart had been unfaithful and he was the one that was being extorted by Leslie. It would then appear that Leslie was killed to keep her quiet. Snyder thought that he could kill Leslie and have Bart take the fall for it.

"This would have the effect of keeping Mrs. Prentice quiet. She would be informed that Bart could be killed at any time if she did anything to interfere with Snyder's operations.

"The plan was flawed from the beginning. No one that knew Bart would believe him an adulterer. Matters got worse when you decided to investigate. He panicked. That was one thing Snyder didn't count on. He made another mistake in assuming you wouldn't be contacting someone like me and my associates.

"Snyder decided to kill Mr. and Mrs. Prentice and turn that as a warning for you to back off. The photos you received were to add validity to the threat. With them dead and your family at risk, he assumed you would back off. You didn't.

"Now I have one dead associate. Your family is in danger and hiding. There has been an assassination attempt on you. More people died. I am afraid, Mr. Shea, I believe a lot more people are going to die before this is over."

Connor's desire for sarcasm vanished. The full sense of what Chameleon was talking about sank in. Chameleon's words looked like a warning, but sounded more like a threat. Jill Starling may have got the ball rolling, but it was Connor that gave it an extra push for speed. Now there was a huge mess that needed to be cleaned up and he had no idea where to begin. His voice was almost shy, "Now what? Where do we go from here?"

Chameleon was silent and the quiet caught Connor's attention, "Chameleon, are you there? What do we do now?"

Silence continued and Connor looked to Bill who was still standing beside him. Bill smiled and reached forward to remove the headset from Connor's head. Connor resisted as he spoke louder, "Chameleon? Are you there?"

Finally he realized the line was dead and he yielded to Bill. When Bill replaced the headset beside the chair, he ushered Connor out of the CIC and back into the main part of the cabin. When he had closed the door behind them, he looked to Connor, "I'm sorry Mr. Shea, but Chameleon closed the connection."

Connor nodded, "I got that, now what?"

Bill smiled, "For the time being, nothing. Chameleon will be in touch again, of that you can be sure. However, it may be awhile. The question of what we do now is probably the exact question he is asking himself at this very moment.

"This can get very ugly if it is not handled properly. I know he is making sure that whatever he decides will bring this to a desirable conclusion. If there is one thing I have learned about him is that he is meticulous and rarely makes mistakes."

Connor nodded and headed for the main door of the cabin, "I think I need a little air."

"I'm afraid you can't go out there on your own, sir. I will have to escort you."

"Fine, whatever, let's go."

11

Bill had only taken one step before he stopped and raised his hand to the earpiece of his headset. Bill nodded his head a few times unconsciously, and then he smiled and looked at Connor, "Copy that."

Bill lowered his hand and was still smiling, "Well, Mr. Shea, it would appear Chameleon would like you to do a little training. It will of course, be a crash course. It should be entertaining for me if not for you." Bill chuckled lightly.

Connor furrowed his brow, "Training? What on earth for?"

Bill was immediately serious, "Just think of it as a means to assist you in not getting your head blown off. A little instruction now may save your life. Personally, I think it is a hell of a good idea."

Connor nodded quickly. Bill smiled again, "Good, we'll start at the range. We use a few different types of personal defense and assault weapons. You'll be trained in their safe and effective use." Bill continued out of the cabin with Connor close behind. Bill put his hand to his earpiece again and spoke, "Range. Bill. Please lay out a selection for instruction. Thanks."

As they walked, Connor took the opportunity to look at the surroundings. Everything appeared as it would if this were someone's private residence. There were a couple barns, and an older pickup truck and car parked near the cabin. The grounds in the clearing looked surprisingly average, and normal; nothing at all interesting. In the woods around the clearing, a variety of apparatus could be seen. There were the ones Connor had noticed earlier, but there were also others that looked completely different. Everything however, had the distinct look of training tools and appeared well used.

Connor returned his attention to the direction they were walking. To his surprise, they were heading to what appeared to be a beat up old shed. The building was no more than eight feet square. Connor's curiosity piqued as he kept following.

Bill took the handle on the door and pulled it open. The inside of the shed was dark. Only small areas that were exposed by the outside light were illuminated. Bill continued inside and as he did he half turned to Connor, "Watch your step, Mr. Shea, there is a set of stairs just inside the door."

When Connor stepped into the building and the door closed, a light came on. It was much like a refrigerator light, only this one came on when the door was closed. Directly in front of them, was the staircase Bill mentioned. As they made their way down, the light in the shed went out and lights below started coming on. At the bottom of the stairs was a landing with another door. This area consisted of raw concrete and the door was steel. Bill reached out and pushed the button beside the door.

A red light above the door was on, but within a few seconds it turned green and Connor could faintly hear a lock unlatch. Bill pulled the door open. As he did, light from the other side of the door could be seen and the light in the landing went out. Connor was sufficiently impressed. He could certainly see how it would be very difficult to see anything from outside of the shed that would in any way indicate this space lay below the surface.

As they passed through the doorway, Connor saw an eight foot wide walkway that led to another door at the far end. To the right were a couple of doors and beside one of the doors was a window. To their left as they entered were six cubicles lining the full length and they all faced what appeared to be a long tunnel.

The tunnel was the full width of this area and was easily one hundred yards to the far end. From each cubicle there was a line along the ceiling that stretched almost the full depth of the tunnel. Hanging from each was a fresh silhouette target ready for use.

Connor smiled broadly when he realized that he would have the opportunity to fire some very specialized weapons. He had fired guns in the past. He had even gone hunting a few times, but weapons were not something he felt a need to keep around. But here and now he felt like a kid in a candy store and could hardly wait to get started.

As they walked full into the walkway, another man appeared from the windowed room. He was a stocky looking man that Connor estimated to be in his early forties. He wore a plaid shirt, blue jeans and black boots. His salt and pepper hair seemed to make the wrinkles in his face more pronounced. He was clearly a man who had seen far too much in life.

Bill smiled and pointed to him, "Mr. Shea, this is Dan. He is our range officer. He will be your firearms instructor."

Connor smiled and reached out his hand, "Nice to meet you Dan, I'm Connor Shea."

Dan nodded without taking Connor's hand, "Mr. Shea, follow me and we will get started." Dan's voice was deep and colored with the noticeable effects of years of alcohol and tobacco use.

Dan turned away from the two of them and started walking towards the far end of the range. As Connor followed, he noticed a different weapon lay in every other cubicle. He assumed he would be starting at the far end and working his way back down the row towards the door they had originally come through.

Bill pointed to the windowed room, "I'll be in here until you are finished. Have fun."

Connor smiled and nodded without altering his course or speed.

Dan stepped into the third from last cubicle and waited for Connor to join him. His expression was unwavering. On the counter lay a pistol with the barrel pointed down the range with the slide fully back. Next to it were two magazines.

When Connor was in the cubicle Dan picked up the pistol, "This little beauty is the Beretta M9 nine millimeter semi-automatic with a ten round magazine. It is a very commonly used sidearm and as such most of us have been using it or a variation of it for most of our careers."

He turned the weapon so that Connor could see the side of it, "This little switch allows the weapon to be easily disassembled for cleaning and this button releases the magazine. Be very careful when using this weapon in close quarters. A trained operative could drop the magazine and remove the slide while you are holding this weapon in your hands and pointing it at him. That could lead to an unfortunate conclusion."

Dan hesitated for a moment to allow those words to sink in. The broad smile Connor was wearing shrank. Dan nodded knowing Connor understood and he reached for one of the magazines and held the open end pointed towards Connor, "Alright then. This magazine is empty and so is the chamber, but it is never wise to assume any weapon is empty, ever. Watch me and my hands as I insert the magazine; Pay close attention." Dan continued to point the Beretta down the range with the barrel pointed slightly upwards. With his other hand, he inserted the magazine and released the slide. "This weapon is now loaded and ready to fire. Did you see what I did? Do you have any questions?"

Connor nodded, "Looks simple enough."

Dan just nodded and released the magazine, secured the slide and placed it back on the counter. "Alright Mr. Shea, give it a try."

Connor moved forward and did precisely as he had seen Dan demonstrate. Dan smiled for the first time, "Very good Mr. Shea. Just

Deadly Truth

like an old pro. Now remove the magazine and secure the weapon."

Connor mimicked Dan again. When the Beretta and magazine were on the counter Dan reached forward and removed the empty magazine. "Alright, Mr. Shea, load your weapon."

Connor was far more nervous. It wasn't a big deal working with an empty magazine, but a full one put an entirely different feel on the process. He didn't let the insecurity stop him though and he prepared the weapon the same as he had done the first time. He stood still with the weapon pointed down the range.

Dan nodded, "Very good, Mr. Shea. Secure the weapon."

Connor repeated the process and placed the weapon back on the counter. Dan nodded again and pulled two sound cancelling headsets from the hooks on the wall of the cubicle and handed one to Connor. "You are going to need this. Put them on and prepare the weapon."

As Connor complied, Dan pushed a button on the side of the counter and the silhouette target started its way down the track. At about fifty feet it stopped. Connor was holding the weapon in a ready position and looked towards Dan, "Really? That seems a long way off?"

Dan smiled, "It does, doesn't it? Fire now."

Connor concentrated on the target and regulated his breathing before he fired five rounds fairly quickly, and then lowered the weapon. Dan chuckled and pushed the button to bring the target back to them. Connor was shocked to see that not one round had hit the target. Dan saw the look on his face and smiled broadly, "Not as easy as it looks on TV is it?"

Dan pushed the button again and moved the target back out to twenty feet this time.

"Alright, Mr. Shea, empty your weapon on the target."

Connor fired five times before the weapon grew silent. Dan pushed the button on the counter again to retrieve the target, "Secure your weapon, Mr. Shea."

Connor complied and then looked at the target. He had at least hit the paper this time. One round had gone over the shoulder, one round was in the chin and the other three were fairly close together in the middle of the chest area.

Dan nodded, "Good. I'm calling those four kill shots."

He reached his hand under the counter and pulled out a box of cartridges and placed it on the counter. He opened the box as he retrieved the empty magazine from his pocket. "Pay attention, Mr. Shea, this is how you reload a magazine." Connor watched intently as Dan pushed the first five rounds in, then he handed the magazine to Connor, "Finish it."

Connor complied immediately. Dan nodded again when Connor had finished, "Very good, Mr. Shea. You can reload the other magazine as well. There is the remainder of this box of cartridges and another full box below on the shelf. Empty both boxes. Adjust the distance of the target. Practice, practice, practice, this is all the training you are getting with this weapon, so use your time wisely. When you are finished we'll move on to the MP5. I think you will really enjoy that one."

For the next couple hours Connor trained on the MP5 and the AA-12 Combat Shotgun and fired hundreds of rounds of ammunition. When he had finished, he and Dan joined Bill in the range office. For the next half hour they ate and discussed the weapons Connor had been using.

Several other weapons had been laid out in other cubicles, but Connor would not be taking lessons on those. Dan told Connor that for the amount of time he would be with them, the three weapons he had learned would be sufficient and he informed him that in spite of how much he now knew of those three weapons, there was still more he could learn. That was, however, far more advanced training and Connor would not be receiving that.

After they had finished eating, Dan took Connor back out to the first three weapons. There were several hundred more rounds sitting with each weapon. Connor smiled, and Dan snickered, "Take your time, Mr. Shea. Practice some more. Practice disassembling the weapons and reassembling them. Practice loading and securing, and lastly enjoy blowing those paper tags to hell. I'll be in the range office with Bill. Have fun."

Connor fired round after round after round. His initial enthusiasm was now being replaced with growing fatigue. Dan and Bill had been watching Connor closely for just this sign. Finally, they left the office and went to Connor. Bill tapped him on the shoulder, "Alright, Mr. Shea, I think that is enough for today. It has been a long one. I think you could use a little sleep. Tomorrow we will move on to bladed weapons, hand to hand, some agility work and the ever-enjoyable obstacle course. You think you are tired now, just wait until tomorrow."

Bill smiled and slapped Connor on the shoulder.

Connor half smiled, "I'm gonna be a full blown soldier of fortune in no time."

Bill belly laughed, "Not even close, sir, not even close." Bill composed himself, "Seriously though, with this training your chance of survival if we see action is about one in one hundred. Without the training your chances would be nil. I think it is time well spent."

Connor nodded, and spoke sarcastically, "That's comforting." He paused for a second before continuing, "You guys really enjoy this stuff don't you."

Bill shook his head, "Not really. We do enjoy the work we do, but frankly, I think pretty much every one of us would really prefer if we didn't need to use our training. Unfortunately, the nature of our work puts us in harm's way and we all accept that. We train hard because our lives depend on it, and we pray every day that we don't have to use it."

Connor started walking towards the door they had originally come through, "That sounds very lonely."

Bill followed close behind, "This work is not conducive to romantic relationships and families if that is what you mean."

Connor half smiled, "Yeah, that too."

***

Angela, Elaine, Simon and Janet Elaine laughed and talked over dinner. As promised the food was great and the variety was unexpected. Even as picky an eater as Janet Elaine was, she managed to find a veritable feast to her liking.

With their meal now finished and nothing but time on their hands, the family chose to simply sit and enjoy each other's company. The whole while, in the back of Angela's mind, her thoughts were of Connor.

She had no idea where he was or what he was doing. She couldn't even be sure he was still alive, but she assumed that if anything bad had happened, they would tell her. Still it was all she could do to mask her concern in front of the family.

Elaine could see the pain her daughter felt. She wanted desperately to talk to her and try to reassure her, but she knew that there were no words she could use that would accomplish that. She knew that the best thing to do at this time was simply to be together as a family and make the most of the situation.

Samantha came into the mess hall and walked casually up to the table. Her smile was as warm as ever as she looked towards Elaine, "I hope you enjoyed your meal."

Everyone nodded and gave thanks.

Samantha nodded, "That's great. Next door is a rec hall. There is a TV, some movies, some books, games and some arts and crafts stuff." She paused as she looked towards Janet Elaine, "How would you like to come with me and we can make something for Mommy?"

Janet Elaine smiled broadly as she looked to Angela in anticipation. Angela smiled back warmly, "Of course, my dear. You run along and have fun with Samantha. Grandma and Grandpa and I will be over in a few minutes."

Janet Elaine wasted no time leaving the table, taking Samantha's hand and walking out of the mess hall.

When the door closed, Elaine looked to Angela, "How are you holding up, dear? I know how hard this must be for you. Try to have faith that everything will work out fine."

Angela nodded and smiled, "I know Mom. I just can't help wondering why this kind of stuff keeps happening to us. When will it ever stop?"

Elaine had no words to offer and instead reached her hand out to Angela's head and drew her into a hug, "I don't know, sweetheart. I have no idea."

Angela pulled away from her mother quickly, "Janet. I have to call Janet. She must be worried sick." Angela pulled out her cell phone and looked at the screen. There was no cell service on the island and she groaned with frustration. Elaine raised her hand and gently pushed Angela's down, "You know we can't contact anyone until this is all over. You know that, Angela."

Angela nodded, "I know, but its Janet."

Elaine nodded knowingly, "I know dear, but no one."

Angela's frustration came through her voice, "Doesn't matter anyway, there is no service here."

***

Janet stared at the newspaper with shock enveloping her face. Mike sat across the table from her enjoying a fresh cup of coffee. The look on Janet's face gave him instant concern. "What is it Janet?"

Janet shook her head, "I can't believe it. Bart is dead and now Leigh Ann is dead; murdered." She continued to stare blankly at the newspaper when a single tear escaped her eye and made its way down her cheek.

She raised her head to look at Mike, "I have to see Angela. She must be a mess."

Mike nodded without saying a word. He usually had some comment or other about just about everything, but he had nothing to say at this moment.

Janet rose from the table and went to the phone and tapped in the number for the Shea's house. The phone rang repeatedly over and over without being answered. Frustrated, Janet ended the call and tapped in Angela's cell number. A recording answered quickly, "The customer you are trying to reach is out of the service area. Sorry for any inconvenience."

Janet ended the call abruptly. She stood for a moment staring at the phone before putting it down and picking up her address book. She found Connor's office number and tapped it into her phone. The phone rang repeatedly for an unbearable length of time before Janet gave up and ended the call. She looked towards Mike again, "They aren't answering their phones. Even Connor's office isn't answering. Something is very wrong. I have to go to the house."

Mike nodded compassionately, at least as compassionately as he was able. Janet expected a little more from him and shook her head as she headed out of the house.

When he heard the door close, Mike reached across the table to pick up the newspaper. The story of the Prentice murders were headline news. He read the story carefully without emotion. When he was finished he put the paper down and rubbed his chin in thought.

***

Janet arrived at Angela's house and rushed to the front door. The door was locked and that surprised her. She rang the doorbell repeatedly without response. She cursed under her breath as she reached into her clutch, pulled out her set of the house keys and opened the door.

She walked throughout the house calling for Angela. Silence filled the space where an expected response should be. Everything in the house appeared to be in order. Nothing looked out of place, except in the kitchen.

A meal was on the counter. It was strange for the dishes to not have been cleared away. Janet's concern was increasing as she reached for the house phone. First she called Angela's cell, but was only met with the same out of area message.

Next she dialed Connor's office. The phone rang repeatedly before the answering service finally answered, "Xavier Holdings. How may I help you?"

Janet controlled her voice, "I would like to speak to Connor Shea, please."

The woman on the end spoke matter-of-factly, "I'm sorry, the offices are closed for the next two weeks. If you would like to leave a message, I will forward it to Mr. Shea on his return."

Janet hung up. She knew his offices were rarely closed during normal business hours and today was not a holiday.

She stood at the counter thinking for a moment before tapping in Elaine's number. If anyone would know where Angela was and what was going on, it would be her. The call was met with only the sound of the phone ringing.

Worry was now replaced with panic. She couldn't recall a time when she ever called the list and was unable to reach someone. Her hands were shaking as she dialed her home number.

Mike answered quickly, "Hello?"

Janet's despair filled her voice, "They are all gone. There is no one here. I tried Elaine's and Connor's office and everything. They aren't anywhere. I am really scared."

Mike talked in a calming manner, "Alright, Janet. You need to come home now. I'm sure they are fine and that there is a very logical explanation for this. Angela will call you as soon as she is able. You know that. Given the news of the Prentice's, they are probably shook up and needed to get away for a bit."

Janet calmed down a little, "Alright, Mike, alright. I am on my way home. We have to find out what is going on. I am really scared."

Mike nodded into the phone, "I know you are, sweetheart. I know. Come home."

Janet nodded in response, "I'll be there in a few minutes. I love you."

Mike smiled, "I love you too. See you shortly."

Mike ended the call and then searched through his address book. He found the number of Richard Johnson quickly and hit send.

Mike remembered Richard from when he was security for Angela's corporate offices. He had also been instrumental is tracking down Angela's biological father all those years ago. Mike was sure that if he talked to him and told him what was going on, he would have a much better idea of how they should proceed.

Richard answered on the second ring, "Hello, Mike. What can I do for you?"

Mike chuckled, "Really, you have me in your address book after all this time. Cool. Anyway, I need your opinion on something concerning Angela and Connor Shea. Do you have a couple minutes for a little chat?"

Richard smiled into the phone, ignoring Mike's surprise, "Certainly. How are Angela and Connor these days? I haven't seen them in some time."

Mike nodded lightly, "Well, up until a day or so ago I would say they were outstanding, however, something has come up that concerns Janet and me. You heard about the Prentice murders I trust?"

Richard was hesitant. He remembered all too well the troubles Angela has experienced in her life and didn't like the sound of where this conversation was heading. "Yes, Mike. I have read a bit about it. Why? Don't tell me Angela and Connor are somehow mixed up in this."

Mike sighed noticeably as he began to update Richard on the events of the last several days.

***

Mike had finished talking to Richard by the time Janet got home. He was still sitting in the same spot as he had been when Janet left. The worry on Janet's face was clear.

Mike cleared his throat to speak, "Sit, Janet, sit. Catch your breath."

Janet just nodded as she continued into the kitchen and sat next to Mike.

Mike smiled again, "I was just on the phone with Richard Johnson. You remember him, I imagine? Anyway, I told him everything we know and he said that we shouldn't worry. He would make a few calls and see what he can find out and he will get back to us." Mike paused for a moment, "Richard does have connections. I think he will be more effective than us in finding out what, if anything, is going on."

Janet nodded quietly for a moment before she spoke, "Maybe I should call my Dad. He has connections too. He could find out everything."

Mike shook his head immediately, "No. I like your father and all, but his people are…" Mike cleared his throat, "I'm sure Connor would prefer to take it easy and go slow. If there is anything wrong, Richard will find it. If things get, err, nasty, we can call your father. Is that okay, Janet."

If Janet's father was anyone other than who he was, she would have been offended, but he wasn't anyone's normal father so Janet understood what Mike was trying to avoid saying, "Alright, Mike. I won't say anything to him… for now."

Mike smiled and nodded, "That is all I ask. This entire conversation is probably for naught anyway."

Janet nodded as she left the table.

12

Three days had passed since Connor had arrived at this camp. As much as he was enjoying this testosterone amusement park, he was missing Angela and Janet Elaine. He was also becoming anxious about when they would be moving against Xenium.

Every time he asked Bill about it, he would get the same response. "Soon. Chameleon is working out the details."

That answer was losing credibility with Connor. In fact he was losing faith that these people would actually be able to do anything positive to bring this situation to resolution.

Connor finished dressing and headed into the main part of the cabin for breakfast. Bill was already eating when Connor sat down.

Bill looked over and smiled, "Good morning, sir. Chameleon said he would be calling you today. I hope you had a good sleep. Today may be busy."

Connor looked at Bill suspiciously, "Really? That would be awesome. Obviously you have already talked to him and know what is going to happen?"

Bill nodded, "I have been talking to him several times a day since you arrived. I have let him know how you are progressing in your training and you're over all spirits. I do know he has something in the works and wants your input."

Connor smiled, "Finally. This is fun and all but I am really missing my family."

"Of course, sir, we do understand, but you were told at the outset it may take awhile. Frankly, I am surprised things are happening this quickly. More often than not, operations of this nature take weeks to plan and then weeks more of specialized training before we can even begin. You should consider yourself lucky that we are moving so quickly on this one."

Connor wanted to say something further, but refrained and smiled instead. He sat quietly for the rest of his meal, not offering any conversation, nor joining in the conversation of the others at the table.

Finally someone came out of the CIC and summoned Connor, "Mr. Shea, Chameleon is online and would like to talk to you."

Connor nodded as he rose from the table. He took his coffee mug over to the counter and poured himself a fresh cup before following the man into the room.

The refilling of his cup was more a control move than any real desire for more coffee. Connor didn't know if anyone caught it, but he felt pleasure in making it appear as if he would do things in his own good time and not simply respond to a beckoning.

Connor sat in the chair facing the screen and put on the headset that hung on the side of the chair. The coffee had been placed on the small table beside the chair. He doubted he would be drinking any of it at the moment.

"Good morning, Chameleon. I hope you have some good news for me?"

There were a few moments of silence then Chameleon came online, "Good morning, Mr. Shea, I hope you are finding our hospitality acceptable."

Connor realized Chameleon hadn't been online when he had first spoken, "As acceptable as can be expected given the circumstances. I do hope you have some good news for me."

Chameleon chuckled, "I'm not sure it is good news, Mr. Shea. Snyder and Xenium are still very much looking for you. It would appear they would really like you to vanish, permanently. It also appears we have angered them."

It was Connor's turn to snicker, "No doubt. All I want is for this whole mess to just go away. I want my life back and I want my family back."

Chameleon was silent for a few moments before he continued, "I do understand, Mr. Shea. I truly do. Unfortunately at the moment that is not a possibility. The organization involved in this has a very long reach. It isn't simply a matter of Snyder and Xenium. There are individuals on three continents with a hand in this pie.

"I have managed to identify the main players and their extent of involvement. Many of these men I have had dealings with in the past. They know me and what I am capable of. I believe that will be to our advantage as we move forward. Many of the Europeans are sensible individuals and I am certain I can settle them down without incident.

"I am only familiar with a few of the people working in South and Central America and locally. The ones down south are a vicious bunch. If they think for one minute we are in a position to threaten them, they will remove the heads of everyone around them without hesitation just to silence them.

"The locals are loosely connected to a relatively smaller organization. They are a nasty bunch in their own right, but they are not targets that will pose much of a threat to my team. I have amassed information on their global operations, but only in very general terms. I cannot cite specific dates, locations or give many names. However, there is sufficient information to act.

"I will also be sending copies of the information to the various national investigation services in the various countries. I expect that will alert the respective organizations involved and they will become very busy in protecting themselves. Hopefully, that will be sufficient to curtail their operations, at least for the time being."

Connor nodded, "Alright that sounds good, but what about me and my family?"

Chameleon was quiet for a moment. Connor was anxious, "Chameleon? My family?"

Connor could hear Chameleon take a deep breath, "The major syndicates will not pose a problem like I said. They have too much at stake to expose themselves in a relatively minor business problem. I honestly believe they will be willing to walk away from their investments rather than risk further investigative impairments.

"However, the locals, the Mexicans and the Peruvians are a whole other matter. They are not going to back down. This is their whole business and you are a serious threat. We will have to deal with them much differently. I'm afraid, you will be in harm's way. Do you understand what I am saying, Mr. Shea?"

Connor responded solidly, "I do. I am ready. I will do whatever I have to do."

Chameleon was less sure, "Mr. Shea, you have been training quite heavily for the last several days, but believe me, the real deal is much different than anything we can simulate. I do not believe you have the first inkling of what you will be witnessing or doing. I would not be so anxious to jump into the fray, as it were. We are doing nothing short of declaring war on individuals that have no morals, and no rules. They will stop at nothing to protect their interests."

Connor was silent for a moment before he spoke, "I do understand, Chameleon, I really do. I know I don't really know what to expect, but I do know that I have to do something or my family and I will never be able to enjoy any kind of normal life."

Chameleon sighed, "Alright Mr. Shea. You are their principal interest.

You are the one they are focused on, so I intend to give you to them."

Connor was a little shocked and attempted levity, "Seriously, you want to hand me over to them? This is your great idea? I don't think I like this plan."

Chameleon chuckled at Connor's attempt, "Not exactly, but I will keep that in mind if things get too ugly."

Connor laughed, "Okay, what is the plan?"

Instead of Chameleon responding through the headset, his voice boomed over the loudspeakers in the room, "Clear the CIC, Mr. Shea and Bill remain, all others exit. Thank you."

There was no hesitation in the room. Those that were monitoring computers or working within the room left their stations and exited quickly. When the door was closed, Bill walked over and ensured it was locked before he spoke, "We are secure."

Chameleon continued over the loudspeaker, "Alright, this is going to require some careful maneuvering. There is no margin for error. Is that understood?"

Bill nodded, "Understood, sir."

Connor nodded silently.

Chameleon spoke slowly and deliberately, "Mr. Shea, you will be contacting Snyder. I will provide you with the number. You will arrange a meeting. I will give you the location. We will be returning you to your home to make this happen.

"You will make the call from your house phone. This will show them that you are in play once again. Things are going to get ugly from there on out. Are you prepared to put yourself in the line of fire? Are you prepared to possibly turning Mrs. Shea's family home into a battlefield? Are you prepared to possibly widowing your lovely wife?"

Connor was silent for a moment as he considered Chameleon's questions, "Are these the only options? Have you looked at every possible scenario?"

Chameleon chuckled, "This is what I do, Mr. Shea, so yes. I am only interested in ending this as quickly and as cleanly as possible. Law enforcement will also be involved. The odds are that you will survive and your home will remain standing. I say should because these things, once started, tend to take on a life all their own, and sometimes the unexpected happens needing a contingency that hadn't be planned for. We are prepared to begin operations in one hour. Are you ready, Mr. Shea?"

Connor didn't hesitate this time, "Yes. Let's get this going. What is the plan?"

Chameleon cleared his throat.

***

It was just before noon when the choppers landed at the house. Connor, Bill, Lance and another man exited the first helicopter. The second chopper contained four heavily armed men. All of them, except Connor were dressed in full black field gear.

The four from the second helicopter joined Lance and the other man from Connor's helicopter. They did a quick overview of their weapons and a map of the grounds before splitting up and heading to what would be their defensive positions.

Connor and Bill continued to the house, and were inside within seconds. The weapons Connor had chosen was the Beretta which was holstered under his sports coat along with a MP5.

Without speaking, the two split up, weapons drawn and began the task of checking the house for intruders. Once satisfied the house was clear, Connor made his way to the security systems room and reviewed the recordings for the last few days.

The video monitors recorded a very worried Janet wandering around the house. Connor spoke sympathetically, "Damn. Janet. She must be worried sick. I doubt anyone told her anything."

Bill saw what Connor was looking at, "Is she clean?"

Connor chuckled, "Who, Janet? She can be pretty obnoxious, but yes, she is fine. She is Angela's best friend in the world. I would really like to let her know everything is okay so she doesn't worry."

Bill stared at the screen blankly for a few moments, "I will contact Chameleon and he can get word to her. Will that be satisfactory?"

Connor nodded, "Thank you."

Bill nodded his satisfaction in return before turning and beginning the electronics sweep of the house to ensure there were no hidden transmitters. Every check was backed up by a different check until Bill was satisfied that there were no listening devices in the house.

Bill moved back to the door they had come through and waved in Lance and the other man. Without speaking the two quickly went through the house ensuring all doors and window were secure and alarms were properly set. Once that was completed, they returned to the outside of the house and took their positions.

The house and the grounds had now been thoroughly checked for vulnerabilities. The team members set up their patrols and stations. The majority of the men were in the back, with only two men moving to positions at the front of the house. Chameleon's initial assessment of the house proved correct and the expected entry point, if there was going to be one, was through the back.

Connor went to the sitting room and picked up the phone and dialed the number Chameleon had provided. The phone rang several times, but was never answered. After a dozen rings or so, Connor hung up. And spoke into his headset mouthpiece, "The call has been made, no answer."

Chameleon responded, "Copy that, Mr. Shea. Hang tough, I'm sure we'll be hearing from him soon."

Connor nodded instinctively and turned to Bill, "I might as well put on the coffee and have a bite to eat. We have some time to kill."

Bill smiled, "Sounds good. I could eat."

***

Two hours passed before Connor's headset filled with Chameleon's voice, "Are you still with us Mr. Shea?"

Connor laughed, "Yes, still here. What's happening?"

Chameleon spoke without emotion, "Federal and local law enforcement have been notified. Interpol has been notified, and federal authorities in Peru and Mexico have been notified.

"Our surveillance teams have spotted a significant increase in traffic to a warehouse at the docks that is owned by the local syndicate connected to Xenium. There also seems to be an increase in security traffic at the Xenium facility. At this moment all traffic has been inbound, and nothing outbound. It also appears strategic response units and federal officers are gearing up for action as well. Things are going to be getting busy pretty soon. I hope you are ready."

Connor sounded cavalier, "I was born ready." And he chuckled. He knew there was no turning back now.

"Very well, Mr. Shea, I expect you will be hearing from Snyder soon. Keep positive and this should all be over in a few hours."

"Copy that. Standing by."

Minutes later the phone rang and Connor deliberately waited for three rings before he picked it up, "Hello?"

The voice on the other end was deep and confident, "Hello, Mr. Shea, I expect you know who this is. You have been a busy boy. I think we have a problem that needs to be resolved. Wouldn't you agree?"

Connor nodded and remained calm, "I do. I am not interested in your operations, Snyder. I was only interested in clearing Bart's name. Now that he and Leigh Ann are dead, I don't see any need to pursue this any further. Things are getting needlessly out of hand. Can we meet and talk?"

Snyder was silent for a few moments, "You want to meet? Just like that? Excuse me if I am a little confused. Why would I want to meet with you?"

Connor responded in his best professionally toned voice, "I think it would be in the best interest of both of us. This mess can go away if we are willing to work together. What I would like to propose is best said in person rather than over an unsecure phone line. Wouldn't you agree?"

Snyder was silent again for a short time, "Where would you like to meet?"

Connor smiled into the phone, "I don't think either of us want to be seen talking together. The fairgrounds are shut down at the moment for renovations. We could meet at the carousel. I know they aren't working on that area of the park at the moment. Say, in one hour."

Snyder thought carefully before responding, "One hour, then. I trust you will be alone. No cops."

Connor continued smiling, "I swear, no cops."

The phone line went dead and Connor hung up before turning to

Bill, "As you have probably heard, we are a go."

Bill smiled, "It would appear so." He raised his hand to the earpiece of his headset, "We are a go. Delta team get ready."

There was an almost immediate response, "Delta team in position. We are green."

"Copy that." Bill turned to Connor and held his earpiece again, "Chameleon, we are green. Delta team is in position. Bravo and Charlie are locked down."

Chameleon answered quickly, "Copy that. I am contacting law enforcement and getting the right tips to them. Bravo and Charlie advise when they are on the move."

All that came back across the headset was, "copy that" from some unknown voice. Bill nodded to Connor, "It is time to roll, Mr. Shea. Some of Alpha team will remain here. The rest will form Echo. I'll ride with them and we will leave now. You leave in ten minutes. Let's get this party started." He patted Connor on the shoulder as he walked out the front door.

13

Connor arrived at the amusement park and made his way cautiously through the gate nearest to the carousel. His heart rate increased with each step he took. He knew Echo team was here somewhere, but he couldn't see any of them. He knew that Snyder would not come alone. That was the point of Echo, to track down and eliminate any of Snyder's people that may already be here.

This was a dangerous game, and Connor knew there were many things that could still go wrong. He knew what a mistake would cost. Seeing his family safe again was the most important thing to him, so mistakes were not an option.

Connor expected Snyder to be armed and he believed there was a very real chance Snyder would try to kill him. But Connor was armed as well and prepared if Snyder tried anything. Even so, there was still a possibility he would not see Snyder's move early enough to react and prevent it.

He had never before been in a situation like this and had no idea how he would actually react if faced with such a scenario. Connor shook his head lightly. He needed to stop second-guessing his abilities. Doubt right now was more dangerous than a mistake. All the thoughts running through his mind were counterproductive. He knew he was ready. He knew his abilities. He was anticipating Snyder's moves. He was ready.

As Connor approached the carousel he could see a man sitting in one of the seats. Connor was pleased that he had chosen that place as opposed to one of the horses. While it would be fun to sit on the horses, it would expose him too readily to an outside shot.

The man in the carousel looked towards Connor. Connor recognized him as Snyder from the photo he had been shown earlier. Connor smiled lightly; so far things were looking good. He took a deep breath and exhaled slowly as he drew closer. He nervously scanned the surroundings. If there were people ready to attack, Connor couldn't see them. He hoped quietly that Echo had already eliminated any threats.

As Connor came within a few feet of Snyder, a rather large man came from behind the bench and walked towards Connor. Connor stopped in his tracks and looked to Snyder, "I thought this was going to be a friendly meeting."

Snyder smiled, "It is. My associate here is going ensure that is the case. I do not like surprises, Shea."

The large man pulled an electronic wand from under his coat and ordered Connor to raise his arms. Connor complied hesitantly.

Immediately the wand identified the gun Connor had concealed under his coat and the man reached in and pulled it from its holster and showed it to Snyder.

Snyder shook his head, "My my, Shea, so much for this being a friendly conversation."

Connor was glad he had decided to the leave the MP5 in the car. The man put the weapon is his belt and ran the wand over Connor again. When he was finished he turned back to Snyder and nodded his head.

Snyder smiled, "Come join me, Shea. Let's have a chat. My associate will stay close to ensure there are no other surprises."

Connor's smile was barely more than a sneer as he climbed onto the carousel and sat across from Snyder, "I was just being careful, Snyder. Now it would appear you are the only one here with a weapon."

Snyder took hold of the lapel on either side of his jacket and opened them wide for Connor to see inside, "I'm not carrying, Shea. You can relax. We can have our little chat now that I know you are unarmed and have no wires. So what is it you would like to discuss?"

Connor remained as composed as he was able considering how vulnerable he now felt, "I would like to find an amiable way to resolve our mutual problem. As you are aware, I have been trying to clear Bart's name, but frankly, now that he and Leigh Ann are gone, there is really no point."

Connor hesitated for a moment and Snyder waited patiently for Connor to continue, "I am a businessman, Snyder. I always have been. When I come across an enterprise that interests me, I like to get involved. Your business looks very intriguing to me. I have resources that could be of use to you."

Snyder chuckled lightly, "I see. So you want to make a business proposition, is that it? Well, Shea, as interesting an idea as that is, I find it very unlikely you would actually join us. Besides, I have associates with all the reach and resources I could possibly need. I must say I am curious, though. I would like to hear more about your suggestion. I think it would be helpful if you tell me what exactly you think you know about our business. Then you can tell me what you think you can offer to improve it."

Connor wanted to swallow, but didn't dare. He could feel his heart rate increasing and tried to use the techniques he had been taught to keep it under control. At this moment, a fast heart rate, sweating or other miniscule twitches could tip his hand.

He focused hard and tried to sound confident. "Xenium has taken the sperm donor principle to the next level. You are managing all aspects of the process. You have access to viable sperm or egg donors and you have capable surrogates to carry the in vitro fertilized eggs to term. From what I can see your costs are quite minimal, and your clients appear to be willing to pay handsomely."

Connor took a breath before continuing, "It is really quite a nice operation. You give a couple the opportunities to provide either the sperm, or the egg, or both and you have willing individuals to carry the child through term. This frees the parents to prepare for their new child without the inconvenience of actually having to carry it. Brilliant really. I'm surprised no one else is doing it already. With my resources we could expand the operations further."

Snyder stared at Connor for a few moments. The look on his face suggested he was debating whether or not he wanted to believe what Connor was saying. With what has happened over the last several days, he was finding it difficult to believe Connor was actually looking to join forces.

"So Shea, you are willing to forget about Jill and Bart and Leigh Ann, and put up significant capital and expertise to expand our operations. I have a man over here that is armed and fully prepared to kill you and you want me to believe none of that matters to you? You want me to believe you just want to make some money with us? That is what you are telling me?"

Connor nodded without hesitation.

Snyder shook his head, "I have checked you out quite thoroughly and I doubt you are the kind of man that would be involved in an operation like ours. The... let's say... hidden costs of this business are quite, hmm, significant. I am not naive enough to think you would be interested in being involved in the occasional asset disposal this business requires."

Connor knew it was critical at this point to remain as composed as possible, "I see. I understand. You know your business far better than I. As such, you know what assets you do and do not need. I am not so egotistical to be insulted at this point.

"I am quite happy to just walk away. I have no interest in making life difficult for you. I don't need that in my life. I am willing to pay to have you leave us alone and forget we ever met, if that is what is needed."

Snyder laughed, "Now, Shea, that makes much more sense to me. That sounds more like something Connor Shea would say. Of course the answer is no. You are a loose end that I really can't have hanging around. I'm sure you can understand that. It isn't personal. It is simply business. Unfortunately you have brought your family into this and they too are issues I can't have all of you running around. I am sorry, Shea, but you really should have minded your own business."

Snyder looked to the man in the black jacket and nodded. The man approached Connor and as he did he pulled Connor's own weapon from his belt and aimed it at Connor's head.

Without a sound the man reeled and fell to the ground. Blood escaped his chest as he lay motionless. The suddenness of the shot caught Connor by surprise and he gasped. During that moment Snyder rose from the bench and started running. Connor quickly recovered, composed himself, and jumped off the carousel.

He grabbed his gun from the dead man and ran after Snyder. He raised his gun and fired. Snyder took the shot in the leg and fell to the ground. Connor arrived beside him just as Snyder was pulling a gun from a holster strapped to his calf.

Connor didn't hesitate and fired his weapon again. His round caught Snyder in the chest. Snyder rolled from the impact and rested face down on the ground. His weapon lay loose under his hand. Connor stood over him, his weapon pointed at Snyder's head. He kicked away the gun Snyder had drawn before kneeling and placing his fingers on Snyder's juggler to check for a pulse.

Bill was approaching quickly and called to Connor, "Don't touch him. No prints."

Connor retracted his hand and looked at Snyder, "Nice shot, Mr. Shea."

Connor chuckled, "Not really, I was aiming for his shoulder."

Bill chuckled, "Well, it is better this way, no loose ends. But we need to clear out of here, now. The police will be here soon and we don't want to have to explain all the bodies lying around this park."

Connor nodded as he stood. He hesitated as he pointed his weapon at Snyder's head and stared down the barrel. Bill stopped and looked towards Connor, "With all due respect, Mr. Shea, if you take that shot, you will be crossing into a place you really don't want to go. He is gone. You killed him honorably, don't go psycho on me."

Connor chuckled and looked to Bill, "I have no intention of pulling the trigger, Bill. I am satisfied."

Bill smiled, turned and started walking. A gunshot rang out and Bill turned quickly with his weapon drawn. He saw Connor looking down at what was left of Snyder's head. Connor had taken the shot after all, "That's for threatening my family."

Connor put the weapon in his holster and walked in Bill's direction. Bill stared at him and Connor spoke calmly, "What do want from me?" Connor didn't miss a step. Bill shook his head and followed him out of the park.

Connor walked to the driver's side of his car, but Bill called out to him, "I'll be driving now, Mr. Shea, we are not finished yet."

Connor looked at Bill with surprise, "What? What do we have to do now?"

"Clean up. Please get in the passenger side quickly. We have to move. The police are on their way."

Connor nodded and ran around the passenger side of the car. Bill brought it to life and pulled quickly away, being careful not to squeal the tires. Half a block in front of them was the vehicle holding the rest of Echo team.

The two cars moved quickly, but cautiously through the streets to an area of warehouses. There didn't appear to be much activity as the two cars pulled through an open door of one of the buildings. The door closed rapidly behind them as both vehicles continued through the warehouse and then out the other side into the back of a forty-foot trailer and came to a stop.

The back doors of the trailer were closed quickly by some unseen individuals and secured. Within seconds Connor could feel the movement of the trailer pulling away from the building. He smiled as he realized they were now concealed and moving to a more secure location.

Bill held his hand to the earpiece of his headset, "Chameleon, Echo. We have six pikes down, zero angels, loaded and moving."

Bill nodded a few times before speaking, "Copy that."

He removed the headset and handed it to Connor, "He would like to talk to you."

Connor smiled and put the headphones on, "Connor here."

Chameleon spoke confidently, "Congratulations on a successful mission, Mr. Shea. I wanted to let you know that all the various agencies responded to the tips they have received from me. The Europeans are shutting down quickly and quietly. The surrogate slaves have been found and released. The syndicate that was holding them went down without a fight.

"The Mexican and Peruvians are currently in firefights with their federal agencies, but I don't think they will be around much longer.

"A raid on Xenium was successful and the feds are busy sorting out what exactly they have. All of these agencies are going to be a tad busy piecing together what exactly has happened. As we speak, each of them has been informed of the others operations. There will be a lot of questions, but the entire Xenium organization has been shut down, and it is all thanks to you."

Connor beamed, "Thank you, Chameleon. Thank you for doing all of this and thank you to all your men. I don't really know how I can repay you."

Chameleon chuckled, "You are welcome, Mr. Shea, but don't worry, I know exactly how you are going to repay me. This isn't over quite yet. You are currently on your way to a facility where you will change your clothes and clean up. I don't want you going home covered in blood and gunpowder residue.

"I can guarantee you will be getting a visit from the police. They will have some questions for you. Bill will be briefing you on all of that while you are in transit. Pay close attention. The next few hours are critical for you. If all goes well, your family should be home tomorrow evening. Is that clear, Mr. Shea."

Connor nodded, "Perfectly, Chameleon. Thank you again."

The radio went dead and Connor removed the headset and returned it to Bill. Bill took it and held out his open hand again. Connor looked at it for a moment, and then he smiled and removed the gun from under his coat and placed it in Bill's waiting hand, "Guess I really won't need that anymore. I hope."

Bill smiled cautiously, "I don't think so, sir. We will be arriving in about twenty minutes. I need to go over a few things with you. Please listen carefully. We really don't have time for me to repeat anything."

Connor nodded and smiled.

14

When Connor arrived home Alpha team was gone. The house was locked and completely empty. This is the first time in several days that Connor felt completely alone. It felt good but at the same time a little empty.

He headed into the kitchen to get something to eat. As he prepared a snack and ate, he recalled the events at the park. He remembered how nervous he was. He remembered how scared he was when he lost his gun. But more importantly he remembered looking down the barrel and watching Snyder's head as the bullet entered it.

He recalled how it seemed to jump slightly off the pavement. He remembered the blood and the mess. He remembered the sound the gun made when it went off and he believed he could even hear the sound of the skull shattering.

At this moment he felt a shiver run through his body. It felt cold and uncomfortable. He tried to ignore it, but it came in waves, over and over again until finally he threw himself face down in the sink and emptied the contents of his stomach.

The image of the head flashed through his mind again, and again he heaved. He couldn't get the image out of his mind and every time it flashed through his mind's eye his stomach heaved violently.

Even after there was nothing left to throw up, the images continued to flash and his body continued to convulse. He didn't believe he was feeling guilt, yet there was no mistaking his reactions. Mercifully he finally sank to his knees and passed out on the floor.

His sleep was not restful. Images of the last several days continued to flash through his mind. Images of the training, images of the park, and imaginary images of what he thought the captive surrogates were going through, images of the man in the park being felled by the high caliber sniper round, the images of Snyder, and as they repeated the sound of knocking filtered into the images.

The images repeated in random order over and over then bells started finding their way into the dreams. Connor convulsed on the floor as the images flashed and flashed and flashed through his mind. Connor felt someone grab him and his mind searched for whom it could be. Finally he realized it was someone outside of his mind.

He woke with a start and standing above him was detective Davidson. There was a distinct look of concern on Davidson's face, "You okay, Shea. You look like crap."

Connor's eyes darted around as he tried to focus and get his bearings. Finally he nodded, "Yes, detective, I am fine. A really bad dream is all, thank you."

Davidson nodded, "Do you often have naps in the kitchen below a sink filled with puke?"

Connor pulled himself together and chuckled convincingly, "Well detective, to be honest with you, far more than I would like to admit. You do know I own a bar, right?"

Davidson laughed knowingly, then became instantly serious, "That must be great booze, can't smell that at all."

By this time Connor had regained his feet and was looking down the front of his clothes. To his delight he was clean. The counter area too, was clean. The entire mess was totally confined to the sink. He smiled as he reached for the faucet, "My aim is certainly improving." He turned on the tap and began rinsing the sink and wished quietly that the memories would go down the drain as well.

Davidson smirked, "I have seen a lot of things in my day, Shea. I have seen this type of thing before as well, so what say we stop pretending you had too much to drink and move this conversation forward, shall we." He pointed towards the doorway into the kitchen, "You remember Williams I'm sure."

Connor nodded towards the other detective, "You are looking well, Williams."

Williams chuckled, "Thanks. You look like you have seen better days. Where is your delightful wife? I hear you have a daughter now too?"

Connor nodded. Color was starting to come back to his face, "Yes, I have a daughter. Her name is Janet Elaine. She and her mother and Angela's parents are out of town for a few days. Angela and I had been on vacation for a couple weeks and I needed some alone time to get caught up."

Davidson nodded, "I see. I came to see you a couple days ago. I stopped by your office and no one was there. I came by here and there was no one here. Where were you Mr. Shea?"

Connor chuckled, "You were coming to see me? Why?"

"Where were you Mr. Shea?"

"I was here or at the office most of the time, but yes I did go out from time to time. Sometimes just for a drive along the coast, sometimes for a meal, sometimes to just go somewhere quiet and think. Why, detective? Was I to check in with you or something? What is this all about?"

Davidson searched Connors face for tells. He was sure that if Connor lied he would be able to see it in his face. "No Mr. Shea, you didn't need to check in with me. I am wondering why you are so defensive, though."

Connor laughed, "Gee, I don't know, detective. It feels like you are interrogating me. What is on your mind?"

Davidson looked to Williams for a moment, "There was a shooting in the amusement park a few hours ago. One George Snyder was gunned down. Do you know him Mr. Shea?"

Connor nodded without hesitation, "Yes, I had a conversation with him just today on the carrousel. I assure you detective he was very much alive when I left."

Davidson continued, "Do you own a nine millimeter, Mr. Shea."

Connor shook his head convincingly, "Nine millimeter? That is a gun, right? No, detective I don't own a gun. You would have already checked that and know that I don't. I don't like guns. They scare me. Why?"

Williams spoke quickly, "I see. We did find your fingerprints and Mr. Snyder's prints on the carousel. Perhaps you can share what you were talking about?"

Connor's expressions remained calm, "I am still trying to find Bart and Leigh Ann's killer. Snyder worked for Xenium and Genstar and knew Leigh Ann. I was hoping he would have information that would help me. He didn't. I left."

Williams chuckled unpleasantly, "And you had to meet him in a closed amusement park to find that out? Why was that necessary?"

"Frankly, I have no idea. It was Snyder's idea. I didn't argue the point or question him about it, I just wanted information."

Davidson smiled, "I see. Have you had any further luck in finding the killer, Mr. Shea?"

Connor shook his head in feigned sadness, "I'm afraid not, detective. Every lead I had went cold. I even had a storyboard up in my office to try and make sense of everything, but that proved to be pointless too."

Davidson's smile remained fixed, "Yes, I did see your office. I didn't notice much on the board aside from information about all the victims. I was, however, surprised no one was working when I was there."

Connor smiled, "I gave them all a two week vacation and a bonus. Going into those offices again and spending time there, I realized how much they do and how little acknowledgement they get from me. It seemed the right thing to do."

Williams nodded, "Interesting your timing and all, Shea. In fact, many of the recent coincidences are interesting, wouldn't you say?"

Connor shook his head with genuine surprise, "Coincidences? What do you mean?"

Williams continued, "It just seems interesting that you thrust yourself into this investigation and as you did, very important persons of interest are killed. Do you have any comments about that Mr. Shea?"

Connor shook his head, "I'm afraid I don't, detective. They are just that, coincidence. Clearly someone is being very careful to plug all the holes and cover their tracks. I must have been getting close to something."

Williams smiled, "That is pretty much what we were thinking too, Mr. Shea. When do you expect your family to return?"

Connor brow furrowed, "I expect them tomorrow night, why?"

Williams nodded, "So it is pretty safe to assume that the killings will stop now. All the tracks and leads have been covered?"

Connor shook his head, "I don't like your tone or insinuation, detective. I want to know what is going on just as much as you. I assure you I had nothing to do with any of this. I would think you would know me well enough by now to trust that I am not the person you suspect me of being."

Connor's eyes locked on Williams' and he didn't flinch. Williams laughed and shook his head, "Very well, Mr. Shea. We are leaving for now. I assume you won't be going anywhere. We may have more questions for you since it appears that you may be the last person to see Snyder alive and all. Please, no more vacations for a while. Thank you."

Davidson and Williams turned from Connor and left.

Connor shook his head and his concern managed its way to his face. When he heard the front door close, he turned back to the sink and continued cleaning up. As he did, he replayed the conversation with Williams and Davidson over and over in his mind. Things didn't make sense.

A few moments later the cell in Connor's pocket rang, and he answered it quickly, "Hello?"

Chameleon was on the other end and sounding very confident, "Hello, Mr. Shea. I see the police have been by. I hope that went well."

Connor nodded, "Yes, I think so. They seem to be inordinately concerned with me. Do you have any idea why that might be?"

Chameleon belly laughed, "Oh yes, Mr. Shea, I know exactly why that would be."

Connor began feeling uneasy, "Where is my family?"

Chameleon was sincere, "They are fine. They will be home tomorrow evening as planned. They have been enjoying the sun and the pool and great food. It has been a very nice time for them, aside from being worried about you of course.

"Tomorrow they will return and see that you are fine and that things are back to normal again. I expect it will be you now that will have to do the worrying and you will have to worry for the rest of your life."

Connor was instantly alert, "What the hell are you talking about, Chameleon?"

Chameleon was silent for a few moments before he spoke, and when he did, Connor could hear his smile in his voice, "Think carefully about everything that has happened Mr. Shea, think carefully. Where did all the information you had come from? The operation we were on was us alone. Snyder is dead at your hand. The gun you used is in my charge. Are you noticing anything here?"

Connor began to sweat, "What are you saying, Chameleon. All of this was a setup?"

Chameleon laughed, "Oh my dear, Mr. Shea, it most certainly was. It is a brilliant one too if I do say so myself. I own you, Mr. Shea."

Connor shook his head in disgust, "No man owns me, Chameleon; no man."

"Really Mr. Shea, really? I have the weapon that killed Snyder. If I make it find its way into the hands of the police they will pull your prints. Your prints, the motive they believe you have and the weapon in their possession, you will be toast."

Connor grew angry, "I will tell them everything. I will help them track you down."

Chameleon laughed loudly, "Let's look at this whole thing together, shall we. Jill Starling worked for Genstar and discovered some unpleasant information about Xenium. It has been suggested that she confronts Snyder about it and Snyder kills her. It only appears that way, Mr. Shea. She is dead, of course, but Snyder didn't kill her. Mr. Prentice is set up to take the fall and is arrested. Where did those pieces of information come from Mr. Shea? Oh, right, it all came from me, shocker.

"Then Mr. Prentice dies in jail and Mrs. Prentice is shot in her bed and Snyder is gunned down in an amusement park. Isn't it interesting that you kept insisting on seeing Mr. Prentice and then he ends up dead?

"Isn't it interesting that you are the one that finds Mrs. Prentice in her bed, dead? Isn't it interesting that Snyder is gunned down and the only fresh prints at the scene other than Snyder are yours?

"Isn't it interesting that you hold a significant quantity of Genstar stock?"

Connor was horrified by what he was hearing. Everything Chameleon was saying was true. He was the center of everything and every lead he had given the police was misdirection. He knew how guilty he could be made to look.

Connor thought for a second before he spoke. His tone was matter-of-fact as he thought he knew what the answers would be, "What about my offices? They were all shot up and blood everywhere? What about the international raids? What about the bodyguard at the park that was sniped? What about Snyder's other people at the park? All of it was staged and fake?"

Chameleon was silent for a few moments, "Yeah, that pretty much sums it up. Your office was back in tip- top shape in about thirty minutes. The cops did show up there, but there was nothing for them to find or see.

Your whiteboards were modified to show only what we wanted them to show. The only people that are actually dead are Starling, the Prentices and Snyder. None of my people have died at all. No police agencies anywhere in the world were notified about anything."

Connor shook his head in disbelief, "For the love of God, man, why?"

Chameleon took time before answering. Connor sat down on a chair in the kitchen and waited for a reply. Finally Chameleon started, "Revenge, Mr. Shea, simple, old-fashioned revenge. Of course it didn't start out that way. Jill was a problem that needed to be dealt with. That was all.

"When you came into the picture... well that was just a pleasant surprise and a real bonus.

"Back in the day you were a very busy man and you worked very hard to build your empire. My associates and I made a lot of money helping you in your growth; A lot of money.

"Suddenly one day you decide to retire. Just like that, bam, we lose a very significant source of income. Yes we have other clients, but I don't care who you are, you are going to miss millions of dollars a year.

"And that was just the monies you paid directly to us in fees. We also made many more millions on the stocks we purchased based on the moves you were making. As you can imagine, we are talking about a butt load of cash that suddenly just vanished. One cannot recover from that kind of loss on a moment's notice. We needed to expand our horizons as it were.

"Actually, it was because of you and your wife that I heard about Genstar and then came across Xenium. That was the ideal business for us to be involved in. We already had the international network in place for distribution, and access to all the, er, raw materials we needed. It wasn't too difficult to line up a crew of... let's call them, manufacturers. Everything was in place and the money was fabulous and far less dangerous.

"Of course, Prentice had no idea to what extent Xenium was involved in the new business model. It wasn't until that bitch, Starling, came along and made a nuisance of herself. She decided it would be an excellent opportunity to make some big money fast.

"She was mistaken, and it cost her life. Snyder started to get a little troublesome when Starling died.

"I believed I could secure Snyder's silence with Mr. Prentice in jail, so that was a no brainer. I wasn't counting on you coming out of the woodwork and contacting me to investigate the Starling murder.

"I am charging you significantly for my help and you will pay it. Why? Because, for the rest of your natural life, I have a gun with your prints on it. The ballistics of that gun match the bullets that killed Snyder, plus there is a money trail from you to the Caymans.

"So by 10:00 a.m. tomorrow I expect to see eight million dollars in my account. I don't think I have to remind you that your family actually coming home tomorrow will depend on you ensuring there are no delays with the deposit. When it has arrived, I will give the all clear and your family will be returned. They will be none the wiser. It will stay that way as long as you behave. Do you understand, Mr. Shea?"

Connor sat stunned for a few moments before he could answer. His voice sullen, "Understood, Chameleon. The money will be there. What guarantee do I have that you won't come back looking for more in the future?"

Chameleon laughed from his belly, "None. In fact, I expect I will be in touch with you fairly regularly."

The phone went dead, and Connor put it on the table. He sat quietly staring off into space for almost half an hour before he was able to pull himself back. He looked at the phone, then picked it up and called his banker. It was late in the day and he hoped he was still there. The phone was answered, "Hello."

"Hi Tom, Connor Shea. I need you to do something for me."

"Of course, Connor, what is it?"

"I need eight million dollars to find its way to an account in the Caymans. Can you manage that?"

Tom was silent for a few moments, "You know what you are asking, Connor? Any movement of that much cash is going to cause considerable attention and generate a lot of questions. What is this about, Connor? You know you can trust me."

Connor was quiet for a few moments, "I know I can trust you or I wouldn't have called. This has to be done quickly. It has to be in this account before 10:00 A.M. tomorrow and it has to be done so as not to attract attention. Do you understand what I mean, Tom?"

Tom was silent as he thought things over, "This will cost you, Connor, you do realize that?"

Connor nodded slowly, "I expected it would, how much?"

"My fees are minimal as usual, but the others… hmmm. I'm guessing fifteen percent."

Connor sighed, "Well it has to happen, Tom. Do what you have to do to make it happen. Call me when it is done, please."

Tom replied quietly, "I will take care of it Connor. What on earth have you gotten yourself into?"

Connor shook his head, "Thanks, Tom. You are a good man. I would tell you if I could, please know that, and please don't ask again."

Tom was sincere, "Of course, Connor, of course, consider it done."

Connor hung up the phone and placed it back on the table.

He replayed the last several days in his mind. He thought about all the things he had done, all the information he had received and all the things he had done as a result of the information he had received.

Sifting through it all he hoped he would be able to find some way out of this mess. He was not prepared to go down for these murders, nor was he prepared to put his family in any further jeopardy. There was a solution; he knew it. There always was, he just had to find it.

The hardest part was always to detach from the issue and simply look at the whole picture from the perspective of someone else looking in. Seeing how everything unfolded usually gives a clue to how it happened and suggests plausible methods of resolution.

Connor picked up his phone and went into his office and sat at his desk. With a pencil and paper, Connor mapped out each event in order. On recipe cards he wrote some details and the source of the details and numbered them to correspond with the timeline.

He thought about the chopper that had taken him to the camp. He researched what type of helicopter it was, determined its normal airspeed and used that against the time he was in the air to give him a rough idea of how far they had gone.

He recalled the sensations of movement to try and determine which direction they had gone, or at least what direction they had started going in. He did know full well that flying gives sensations that can't necessarily be counted on. With his head covered those sensations would have been exasperated. Still, with his computer open, he used online satellite imagery to review the terrain, using his own time and speed estimates.

As he looked he recalled how the camp looked from the ground and imagined what it would look like from the air and focused his attention on terrain that matched his memory. Incredibly there was only one area that met all the parameters. Just one.

Connor was very pleased. At least he believed he knew where they were based. Given the established infrastructure, he doubted they would move operations, and if they did, it would take some time to do so.

Next he pulled up real estate records and found that property in the registry and from that determined the name of the owner of the property. He wrote those details down.

From there Connor looked up the prospective details and the principles on record for Genstar and Xenium. He hoped there would be a connection between the two and it would match the property owner. He wasn't really surprised when no connection readily presented itself. That would have been rather sloppy and these people weren't sloppy.

Next he focused on the faces he had seen. He wrote down as detailed a description of each as he could and the alias they had given him. He included any identifiable marks on their body or inflections in their speech. He wrote down anything and everything he could recall.

Then he turned back to the computer and researched the warehouse where they had gone after the park. It didn't take long to get those details. The owner of the building was someone Connor knew from his past, and not someone he would ever suspect in being involved in anything like this. Still he wrote down the information. It could prove useful.

Next was the actual ride in the trailer. As with the helicopter, he tried to remember motion and time. He wrote down minute calculations and turn details as best as he could recall. Then he opened an online street map and compared his notes to the real world. He was surprised how closely his estimates mated with actual streets. He knew he could be off by seconds at any point along the route, but from what he remembered he was able to lay out a plausible course. At least it was something.

Lastly he prepared a list of email addresses and phone numbers that had been used in his communications. He doubted any of that information would lead anywhere. He was certain Chameleon would employ security that was at least as sophisticated as his. It was more likely that Chameleon's systems were far more secure.

Connor was starting to feel better. The time he had just spent was very productive. He was able to create a reasonably detailed mapping of the events as they had occurred from his perspective. He went to the bar in his office and poured himself a drink before returning to his desk.

His next concern was security. He considered his home, Elaine's home, his offices downtown and Too Shea. The security of all those places needed to be addressed and the people associated with him needed to be safe. He wrote down everything he could think of that should be done to beef up security. The list was long. The exercise illustrated the complete lack of security most people exist in and how vulnerable they are.

By tomorrow the money will have found its way to Chameleon. Chameleon should then be satisfied and feel relaxed in his control. Connor would need that complacency within Chameleon before he dared try anything.

The next thing he needed to figure out was what he was going to do with the information he had now accumulated. That was going to take some time to plan. Police involvement at this point was unwise.

Whatever he decided to do would have to be well below the radar. He knew he wouldn't be sleeping until his family was home. He would spend this time in productive work towards cleaning up this mess. He realized that cleaning up this mess was something he was committing himself to.

15

By morning Connor had assessed every contingency he could think of. He knew full well the skill level of Chameleon and his organization. But he also knew that Chameleon had exposed himself and his operations to Connor. In his arrogance he was sure Connor would be too afraid for his family or incapable to try anything.

In reality, Connor was planning to use ideas from Chameleon himself to take him down. There was a certain satisfaction at the thought of that. At the same time, he knew that once he began, Chameleon would know about it and would react. That was going to be the part that required the greatest planning. He absolutely needed to ensure the safety of those that meant the most to him. Those would be Chameleon's first targets.

Shortly after 10:00 A.M. Connor's burn phone rang. Connor knew who it was immediately and answered it, "Good morning."

Chameleon chuckled, "You are certainly in a good mood for a man that just lost eight million dollars. I'm pleased you are handling it so well, Mr. Shea."

Connor responded instantly, "It's just money, Chameleon, not that I have much left. I am excited to be seeing my family again."

Chameleon remained nonchalant, "Yes, I am sure you are, Mr. Shea, I'm sure you are. They will be arriving home this evening as promised. I thank you for being so careful in the transferring of the funds. Questions can be such an inconvenience."

Connor pulled his emotions under control, "Business is business, Chameleon. I think we are both men of our word. Perhaps one day we can get passed this and maybe work together again."

Chameleon was silent for a few moments, "Really, Mr. Shea. I find it hard to believe that you would work with me again after what I have put you through."

Connor chuckled, "You haven't actually put me through anything. Several people have died and that is unfortunate, but my family and I are fine. Nothing that you have done has put them in harm's way. You have taken money from me, but you also provided me with several days of training I would not of otherwise received.

"Overall, I have no ill feelings. Seriously. I will have to talk to my wife, of course, but I may be re-entering the corporate world to recover from this financial inconvenience. I did know going in that this was going to be expensive. I am not opposed to that. Would you be opposed to making money with me again?"

Chameleon was decidedly cautious, "I will have to think about that Mr. Shea. It is an interesting offer. Money can always come in handy. I do recall how good you were at making it. It is a possibility, Mr. Shea. You do know how to contact me. We'll see how things go. Goodbye Mr. Shea."

The phone went dead. Connor turned it off and tossed it unceremoniously onto the desk. There was a definite smirk on his face. He was hoping Chameleon's greed would overshadow his common sense. He was glad to see that. It too could be useful when the time came.

Connor's musings were interrupted by the ringing of the main house phone. He chuckled lightly at having been startled by it, "Hello?"

Janet sounded frantic, "Connor? You are home? I am so glad to hear your voice. I got a call from some random dude. He tried to convince me all was well. What the hell was that about? Is Angela there? I need to talk to her."

Connor remained composed, "Hi Janet. It is nice to hear your voice too. No, Angela isn't here at the moment. I do expect her home this evening though. I'm sure she will call you then."

Janet wasn't appeased, "Don't give me any crap, Connor. What is going on? Where have you guys been? Why isn't she home? What about Elaine and Janet Elaine? Where is everyone? There is no way she would have taken off without telling me."

Connor was cautious, "Yes, Janet, I understand. It has been a busy few days and I am a little tired. If you don't mind, I would really like to lie down. I will let Angela know you called."

Connor hung up before Janet could say another word. He stared at the phone for a couple moments knowing full well that Janet would not be satisfied. At this point he hoped she would be angry enough to stay away until she heard from Angela.

***

Connor spent the rest of the day preparing for the return of his family. He tidied what needed tidying, and then started preparing dinner. He was not much of a chef. Actually, he wasn't even a borderline cook, but this was something he wanted to do for them.

As he progressed through the preparations he realized that more likely than not, they would be going to Jack's to eat. He chuckled to himself, but continued to work. It may not be edible, but at least they will know he made the effort. He was certain that would mean something.

It wasn't long before he realized it truly was not working out. He picked up the house phone and called Jack's to make a reservation. He didn't know exactly what time they would be home, but he had a rough enough estimate to plan with confidence.

Once that was done, he returned to the kitchen and continued his pointless efforts. His mood was solid and unwavering and his excitement grew as the clock ticked by. Eventually he completed the meal that wouldn't be eaten and set up the table.

Time passed increasingly slowly, and eventually the time of their expected arrival came and then went. Connor wasn't worried. He knew they would come, they were just a little late. Janet Elaine can be difficult if she is having fun.

Minutes passed into hours and still no sign of them. The hours passed increasingly slowly and genuine concern grew within him. He started pacing around the house. He needed to be up to something and he couldn't find anything to occupy his mind.

The sun set and full darkness fell across the house. The moon rose high. The hours passed and the moon sank giving way to dawn. Still there was no sign of them. He wanted to contact Chameleon and find out what was happening but he knew that would do nothing more than give Chameleon pleasure. Yet he had to know what was happening. It has now been two nights and two days without sleep. That alone was starting to play tricks with his mind.

The clock in the hall chimed out 9:00 a.m. and was quickly followed by the chime of the doorbell. Connor raced to the door, fully expecting to see Angela on the other side. Instead, it was Davidson and Williams. Connor's heart sank. He was afraid of what they were about to tell him.

Davidson spoke pleasantly, "My God, Shea, you look like shit. Even worse than the last time I saw you. Are you okay?"

Sudden relief came over him, "Yes, I am. I was expecting Angela back last night. They haven't arrived yet."

Davidson nodded, "Why don't you call them and find out where they are?"

Connor was almost disgusted, "Really, detective, do you think that is something I should do? Do you not think I would have already done that if I could?"

Davidson snickered, "Panic makes people do some rather strange things, Mr. Shea. May we come in?"

Connor shook his head, "Frankly, no. I have answered your questions and I really don't have anything further to say."

Davidson nodded, "I see, so that is how it is, is it? Suddenly all cooperation is out the window?"

Connor raised a finger to his lips to indicate a need for silence and nodded his head towards the inside of the house. Davidson understood immediately. Connor spoke again, "Yes, detective. I think I have been more than helpful and cooperative. There is really nothing more either of us can do.

"I would like to get my life back to normal as soon as possible, if you don't mind. Two very dear friends are dead and I would like my family back safe and sound in my home once again so we may properly pay our respects."

Davidson nodded, "Very well, Mr. Shea. We were really only coming over to inform you that we have officially been removed from the case, again. It was going nowhere and the Captain wants us to work on other cases. I was just going to let you know that. That was all. If there is anything I can do, please let me know. Sorry to have bothered you. Good day."

Williams and Davidson turned and left. Connor quickly shut the door behind them. Within in minutes his cell phone rang. Connor answered it quickly, "Hello?"

Chameleon's voice was as sure as usual, "Hello, Mr. Shea. It would appear I misinformed you on this little matter. Your family wasn't coming home last night after all. They will be there within the hour, though. I can imagine you were a little concerned about their whereabouts, am I right? That must have been awful for you. Like you, I certainly wouldn't want anything to happen to them. That would be just awful."

There was no question in Connor's mind as to what Chameleon truly meant. He wanted to get angry but knew that would only give Chameleon pleasure, "Yes, it would be unfortunate. I would be lost without them. I appreciate your calling and letting me know. Thank you."

"You are most welcome, Mr. Shea. Have a pleasant day."

The phone went dead. Connor cursed under his breath.

The house phone rang and it startled Connor. He answered quickly and barked into the receiver, "Hello?"

Janet sounded angry, "You said you would have Angela call me when she got home. I haven't heard from her. Did you forget? That isn't cool, Connor."

Connor rolled his eyes, "Hi, Janet. No, I didn't forget. They aren't home yet. They didn't make it home last night. I expect them in the next couple hours. I will let her...."

Before Connor could finish the sentence Janet hung up. Connor shook his head. He knew Janet well enough to know she was now on her way over. She wasn't satisfied waiting for a call, she would be determined to be here the second Angela walked through the door.

Connor sighed as he went upstairs. This was probably the only chance he would get to have a shower for the rest of the day.

***

When Connor came back downstairs, Janet was already in the house. She didn't look happy. All Connor could do was smile at her, "Hi Janet. What a pleasant surprise. How are you doing today?"

Janet's expression suggested that she was going to rip a strip off him, but instead she huffed and shook her head before she spoke, "I am glad you have had time to shower, Connor. I am half worried to death and you are relaxing and taking it easy. Nice."

Connor maintained composure, "I am sorry you have been worrying needlessly. They are all fine and healthy and should be home soon. There is no need for all this worry."

Janet wasn't ready to stop chastising Connor, but she realized there really was no point. Angela and the family are fine. She will be seeing them shortly. That was all that really mattered. Even still, she wanted to blame someone for her worries, needless or not, and Connor was the only one convenient.

Connor walked casually past Janet, "I am going to put on some coffee, would you like some?"

Janet answered angrily, "Yes. I do." And she stomped after him into the kitchen.

***

Connor was on the back deck and watched as the black helicopter landed. Janet Elaine was the first one through the door yelling, "Daddy, Daddy. We're home."

Angela, Elaine and Simon followed without quite the same exuberance, but were smiling and conversing as they made their way to the house.

Connor held Janet Elaine in his arms as Angela approached him. He used his free arm to pull her into as warm a hug as he was able, "It is nice to have my girls home. I have missed you so much."

Angela wrapped her arms around Connor in return, "We have missed you too, sweetheart." Her voice became a little more guarded, "Were you able to complete your project?"

Connor shook his head, "Things didn't work out the way I had hoped. I'll talk to you about it later."

Janet pried Connor away from Angela and took her in a hug, "Where the hell have you been girlfriend? I have been worried sick. Why didn't you call me before you left? I am so mad at you? I have really missed you. I love you. What the hell were you thinking?"

Angela laughed warmly, "I am sorry Janet. It was last minute. I didn't have time to call and the compound didn't have cell service. I am sorry. You must have been frantic."

Janet straightened up. Angela was fine. Everyone was fine. She now needed to look strong and satisfied.

Connor spoke, "All of you must be starving. What say we go for a nice brunch?"

Elaine spoke quickly, "Frankly, Connor, I am exhausted. I would rather just stay here if it is all the same to you."

Angela and Simon mirrored the sentiment, and Connor chuckled, "Sure. That is fine. I want to hear all about your trip. Where did you go and what did you do?"

Janet nodded her head, "Yeah, girl, what Connor said!"

Angela raised her hand to Janet Elaine's hair and brushed it lightly aside, "Sweetie, why don't you go upstairs and change. I need to talk to Daddy for a few minutes, okay?"

Janet Elaine groaned, "I don't want to, Mommy. I want to stay with Daddy."

Angela remained firm, "You can see Daddy later. We aren't going anywhere. I just have a few grownup things I need to talk to him about. Please, Angel."

Janet Elaine conceded, "Okay, Mommy. Come up and play with me Daddy when Mommy is finished being a grownup."

Connor put Janet Elaine down and smiled, "Yes, princess, I will be up shortly. I love you."

Janet Elaine wore a broad smile, "I love you too, Daddy."

She turned and ran up the stairs to her room.

Angela turned her attention to Connor, "I want to hear everything that happened."

Connor put his arm around her and led her towards the kitchen with Elaine, Simon and Janet following behind, "First I want to hear about you. I want to hear all about what you guys did."

Angela smiled, "It really was quite nice, Connor. It was a private compound near the beach. Much smaller than this place but aside from some staff, we had the whole place to ourselves. There was a pool and it was a very short walk to the beach.

"There were two men with us at all times. They were nice, but extremely professional. Groceries and clothes arrived early the first day and we just lay about the whole time. The meals were cooked for us, and the place was cleaned for us. It was fabulous. Almost like a hotel, only far more intimate. Janet Elaine had a great time with Grandma and Grandpa." Angela giggled at that.

Connor nodded, "Sounds great. I would really like to know where exactly the place was and as much detail of the area as you can give."

While Connor's tone was pleasant enough, but Angela sensed something was not quite right, "What is it, Connor? What has happened?"

Connor nodded, "Let's get you guys something to eat and we can talk. It is important for Elaine and Simon too." Angela nodded suspiciously as they made their way to the kitchen.

As Connor and Angela prepared some food, Connor explained what had happened over the past few days. He spared nothing. He felt it was important they be aware of all the facts and the potentials.

When he was done, Simon was the first to speak, "So what are you going to do now, Connor?"

Connor smiled and shook his head. As he winked he looked at Simon, "Nothing. There is nothing I can do. I am not going to jeopardize any of us. He isn't worth it. Nothing is worth that level of risk."

Janet was about to speak, but Connor put his finger to his lips to silence her. He pointed to his ear then pointed around the house. Surprisingly, Janet appeared to understand.

Simon knew what Connor wasn't saying. His body language, the wink, his facial expression told everyone in the room that this was far from over. But it also told them all that Connor believed that someone was listening and he needed to be careful what was said.

Connor looked back at Simon, "After we have finished, what say you and I go into town and clean up my office. There are things I need to dispose of once and for all."

Simon smiled and nodded, "Sure, Connor. I would enjoy that. Perhaps we can grab a beer or something after?"

Connor chuckled, "That is entirely possible."

***

Connor and Simon didn't speak about anything to do with what was happening on the drive into town. Connor and Simon had to assume the car was bugged and until he had a chance to have all the cars, house and grounds swept for electronic transmitters and/or cameras, every conversation needed to be handled carefully.

Once they were in town, Connor didn't actually go to the office; instead he pulled into the parking lot of the small park near the office building. Without a word, Connor and Simon stepped out of the car and walked casually into the green. A few feet from the car, Connor pulled his phone from his pocket and dialed Richard Johnson.

Richard was one of the people Angela and Connor had rewarded financially for his services when they retired. Since then, they had remained friends. Richard didn't retire though. He continued working freelance with his investigation services, but now had the luxury of being able to pick and choose the cases he involved himself in.

Richard answered on the second ring, "Richard Johnson Investigations. How can I help you?"

Connor smiled, "Hi Richard, Connor Shea. How are you doing?"

Richard's timbre changed immediately to a more casual, friendly tone, "Hey Connor, how are you guys doing? I had a panicked call from Mike the other day. Apparently Janet was quite worried about you guys."

Connor chuckled lightly and then his voice became more serious, "Sorry about that, Richard. That is what I would really like to talk to you about. I could use your services. Can you meet with Simon and me in a hour. Somewhere quiet if you know what I mean?"

Richard didn't hesitate, "Of course, Connor. I sometimes meet clients in Georgia Park. Do you know it? It is pretty close to downtown."

Connor nodded, "Yes, I do know it. That will work."

"Great, I'll meet you in the south parking lot in one hour." The phone went dead.

Connor turned to Simon and smiled as he put the phone back in his pocket, "So far so good. Let's go."

Instead of returning to the car they had come in, Connor and Simon continued through the park and came out to a parking lot on the far side. Just beyond the parking lot was a major street and the men continued to the sidewalk.

Connor was careful when they first came to the park to ensure they weren't followed, but in the event they were, picking up a taxi at this end of the park should be enough to lose any tail that may be following. There was no way someone would be able to get back to their car, drive around the park and pick up a fresh tail of the cab.

Stepping onto the sidewalk and looking up and down the street for a taxi. Connor shook his head, "Of course, we need a taxi and there aren't any."

He had no sooner said that when one came down the road. Simon quickly raised his hand to flag it down. The taxi pulled to the curb and they got in.

Once the car started moving, Connor spoke jovially, "I was beginning to think there weren't any cabs left in town.

The cab driver smiled, "This is not one of the busier roads, so no, not many of us just drive down here. You were lucky I just dropped my fare up the block or I wouldn't have been here either."

Connor smiled. He was even more confident that if they did have a tail, chances were slim that they would be able to get a cab.

The cabby spoke up again, "So where are we going, gentlemen?"

It was Simon that spoke first, "South parking lot of Georgia Park, please."

The cabby chuckled, "Parking lot to parking lot. This sounds like one of those movies. You know, the one where the cop and that guy with the attitude are running around town trying to stop a bomb from blowing up a school. You know the movie I'm talking about, right."

Connor smiled broadly and chuckled lightly. He knew exactly to which movie the driver was referring. He liked that whole series of movies and in fact he liked all the movies with that lead actor in it, "Yeah, I know the one. Great movie, but that is a movie, we aren't doing anything even remotely that exciting. Sorry. We are just going to pick up my friend's car."

The Cabby laughed, "Bummer. Intrigue would really liven up my day."

Simon smiled and chuckled, "Alright, you caught us. We are on a mission to stop an organization that is working with third world gangsters that are smuggling slaves into the country and using them to build a human breeding farm where they sell the babies all over the world."

The Cabby laughed, "Okay, never mind. If that is the best you've got, I'll stick with picking up a friend's car. Sit back, I'll have you there in a few minutes."

Connor looked at Simon and chuckled, "Thanks."

Simon looked back at Connor and smiled. Simon was all too aware that sometimes the truth is far less believable than a lie. In this case he was right. The driver stopped pushing and at the same time, made his day.

Connor just shook his head. The two men remained silent until they arrived at the park. It was Connor that reached into his pocket and paid the cabby. He was generous with the tip and in hindsight, probably too generous.

16

It wasn't long after the cab left that Richard arrived. His broad smile lit his face as he approached Connor, "Good to see you. It's been too long."

Connor returned the smile with his hand outstretched, "It is good to see you too, Richard. I wish it was under better circumstances."

Richard nodded politely as he turned his hand towards Simon, "How are you keeping these days, Simon?"

Simon returned the handshake, "Very well, thank you. I take it you have been well and keeping busy."

Richard smiled, "Too busy for a retired man, but I am enjoying it."

Simon nodded knowingly.

Connor continued more seriously, "You have heard about the Prentice murders, I'm sure? I was looking into the whole thing in an attempt to clear Bart's name. It would appear I have kicked a hornet's nest and they aren't happy. Things are a tad beyond my scope of expertise."

Richard's smile remained, "I have heard about the Prentice's and have actually been doing a little digging on my own since Mike's call."

Connor nodded as he pointed to a quieter area of the park. The gentlemen strolled casually towards a vacant bench as they listened to Connor recount what he had learned and about the events of the last few days.

Sitting, Connor took a deep breath before he finished his thought, "So you see, Richard. I need to find a way to bring Chameleon and his organization down without getting all of us killed. I just can't allow a man like that to continue unchecked."

Richard nodded nervously, "I don't know Chameleon. I have never heard anything about him, but I have heard of an organization similar to what you are describing. I have heard rumors of some of the things they are into, but they are only rumors. I will have to do a little more digging to see what else I can find out. Are you sure you don't just want to take what you know to the police and just let them handle it? They know what they are doing, and are quite capable of dealing with this."

Connor half smiled, "The thought crossed my mind, believe me. I'm afraid that if the police start digging into it, Chameleon would make it his mission to eliminate me and my family before he went down. Besides, the police have to follow the rules of the law. We don't have quite the same restrictions. I think the law will have to be involved at some point of course, but I don't want to put us at risk in the process. These people are very organized and if they see that someone is checking into them, things could get out of hand rapidly."

Richard stood and looked at Connor. "You recall my associate, Eric Jerome?"

Connor nodded, "Yes, I believe I do. He was the one that did the security work for Angela's office? As I recall he had some rather interesting associations in his own right."

Richard nodded, "Yes, that's him. He is, let's say, diversified in his skill sets. With your permission I would like to contact him and bring him on board. I know he has connections that would be of use to us."

Connor stood and moved his hand towards Richard, "Thank you, Richard. That would be great. I look forward to it."

Connor shook Richard's hand again. When the men released, Richard pulled a cell phone out of his pocket and handed it to Connor, "This phone is clean. I will contact you when I have some information for you. I suggest we only use text messages through these phones until we have had a chance to scrub the house, vehicles and your office."

Connor took the phone, ensured it was on before slipping it into his jacket pocket, "Thanks, I really appreciate this."

Richard nodded, "Try to avoid the police for awhile if you can. As a result of my years on the force I am all too aware of how they run when they should walk and walking when they should crawl. Having said that, there are a few that I trust. I may need to include them in this as well. They could be of use and they definitely know about discretion. We'll see how things go."

Connor's voice was matter-of-fact, "Davidson and Williams have been around a few times. I don't think I will be able to keep them away. Davidson knows something is up."

Richard focused, "I know them. They are good men, both of them. I will contact them myself. I'm pretty sure they will play ball. They are dedicated and don't let their egos get in the way of good police work."

Simon stood and reached out his hand, "Thank you Richard. It is good to see you again. I truly appreciate your assistance in this. I will follow your lead and expertise, but please, I need to be involved. Please keep me in the loop."

Richard nodded, "For now, just keep doing what you guys normally would be doing. I will be in touch as soon as possible and we can go from there. I expect Eric Jerome and his team will be by your home soon."

Richard smiled, "Pest control; best bug eliminators around."

The men chuckled as Richard left. Simon and Connor made their way to the sidewalk of the main road to hail a cab. It wasn't long before they were on their way back to Connor's office. Connor knew that if they did have a tail, they would pick it up again at the office.

He also knew Chameleon won't be calling to inquire as to where they went. For him to do so would confirm that he was following them. Connor was certain that was not the kind of information Chameleon would be ready to divulge.

***

The elevator arrived on Connor's floor and the two men stepped into the hallway facing Xavier's main glass wall and doors. Everything appeared as it always had. There was no indication whatsoever that a gun battle had been fought here mere days ago.

Connor glanced to Simon with a surprised look, but continued on to the main door. Sticking his key into the lock, the door yielded and they walked casually into the main reception area.

Connor turned and locked the door behind them. They surveyed the area and couldn't see any sign of blood on the floor, nor was there any sign of bullet holes in the walls. The entire space appeared as if nothing had happened.

Connor shook his head lightly as he walked out of the reception area towards his office, "I swear there was a gun fight and two men were killed. I can't believe it was all staged and I didn't notice."

Everything in the common office area looked to be in place, in good condition with no signs that anything out of the ordinary had occurred.

Reaching his office, he unlocked the door and walked in. Although the door had been locked, it was clear that much of the material Connor had accumulated during his investigation was now gone. He was expecting that. Chameleon had mentioned they had been there. Still Connor was annoyed at the amount of information that was now missing.

What he wanted most at this point was to see what they had left behind. That in itself would be telling. Whatever information Connor had gathered that they considered unimportant would remain and therefore the information they took is the information that would point Connor in the direction they needed to pursue.

Connor and Simon talked superficially as they cleaned the office. When they had gathered everything they could, Connor put it all into a file folder. He would look more carefully at it all later. Before they left, Connor fired up both machines. He couldn't go through this office without at least checking his machines.

With both machines up, Connor looked to his regular business computer first. There was nothing that needed his immediate attention. Then he turned to the TOR machine.

It was immediately apparent that someone had tried to force their way through his security, and it was equally obvious that they had been unsuccessful in the attempt. He smiled lightly to himself at the thought of that.

Once it was online, Connor went through his usual processes and arrived at his webmail account. Opening it, he saw an email from Chameleon. Connor sat back in his chair and stared at it for a few moments before he leaned forward and opened the email.

It was a short email, but the message was clear.

Hello Mr. Shea,

If you are reading this then you are back online. Don't be foolish with your time. I am aware of everything that goes on around you. Keep your nose clean and there will be no need for any further communication from me.

Chameleon.

Connor smiled and deleted the email without responding. He logged out of both machines and shut them down. As he rose from his desk he looked to Simon, "What say we go have that beer now. I don't think there is a need for us to remain here any longer."

Simon smiled knowingly, "I'm in. You're buying."

Connor laughed, "Naturally. I'm good with that."

Simon smiled politely and headed towards the exit without another word.

***

The drive to Too Shea was uneventful and the two entered the pub casually. As usual, Connor was greeted warmly by his staff and the regulars that were in attendance. Connor made a point of talking to each one and shook their hand as he made his way. It was a good business practice, but to Connor, the sentiment was one of true friendship and appreciation.

As Connor was making his way to his usual table, he saw a well-dressed man in his early fifties seated there. There was a definite air of arrogance surrounding the man as he smiled towards Connor. Connor immediately recognized him as Janet's father. The smile left Connor's face as he sat and stuck his hand out, "Mr. Kane, to what do I owe this pleasure."

Mr. Kane spoke confidently, "Please Connor, call me Sayer. We have known each other far too long to be so formal."

Connor's displeasure wasn't missed by Kane but he smiled in a sinister manner as he shook Connor's hand.

Connor remained reluctantly polite, "I must say I am surprised to see you, Sayer. I don't believe I have ever seen you in my place before. I have to assume you have a reason for this visit?"

Kane released Connor's hand and moved it deliberately to Simon,

"Simon, is it? It is nice to meet you. I have heard much about you."

Simon's smile too was only just polite and he gave a casual nod, "Sayer. Your reputation precedes you."

Kane chuckled, "Don't believe everything you hear, Simon. As you well know, there are a lot of myths that are prevalent in this world. Many of those myths have no connection to fact. The tales you have heard about me are myths. They are not true, but I embrace them as if they were. Such a reputation has its uses. That being said, I am someone that you very much need right now."

Simon chuckled lightly as he dropped the handshake. The beers Connor and Simon had ordered arrived as if on cue and were placed on the table in front of them. Kane held his highball glass towards the waitress, "I'll have another too, please, darling."

The server smiled as she turned and left. Connor spent the few moments that Kane was engaged with Simon to have a quick look around. He fully expected to see at least a couple of men that would have come in with Kane. He wasn't disappointed. Not too far away sat two rather large men in clearly over-stuffed suits. They seemed more interested in scoping out the bar and waitresses than on the drinks in front of them.

Kane noticed Connor's interest, "Yes, Connor, they are with me. I too have acquired a few enemies over the years. Tell me one successful man that hasn't. It is a cross we must bear."

Connor returned his attention to Kane, "Alright Sayer, why are you really here. I doubt this is a social call. For as long as I have known Janet never once have you popped by for a visit. I will be polite for Janet's sake, but I would like to know why you are here?"

Kane's fresh drink arrived and he emptied the glass he was holding before handing it to the server, "Correct, Connor. I don't have much time or interest in being social. For that I am truly sorry, especially in knowing how much you and Angela have benefited my little angel. I am fortunate that she has such good people like you two in her life." Kane paused for a moment, "The truth of the matter, Connor, is that Janet told me about your recent, er... situation. Like I said, I am a grateful man and I am here to offer you any assistance I can." He paused again before continuing, "I have certain assets that could be of use to you and I would be more than happy to work with you."

Connor was annoyed that Janet had discussed this with her father. He was suspicious and careful, "Assets, eh? And what exactly would you want in return for the use of those assets?"

Kane took a sip of his drink. He was not at all offended by the insinuation, "Nothing, Connor. Not a damn thing. I owe you and your lovely wife a great deal and this is the least I can do to help you in your time of need. Sometimes, business needs to come second."

Connor nodded politely, "I see. That is very generous of you. I will keep that in mind. I can assure you we have matters well in hand."

Kane chuckled lightly, "Of course you do, Connor. I wasn't suggesting you didn't." Kane paused again for a moment before continuing. It was clear to Connor that he was wrestling with a decision.

Kane cleared his throat, "Let's just say that I have had a few issues with some of my interests. These issues appear to coincide with your situation. I believe we are working the same problem from different directions. The principle is a rather dangerous individual.

"I am merely suggesting that perhaps it would be in our mutual interest to combine our efforts to achieve our shared goal. What would you say to that, Connor?"

Connor was beginning to believe that there was more to the offer Kane was making, but he remained unemotional as he appeared to consider Kane's words. He also knew the implications of working with such a man, whether his reputation was unfounded or not. He wasn't sure he wanted to have that notoriety associated with his activities. Still, Kane did have a wealth of experience in dealing with situations like this.

Connor smiled, "Thank you for your kind offer, Sayer. I will have to think about it and discuss it with the other members of my team. I am sure you understand."

Kane finished his drink in one swallow before he reached for his wallet. Connor stopped him, "It's on the house, Sayer. Thank you."

Kane smiled as he stood, "Thank you for hearing me out, Connor. I consider your family my family. I protect my family."

He stuck his hand towards Connor. Connor stood and didn't hesitate in shaking Kane's hand as he spoke, "I will be in touch, Sayer."

Releasing the grip, Kane nodded and walked casually out of the bar with his two men following close behind.

Connor sat across from Simon, "What do you think? Should I trust him?"

Simon sat in contemplation for a few moments, "I would suggest that you keep him on a back burner for now.

"I am not entirely sure what we are getting into, but it may prove that he could be of use. I know Richard and especially his friend Eric Jerome have experience in this type of thing. I believe we can trust Richard's judgment more than Kane, don't you agree?"

Connor took a sip of his beer before nodding agreement. As he put his glass on the table a thought came to him. He quickly dropped to his knees and looked under the table top. As he suspected, there was an electronic bug attached to the bottom of the table. He cursed lightly to himself as he sat back up. He indicated to Simon what he saw before he spoke, "Thank you for your frankness Simon. I do have to agree with you, but we also know that Janet is a part of our family and I believe Kane's sincerity. I don't think I will call him right away, but I do believe I would like to include him in this."

Simon nodded understanding, "I hate to be the devil's advocate, but I just wanted to be sure you were considering all sides. I agree that Kane could help us and I believe what he says about the effort being of mutual benefit. So we are in agreement then. Next time we talk to Richard we can inform him of the arrangement?"

Connor nodded, "Absolutely."

Connor smiled as he sat further back in his chair and took another sip of his beer. Part of the job of the staff was to wipe off the tables throughout the day, but it was also their job to scrape the bottoms of the tables at the end of the day. Connor knew the bug would be gone before tomorrow, but he would make a point of telling the night staff to expect the little surprise and to be sure to scrape the bug in a beer glass full of water before tossing it.

***

Returning to the house, Connor and Simon noticed a vehicle in the drive. It was a white van that had a logo and the words "World's Best Bug Disposal". Connor smiled as he pulled in behind the van and exited his car.

It took Simon a moment longer before he realized what it was. He looked to Connor, "Richard is apparently all over this."

Connor chuckled and nodded politely as they walked through the front door of the house. Just inside Angela greeted them with a wide smile, "Eric Jerome showed up a few minutes ago. Apparently Richard called and let him know about our pest problem."

Connor nodded, "I am glad Richard has that kind of pull. It would be hard to sleep knowing those little devils were lurking in the dark.

Where is my princess? And grandma?"

Angela pointed up the stairs, "They have gone down for a nap. It seemed like a good idea while Eric and his crew are down here."

Connor nodded as Eric walked into the foyer, "Hello Mr. Shea. It is good to see you again. Richard asked I not waste any time getting over here and dealing with these menaces. I hope you don't mind my not making an appointment?"

Connor shook Eric's outstretched hand, "Not at all. I am just glad you were available on such short notice. It is good to see you again as well. How are things looking?"

Jerome smiled, "The infestation is significant. We have a new piece of equipment that I will be setting up. It works at a very specific frequency and drives them mental. It is far less intrusive than the chemical solution and just as effective.

"It can take a little longer though. I should expect that the little darlings will have had enough in a few minutes though and you will be clear. I will be firing it up shortly now that I have identified all the nests. I will give it a few minutes and then I'll double check that they are indeed gone." He winked to Connor.

Connor looked a little more concerned, "What frequency? Will it cause us grief if we stay in the house?

Jerome shook his head, "Not at all, Connor. You won't hear a thing. The frequency is beyond our hearing range. Most animals won't be able to hear it either, but it is most annoying to the little menaces."

Connor's smile was more relaxed, "Is there anywhere in particular you would like us to be so we are out of the way?"

Jerome scanned the area surrounding them for a moment before he answered, "I think the back deck is your best option. I didn't notice any out there. The things that are out there are the types you want out there. Like I say, it won't be long once I get this bad boy fired up."

Connor nodded as he took Angela by the arm and led her outside to the back deck. Simon followed and they sat on some cushioned wrought iron chairs surrounding a small table and overlooked the backyard area. It was a nice sunny day and reasonably warm, so being out back was not an inconvenience. Angela had been out prior to Connor and Simon's return and the pitcher of cool lemonade was still on the table.

The three sat and enjoyed a cool drink and some light conversation. In the back of their minds they knew that it wouldn't be long before times like these would be few and far between; at least until this whole matter had been resolved.

Jerome strolled confidently onto the deck and sat in an empty chair at the table. The smile on his face exudes pride and accomplishment. Connor chuckled lightly, "I take it you have been successful, Eric? Have a glass of lemonade to celebrate."

Jerome reached for a glass and the pitcher as he spoke, "Yes, all clear. When the wireless devices went down there would have been a lot of static and noise on the receiving end for a few moments and then complete silence. With any luck, Chameleon will believe the RF bug spray was what destroyed them and not us deliberately.

"I have also fixed the cctv so all the security cameras are routed properly and not accessible by anyone on the outside. I have to say, Chameleon's crew were very thorough."

Jerome took a sip of his lemonade before continuing, "We swept the cars and they are clean. The GPS on them has been disabled so the cars can't be tracked. I also had a crew go through your office and scrubbed it, too. There were a few in there and they were encased in a sound cage. That will give the listener white noise without actually disabling the devices."

Connor nodded, "So in theory, it could be a few days before Chameleon realizes something isn't quite right and hopefully we'll be in good shape by then?"

Jerome laughed notably, "That is the theory. We have a lot of work to do and quickly, if we have any hope of getting this guy. I believe Richard gave you a clean phone? Don't use any of the others in the house.

"Richard should be in touch with me later today with what information he has found. We will review it and with a little luck, tomorrow we should have a working plan."

Simon gasped lightly, "Tomorrow? Really? That fast? Isn't there a bit of a risk throwing a plan together that fast?"

Jerome smiled, "Risk? Sure let's go with risk. Risk is an understatement. I will say this though, it is going to be exciting."

Angela looked worried, "I don't like the sound of that at all. What should we do with Janet Elaine to keep her safe?"

Jerome nodded, "Nothing at the moment. We may have deactivated the wireless, but I'm sure he is still watching. Everything we do will have to be done very carefully and deliberately. You, your mom and daughter will be safe and the plan will ensure that, whatever it is."

Connor handed the file folder from the office to Jerome, "This is everything they left in my office after they had gone through it. There is a lot of stuff missing, so these are the things he considers unimportant. I think that is telling, don't you?"

Jerome nodded as he took the folder, "Absolutely. I have been informed of the information you have managed to acquire, so I will compare that to what is in here. I am heading out now. Richard will be in touch later. Try to relax and enjoy the rest of the day. Things are going to get a little crazy tomorrow and probably stay that way until this is all over.

Angela spoke quietly, "Thanks for coming over, Eric. We appreciate all you have done for us."

Simon and Connor nodded their agreement as Jerome stood. He shook hands with each in turn before leaving.

When Connor heard the front door close he looked to Angela and took her hand, "Everything will be fine. Trust me. Trust us. There is nothing that any of us want more than to ensure the safety of this family. Chameleon has no idea what he has gotten himself into."

Angela smiled and nodded as she stood, "I hope you're right, Connor."

17

There was an air of tension in the Shea house from the moment they all awoke. Throughout the morning rituals and dressing no words were spoken. They ate their breakfast is silence. An hour and a half passed before Simon broke the silence, "Alright, the car is here."

Angela looked towards Connor and tears formed in her eyes.

Connor smiled unconvincingly, "It is going to be alright Angela. Everything will be fine. Eric and Richard have everything planned down to the last detail. The important thing right now is to get you, Janet Elaine, Simon and your Mom somewhere safe until this is all over. Trust me, it won't be long and we can finally put all this behind us."

Connor stepped forward and took Angela into a warm embrace and gave her a kiss. After a few moments he stepped away from her and picked up Janet Elaine, "Alright, princess. I need you to take care of Mommy and Grandma, okay. I will see you in a few days. I love you."

Janet Elaine smiled innocently, "I love you too, daddy. Don't worry, I take care of them."

Connor smiled, "That's my girl."

Putting Janet Elaine down, he turned to Simon, "Take care of them, Simon. I am counting on you."

Simon took Connor's hand and shook it, "I will, don't you worry about us. You stay safe."

Connor looked back at Angela quickly and then back at Simon and smiled, "I have several very good reasons to ensure this goes off without a hitch."

Simon nodded and smiled as he released his grip on Connor's hand.

Deadly Truth

They walked slowly out of the house. The waiting driver smiled as he stowed the bags in the trunk of the stretched limo. As they got in the car they noticed an armed man in the passenger seat up front and another in the back.

Angela looked back at Connor as she climbed in. Connor nodded and smiled. Angela feigned a smile in return. The doors closed and the limo began to pull slowly away from the house and down the drive. The windows in the back of the limo were blackened so Connor could not see inside, but he waved anyway. He knew they would be watching.

As the car pulled through the main gate and turned right, Connor went back into the house.

The man in the black sedan parked on the other side of the gate, picked up his walkie-talkie and keyed it up, "CIC, Delta One."

A few moments passed before the voice of Chameleon came back through, "Delta One, Chameleon."

The man keyed up the mic again, "Two females, one male and one child just left Victor in a limo. Victor One is not on board. Repeat, Victor One remains."

Chameleon thought to himself quickly, "They never use a limo. What are you up to Shea." Then Chameleon keyed up his mic and spoke, "Delta One follow but do not approach. I would like to know where they are going." Chameleon paused for a moment and Delta One responded, "Chameleon, Delta One, copy."

Chameleon keyed up his mic again, "Delta Two, remain and keep an eye on things."

A male voice boomed back, "Delta Two, copy."

Chameleon sat in his chair in the CIC and stared at a blip flashing on a large map on the monitor on the wall. Chameleon spoke to no one in particular, "How is the signal?"

A man with his back to Chameleon looked to the big screen quickly and then back at the monitor in front of him, "We have a good signal. Delta One is moving and tracking."

Chameleon nodded acceptance.

He picked up his mic again, "Delta One, Chameleon, sitrep."

The speakers in CIC crackled lightly, "Delta One, Chameleon. They do not appear to be in any hurry. The route suggests they are looking for a tail. I have not been spotted."

Chameleon nodded and thought for a moment, "Copy that."

Chameleon continued to watch the blip on the screen as it moved through the city streets. The pattern wasn't logical. It was obvious to Chameleon that Delta One was correct in his assessment. He had to trust that Delta One would be able to maintain contact without being spotted.

***

The limo driver looked to the man seated beside him, "Three cars back, the dark sedan. It has been with us since we left the house."

The man in the passenger seat looked to his side mirror and nods before pulling his radio to his face, "Looks like we picked up a tail. Starting evasive."

There was no response, but the man wasn't expecting any. He then looked back at the driver, "Alright, get us out of here."

The driver nodded and increased his speed noticeably. Both men continued to check their rear views as the limo sped through traffic. A traffic light ahead was red as they approached, but there didn't appear to be any cross traffic, so the driver did a controlled drifting turn onto the cross street.

Looking in his rear view he could see traffic growing behind him, but the dark sedan managed to make the turn. The driver made a left this time across traffic and into a quieter street, travelled a block before making another right.

As they drove, the two men continued to check the rear view. Satisfied, they looked to each other and smiled as they turned left onto another street.

Delta One keyed his microphone, "Chameleon, Delta One. Apparently I was mistaken. They have spotted me. I am holding back slightly."

Chameleon smacked his hand hard on the arm of his chair, "Copy that. Do not lose them. Is that clear?"

Delta One's voice wavered slightly, "Copy."

Delta One scanned each street he passed in hopes of seeing where the limo may have gone. He had been well trained in evasive driving himself and had a pretty good idea what the limo driver would do based on what he believed he would do himself. Still, there was a lot of speculation in trusting ones instinct completely. As he approached another street he suddenly turned hard and cursed when he didn't see the limo in front of him.

A block further along he made another sharp turn and in front of him he saw what looked like the limo stopped in the middle of the road. There was a white van pulled across the road in front of it and another behind it. As he got closer he could see the men in the limo engaged in a gun battle with masked individuals from the vans.

There were a few more shots before the shooting stopped and Delta One could no longer see any of the limo's men standing. A helicopter landed in the vacant lot at the side of the road. The men from the van rushed the limo, pulled Angela, Janet Elaine, Simon and Elaine out and directed them forcibly towards a waiting helicopter.

Two of the men entered the helicopter with them, the remainder ran back towards their vans. One of the men noticed Delta One and turned towards him, aimed his weapon and opened fire.

Delta One cursed as he put his vehicle in reverse and backed away as quickly as he could.

Satisfied, the gunman continued to his van and both vans sped off in opposite directions. Bringing his sedan to a halt just around the corner, Delta One put the car back in drive to return to the limo. As he started to move he could hear the police sirens getting closer. He looked up the street and saw the bodies of the men on the street and thought it best not to linger.

He sped away on the main street and keyed up his mic. This was a call he really didn't want to make. "Chameleon, Delta One. I lost them."

There was silence for a few moments before Chameleon responded. His voice was very controlled, "Excuse me, Delta One?"

Delta One knew that tone. It was not something he wanted to hear. He cleared his throat carefully in order to plan the form of his sentences, "I followed them into a quieter part of town. They were ambushed by two vans loaded with masked vipers. Three angels down. Two females, one male, one child extracted by helicopter.

"Assault vehicles left scene in opposite directions. I was taking fire and had to surrender my position. Police are arriving on scene."

Delta One sat quietly waiting for a response from Chameleon. None came. He knew how angry Chameleon probably was at that moment. Delta One keyed up the mic again, "I expect a crowd of curious onlookers will have started to form. I am going to return and see what I can learn. Delta One, out."

Chameleon answered immediately, "Copy."

Chameleon took a deep breath and keyed up his mic again, "Delta Two, report."

There was a brief pause before the speaker crackled, "Chameleon, Delta Two. Everything is quiet. I have not seen Victor one leave. There has been no traffic inbound."

Chameleon nodded his head and thought for a moment before responding, "Delta Two, Chameleon, stand by."

Chameleon continued to sit in his chair rubbing his chin, deep in thought. After a few moments he keyed up the mic, "Delta Two, Chameleon. Have you noticed anyone else surveying Victor?"

Delta Two looked around carefully before keying up his mic, "Chameleon, Delta Two, negative. There was a municipal crew working here a while ago, but they have moved on."

Chameleon took a deep breath and shook his head before keying up the mic. He strained to keep from yelling, "A municipal vehicle you say? You do realize you are out of the municipality?"

Delta Two slammed the palm of his hand hard into the steering wheel, before responding, "I was aware, Chameleon. I didn't put the two together, sir."

Chameleon took several deep breaths as he fought to keep himself composed, "Copy, Delta Two. Stand by. Please stay awake."

Delta Two keyed up his mic, "Copy."

***

Thirty minutes passed by the time Delta One returned to his vehicle, "Chameleon, Delta One."

It was a few moments before Chameleon responded, "Go, Delta One."

Delta One spoke clearly and precisely, "Confirm, three angels down and transported from the scene. Forensics are on the scene now marking rounds and tracks."

Chameleon shook his head and thought for a few moments, "Understood, Delta One. Return to Victor."

"Chameleon, Delta One, Copy."

Chameleon spoke out loud to no one in particular in the room, "Put up the trace of the route."

Within seconds the city map was up again with the highlighted line of the path Delta One had taken, including his back track, change in direction and then final parking spot before leaving to return to the Shea home.

Chameleon sat motionless staring at the screen for a few moments, "Overlay satellite imagery."

A few seconds later the satellite view of the areas, buildings, streets, and alleys were displayed. Chameleon continued staring at the screen looking at the area where the limo was prior to accelerating and the area it was captured.

The more he stared the less sense the vehicles course made. Clearly they had the intent of going somewhere. Just as clearly they were taking a course that would identify anyone that may be following, and then the high speed course to shake the tail.

There was nothing on this particular side of town that he would consider a destination for the limo. Nothing. It became apparent that the limo expected a tail right out of the gate and was trying to flush it out before heading towards their true destination.

Chameleon was frustrated, "Where the hell were you going?"

Then Chameleon started thinking about the abduction, "Who could have pulled this off? The crew knew what they were doing. The operator must have significant resources to finance such a mission. Who would find it necessary to pull off a mission in this fashion? What did they want from the Shea's that would justify this expense."

The only conclusion that came to Chameleon over and over and over was money. They were not a family of influence in the community or politics, so that wouldn't be a motive. Cash money makes the most sense. Simple extortion. The thought of that infuriated Chameleon. Clearly the operator has money, but is now looking for a quick infusion of fresh cash.

Chameleon thought for a few more moments, "Why? What would require a large sum of money quickly for an established organization."

He thought about his own operations and realized that the most likely scenario is a planned, sudden increase in reach and operations. That made the most sense. Then he thought, "Why the Shea's? There are so many deep pockets around here, why this family at this time? It can't be a coincidence that this mission was executed so close after my operation."

Chameleon nodded to himself as he continued to think, "Whoever did this, must know the family. They must have knowledge of Shea's investigation and of my operation that followed."

He nodded, "Alright, that must be it. Someone is looking for a large influx of revenue for a particular mission. Given what has been happening for the last little while, I have to believe that I am the ultimate target. So who? Who is behind this?"

As Chameleon considered that question the speaker in the room crackled, "Chameleon, Delta Two."

Chameleon cleared his mind before picking up the mic, "Delta Two, Chameleon, go ahead."

Delta Two responded immediately, "A car has pulled up to Victor. I recognize the two individuals as plain clothes detectives."

Chameleon's brow furrowed, "Copy that. Let me know when they leave."

He knew the police would have to contact Connor at some time to inform him of the abduction. He wasn't surprised they were there. He was more interested in how long they stay.

A few moments later the speaker in the command center crackled again, "Chameleon, Delta Two"

Chameleon was surprised at how quickly Delta Two was calling back, "Go ahead Delta Two."

Delta Two responded immediately, "Another vehicle has entered Victor. It appears to be Janet Kane. She looks to be in a hurry."

Chameleon was surprised by that. He was expecting the police, but certainly not a friend, at least not yet. He thought out loud, "How did she hear about this so fast? There hasn't been time for any reports."

Chameleon keyed up his mic, "Delta Two, keep an eye on the house. I want as much information as you are able to get from your position. Has Delta One arrived yet?"

Delta Two keyed up, "Copy that Chameleon. Delta One has just returned."

Chameleon nodded as he keyed up his mic, "Copy that. Delta One, stand by."

Chameleon spoke out loud to the room, "Do we have ears in there at all?"

A voice spoke immediately, "Negative. Victor is silent."

Chameleon cursed under his breath.

A few more moments passed when the CIC speaker crackled again, "Chameleon, Delta One. Victor is on the move. The two police are in their car, Victor and the female are in her car. They are leaving quickly."

Chameleon keyed up his mic, "Copy that. Delta One, remain on station. Delta Two follow. Don't get too close. If they split, Victor is the priority."

The speaker crackled, "Delta One, standing by."

Then Delta Two spoke, "Roger that."

Chameleon sat further back in his chair with his hands together and his index fingers touching his chin as he thought out loud, "How did Janet know so quickly?"

Suddenly Chameleon sat up straight. He knew Janet's father was Sayer Kane. He knew him as a man with certain influences around town and abroad. He knew this type of operation was something he was capable of and something he would consider without hesitation if it were warranted. Chameleon wrestled with the notion of Sayer Kane being ruthless enough to attack such a close and dear friend of his daughter.

He sat quietly pondering the thought. He finally decided that it was the only thing that made sense given the information he had. The only way to be sure was to confront Kane directly and learn his true motivations.

Chameleon cleared his throat before speaking to the room, "Alpha team briefing in 3 minutes."

He rose from the chair and left the room as he heard one of the men in the room calling through his mic for Alpha team to report to the briefing room immediately.

Chameleon walked briskly through the compound to a small building a hundred yards from the CIC. Inside he continued without hesitation to the front of the room and started the laptop that sat on the podium.

Through his periphery, he watched as the last of the ten men of Alpha team arrived and sat. All the men were dressed in casual civilian attire. Generally, none of this team wore uniforms unless they were on a specific mission where uniforms were called for. Those missions were rare.

They sat in complete silence and after a few more moments, Chameleon turned to face them.

He cleared his throat as he scanned the room, "The target is one Sayer Kane."

He pushed one of the keys on the keyboard and a picture of Sayer Kane filled the large overhead screen that was mounted high up and behind Chameleon. "This is the latest photo we have of him."

The picture was clearly a scanned image from a newspaper. The quality of the image was poor but it was sufficient to identify him.

"Your team leader will distribute copies after this briefing." Chameleon hit another few keys and a list of addresses appeared on the screen.

"These are the most common places Kane can be found. Check them all. If he is not at one of them, check again. He will be."

Chameleon turned again to face the room. "You do not have a kill order. He is to be returned here alive. You do not have a need to discuss anything with him. I will deal with him on his arrival. Note, he is far more aggressive and dangerous than he appears. He always

Deadly Truth

has two heavily armed assets with him in plain sight. However, expect other assets as well that are not as obvious."

Chameleon paused a moment before continuing, "Kane must be taken alive. You are authorized to use whatever means necessary to bring him in."

Chameleon knew he didn't need to be any more specific than that. The team now knew that every other person or asset in the field of operation was expendable. Chameleon looked around the room for a moment and nodded, "That is all."

He walked through the room and out the door to return to the CIC. The team leader moved to the front of the room to address the team and discuss the plan. This was a type of mission they had performed many times in the past, so the precise procedures didn't need to be discussed.

The team leader queued up the printer with copies of the image of Kane and the list of addresses. While they were printing he faced the room and divided the team into small groups. Each group would check out each location and report back with their findings.

When the location of Kane was determined, all the groups would meet. They would form the assault with respect to the specifics of the location, and move forward with the acquisition of the target.

Once the preliminary work was completed, the men left the briefing room and moved to the armory. Once they had taken the weapons and ammunition they would be needing, they proceeded to the cars and headed into town.

The team leader and two other men took a van that contained communications, and an assortment of specialized weapons and equipment. They would be checking out one of the locations themselves while monitoring the communications of the rest of the groups. Once the target was located, the van would serve as the main command post for the assault.

18

Less than an hour had passed when the location of Kane had been determined and all the groups arrived. Each car remained a short distance away so as not to draw attention. The team leader and his group reviewed the location and worked out the strategy for the assault. They knew they needed to execute quickly. Surprise and confusion would be their greatest weapons.

***

The speaker in the CIC crackled, "Chameleon, Delta two."

Chameleon keyed up his mic, "Go ahead, Delta two."

Delta two responded immediately, "All subjects have arrived at police headquarters and have gone inside."

Chameleon thought to himself for a moment before responding, "Very well. Stand by and let me know if anything develops further."

"Roger that, Delta two out."

Chameleon was not surprised of the final destination. He assumed the feds would also be involved and would already be there, and if not, they would be arriving soon. Given the nature of the abduction and the persons involved, he expected several investigative bodies would be included. He chuckled to himself, "The more the merrier. They will be stumbling over each other fighting to be the lead as most of those bureaucracies do."

***

Through the use of satellite imagery and street views from the internet, Alpha team determined the layout and configuration of the small warehouse. It was good fortune that Kane happened to be in a location where collateral damage would be negligible and a direct assault could be executed rapidly.

The two scouts that had been dispatched earlier called in stating the locations of the only two external surveillance cameras. They also reported that no assets were spotted guarding the exterior of the building.

The team leader smiled and shook his head, "This clown has no idea about security. This will be a cakewalk."

The team leader ordered four assets to take up position in the back of the building out of sight of the one camera mounted there. When the assault began, they would remain stationary but prevent anyone escaping through the back.

The team leader ordered another four to take up position out of sight of the front camera. He and one other team member would remain in the command van to coordinate. They waited patiently as everyone formed up and made their way quickly and quietly to their assigned positions.

Once all reported in, the team leader gave the go order. The team in the back remained stationary. The team in front began their assignment. A silenced round was fired and it destroyed the surveillance camera. With that down, they moved as a group to the main man door of the building. Testing the door they found it was not locked.

That was good fortune indeed. Blasting in would have tipped their hand too soon. The first man opened the door slightly and slid in a mirror mounted on the end of a short rod and moved it around to get a view of the inside of the warehouse.

As far as he was able to determine with the view the mirror provided, there was no one within sight of the door. He retracted the mirror and stowed it. He then motioned for his team to follow. One by one they slowly moved through the doorway and took defensive positions as each man in turn made his way in.

Once they were all in, they moved as a group to the wall of the warehouse nearest the door. In front of them was a staircase that led to the second floor mezzanine. At the bottom of the staircase they stopped and scanned the entire warehouse again. The building was completely empty and there were no locations that could conceal forces. Satisfied, the group leader again motioned them forward.

Slowly and methodically they ascended the staircase, careful to continually look around them to ensure they were not detected. The group leader stopped his ascent when he had made it high enough up the stairs to see the layout of the second floor. He scanned carefully and everything looked quiet. A few feet from the top of the stairs was an office with its lights on. He could hear muffled conversation escaping the room.

The front of the office had a wall and a few small windows. From the office, the group leader believed it would be unlikely anyone could see them on the stairs. He smiled lightly as he continued up the stairs onto the landing. Each man followed close behind and together they advanced to a position close to the office door.

There was a window in the office door and another couple of windows on the wall on the other side of the door. The group leader pulled out his mirror again and positioned it to see inside the room. After a careful look he was able to determine that Kane was alone. The two assets they expected to be with him were nowhere to be seen. Apparently the muffled conversation they heard was from a radio or television.

The group leader smiled as he put the mirror away. He indicated for the two men at the back of the line to hold their position. He and the man behind him would be the ones entering the room.

Carefully, the group leader squatted below the height of the window and moved forward slightly. From his position he tried the doorknob. It was not locked. He smiled as he stood and pushed his way through the door. His partner was right behind him. Both positioned themselves on opposite sides of the door with their weapons pointed at a very surprised looking Sayer Kane.

Kane composed himself quickly and laced his fingers together on the top of his desk, "To what do I owe this pleasure?"

The group leader didn't speak. Instead, he motioned with his weapon for Kane to stand and move around to the front of the desk. When he had done so, the group leader motioned for him to turn around and Kane complied.

The second man moved to the back of Kane, tightened click-locks around his hands, and pulled a black hood over his head. When that was complete, the team leader motioned for the other man to escort Kane out of the office.

The two men outside the office did a quick look around the warehouse again before starting down the stairs. Kane, his escort and the group leader followed from behind. They all moved quickly and quietly to the warehouse door and held position there until the van pulled up close. Kane's escort opened the back door of the van and manipulated Kane into the back.

Kane complied without a word. The team leader followed him into the back of the van and sat Kane on the floor with his back to one of the sides of the van. The man that had served as Kane's escort closed the van door from the outside, thumped on it twice, and the van drove off.

All the other men returned to their respective cars and left. They each would take a different route back to the compound to avoid suspicion. The Alpha team leader keyed his mike, "Chameleon, Alpha, target secure, returning to base."

There was a quiet moment before Chameleon responded, "Copy that. Resistance?"

Alpha team leader responded with a tone of gloat, "Negative."

Chameleon didn't let his surprise come through his voice, "Roger that."

He had expected there would have been at least some resistance, and was grateful that he didn't lose assets in the operation.

***

Kane sat in the only chair in the middle of the twelve foot by twelve foot room. There was a bare light bulb lit and hanging above his head that offered very little light. He still wore the hood that had been pulled over his head and his hands were still tied behind his back. He wasn't sure how long he had been sitting in the chair but it felt like hours.

Finally the door to the room burst open and three men walked in. All were dressed from head to toe in black and each wore a balaclava to conceal their face. After they entered the room, the door was once again slammed shut. It was obvious that the noise they were making was deliberate.

Kane chuckled audibly. He had used such tactics himself to intimidate individuals being questioned. He spoke sarcastically to no one specifically, "Is that the best you got? A little door slamming and foot stomping? Please." He chuckled again.

The lead man moved noisily in front of Kane and stood a moment looking at him. Kane spoke again with the same tone, "So, is this when you start beating the man in the hood with a stick or something?"

The man in front of Kane, pulled the hood off, exposing Kane's face to the room. Kane wasted no time quickly surveying his surroundings. The man in front of him reached forward and grabbed Kane by the chin and forced his head forward and his eyes to meet the eyes behind the balaclava.

Kane didn't resist much and he smiled at the face staring at him, "Hi, I'm Kane. To what do I owe this pleasure?"

The man released Kane and stood erect, "Yes, Mr. Kane, I do know who you are. I know much about you and I have heard stories of even more. I can imagine how interested you are in why I have called this little meeting."

Kane laughed, "The thought crossed my mind, Chameleon."

Chameleon's eyes widened.

Kane chuckled at the sight of them, "Surprised? I have heard much about you too. I am sure that is who you are. I know most everyone in this town and I am pretty certain none of them are this stupid."

Chameleon nodded and his smile was visible from under the hood, "Indeed."

Chameleon cleared his throat before he continued. His voice and manner were clearly that of someone in control and completely confident, "I also know a great many people and I'm sure I'm talking to the right man."

Kane's smile continued as he nodded, "So you are interested in discussing a business proposition are you? I have to say your negotiation tactics need a little fine tuning."

Chameleon laughed, "I'm glad you are amused, Kane. I like a man with a sense of humor. So many people this close to death tend to be so uptight."

Kane simply shrugged his shoulders, "If you wanted me dead, you wouldn't have gone to all the trouble of bringing me here. If you were interested in extortion, it is unlikely you would be so sociable. So that just leaves a need for information that you believe I possess."

Chameleon nodded pleasantly, "Very good, Kane, very good. You and I are a lot alike, wouldn't you agree? Perhaps if we got together under different circumstances we could have been friends?"

Kane was expressionless, "I doubt it. My friends are proud people and don't hide behind masks."

Chameleon laughed, "Naturally... Let's just agree to disagree over our respective preferred methodology. I must say I have enjoyed our little banter but time is wasting."

Chameleon turned and took a few steps away from Kane before turning and walking back again. It was clear he was formulating his thoughts, "A very dear friend of mine has recently had his entire family abducted. I believe you may know them. You wouldn't have any knowledge of that would you?"

Kane looked confused, "Abduction? Who has been abducted? I haven't abducted anyone."

Chameleon hesitated for effect, "The Shea's. Don't tell me you don't know them?"

Kane nodded knowingly, "The Shea's. Yes, I know them. Of course, you already knew that. No, I had nothing to do with any abduction. Why on earth would I do that to my daughter's friends. They are like family."

Chameleon feigned more surprise than he was actually feeling, "Really? Interesting. The boldness of the abduction and the tactics used screamed of someone with more than average resources and assets. You are the only one I know of around here like that... besides myself, that is."

Chameleon hesitated a moment, "Why should I believe you, Kane?

You have an inside channel to everything they do. It would be nothing for you to pull this off."

Kane nodded with pride, "You know it! This is something I could have pulled off very easily. But why would I? What possible reason could I have to betray my daughter and my daughter's friends like this? Besides, if I were involved, there is no way you would have been able to pick me up so easily. My operations would be locked up tighter than a drum, don't you think?"

Kane laughed, "Geez, I always thought you were a clever man but it appears the blatantly obvious escapes you."

Chameleon smiled and chuckled unpleasantly, "I would be a little more careful in the choice of words I use if I were you, Kane. My patience isn't infinite."

The smile didn't leave Kane's face, "Listen. I do not know what is going on. I do, however, know that it is something far larger than both you and I know. I too have lost assets recently, and frankly, I thought it was you. I have two very dear associates that accompany me nearly everywhere I go. They were gunned down this morning while I was in a meeting. That is why I was at the warehouse, tidying up a few things before I went underground."

This time Chameleon's surprise was real. He stood staring at Kane for a few minutes before turning and briskly leaving the room. The two men that had accompanied him remained. When the door to the room closed, Kane looked to both men, "Anyone interested in some cards?"

They didn't move and Kane chuckled, "When you guys are looking for work, look me up. I pay pretty good and the benefits are great."

Kane laughed from his belly before clearing his throat, "But seriously, guys. I really need to use the head. Can you help me out?"

Without speaking one of the men pointed to a back corner of the room.

Kane looked in that direction and saw a stainless steel toilet and sink. He looked back to the man that was pointing, "Seriously?" He shrugged his shoulders, "Alright then, can you let me out of this chair at least?"

***

Thirty minutes passed when the door to the room opened and Chameleon walked back in. As he broached the threshold he saw Kane sitting in the chair with his hands tied in front of him, but he was not tied to the chair. He quickly looked at both men and then back at Kane, "Making yourself comfortable are you, Kane?"

Kane smiled, "These gentlemen were kind enough to allow me the use of the facilities. I am very grateful for that kindness."

Chameleon simply nodded as he closed the door behind him and continued towards him, "It would appear that you have indeed told me the truth... well the truth about your associates, anyway. My question then is who. Who do you think is capable of pulling this off and capable of taking out two of your men. Who and Why?"

Kane was about to speak when he caught the look in Chameleon's eyes, "You already know that, don't you? You know who has done this." Kane's brow furrowed angrily, "Who is the bastard? I'll kill him!"

Chameleon continued towards Kane without slowing, then reached down and began untying his hands, "It would appear that there is a new kid in town. I think we may have to do something about this individual. I can only see him being bad for both of our businesses."

With his hands now free, Kane rubbed his wrists, "You have a helluva way of attracting new partners, Chameleon. Why the hell would I work with someone who won't even show his face?"

Chameleon stepped away slowly as he chuckled, "It isn't personal, Kane. Very few people have ever actually seen my face. It gives me a certain level of privacy and freedom I couldn't enjoy otherwise. I'm sure you can understand that."

Kane didn't smile, "I don't work with people I don't know. Especially after they have threatened my life."

Chameleon nodded, "I do apologize for that, Kane. I'm sure even you can understand how it looked. What else was I too think, given the circumstances?"

Kane took a deep breath, "Okay, okay, fine. I am a big enough man to forgive under these circumstances. But trust me on this, you so much as look at me the wrong way and you will be a burning pile of shit in a gutter somewhere. Do I make myself clear."

Chameleon laughed heartily, "I think we understand each other just fine. I do give you credit for making such threats when you have no idea where you are and are surrounded by a small army of heavily armed men with anger control issues."

Kane looked around and chuckled, "Good... as long as we understand each other. Details. I want details. I want to hunt this bastard down and shoot him in the street like..."

Chameleon interrupted, "Calm yourself, Kane. I want him as much as you do. I think we can work together to eliminate this inconvenience, don't you think?"

Kane looked at Chameleon carefully for some time, before he stood and made his way to the door of the room. Neither Chameleon, nor the two men attempted to stop him as he walked through the door into the daylight. Kane squinted a moment as his eyes adjusted to the light and then took a few moments to look around the compound before he turned back to Chameleon.

Kane smiled, "Quite the place you have here. How many souls on site?"

Chameleon stepped forward and put his hand on Kane's shoulder as he directed him to walk towards a building not too far away, "Let's get a bite to eat. You are probably hungry. We can talk over a meal."

Kane nodded and walked with Chameleon, "So tell, how do you eat in that thing?"

Chameleon chuckled, "Don't worry, I ate already. You eat, we talk. Is that better?"

Kane gathered a plate of food before sitting across from Chameleon at the long mess hall table. Without speaking, Kane ate a few mouthfuls as he looked around. The room was clearly large enough to seat forty men, although there were only four of them there at the moment.

After a few more bites, Kane focused on Chameleon, "Alright, what do you know. Spill it."

Chameleon nodded and took a breath before he began, "From what I have been able to gather, the gentleman involved is one Eric Jerome. He has a private security firm that works in several locations around the globe."

Chameleon paused for a moment before continuing, "Apparently, Jerome has quite an extensive military background and training. He was a Seal for a number of years before moving up to the groups that officially don't exist. He retired from the military, about ten years ago and began his company.

"Shea has hired him in the past to do security work for him. Through that, Jerome has become quite knowledgeable about the Shea situations and past. It would appear he is capitalizing on that knowledge. From what I have learned, it is his intention to use extortion to acquire significant cash from Shea to... let's say... diversify his operations.

"What I have not yet determined, is where he is holding the Shea clan or where his base of operations is. We can't move forward with any plan until we get at least that much information. I don't even know if he has contacted Shea yet with his demands."

Kane continued to eat as Chameleon talked. When Chameleon finished Kane stopped eating, "Clearly, I need to step in here and take this man out."

Chameleon laughed, "From what I hear, you are good, but you are no match for this group. They have training you can't even imagine. You and your crew would be slaughtered. I think this is a job for my team. We are trained to deal with individuals like these."

Kane took a few more bites before speaking again, "Very well then, but me and my crew... as it were... are to be included in this operation. I want to take this Jerome character and watch the light leave his eyes as I squeeze his throat with my bare hands."

Chameleon smiled as he carefully considered Kane's words. It was several moments before he spoke, "I'm sure we can arrange that."

Kane nodded, "I will also need to contact Shea and let him know what has developed. Does that pose a problem for you?"

Chameleon hesitated a few moments giving the appearance he was considering Kane's words. The reality was he would rather use as many of Kane's men in this operation as possible. They were far more expendable than his own. After an appropriate amount of time he nodded agreement.

19

By morning twenty men had assembled in Kane's warehouse and were seated in small groups on the floor waiting for their instructions. Each man was unique in stature and character, but they all shared the same eyes - black pools from which the light of innocence and faith had long since vanished.

A closed 24-foot panel van drove through the warehouse door and stopped a few feet inside. The large warehouse door was closed quickly. Two of Chameleon's men left the cab of the van, walked to the front and stood looking over the men assembled.

The closing of the warehouse door was Kane's queue to leave his mezzanine office and walk down the stairs to the warehouse floor. He moved with the strength of a leader; a general about to address his troops.

He stopped in front of the van, with Chameleon's men behind him and his men in front of him he smiled, "Thank you all for coming. As you have all been informed, this operation is voluntary. If any of you are having second thoughts, now would be the time to go home to your girl and snuggle with your teddy."

Kane allowed a few moments for a response. There was none. One might have expected a sigh or a chuckle or even a smile, but there was nothing but a sudden chill in the air. Kane smiled at that, "Very well, gentlemen. We are going for a little training and refresher. We are going to a secure location so we will all be riding in the box. Grab your gear and let's get moving."

Each man rose slowly, grabbed the duffle they had been seated on and moved to the back of the van. One by one they boarded. When they were all aboard, Kane joined them. Chameleon's men pulled the door down and sealed it. Seconds later, the van was moving.

It was about an hour before the van stopped and the back door opened. The daylight was refreshing to the contained men. The van had a translucent panel in the roof that let in some light, but it didn't compare to the sharp brightness of daylight.

As each man focused, they picked up their gear, left the van and formed up in a single straight row, side by side. Kane met up with Chameleon in his ever-familiar black balaclava. With a smile he shook Chameleon's hand. Chameleon's eyes showed the smile was returned.

When he released his grip, Chameleon nodded and walked out in front of the line of men.

"Good day, gentlemen. The next few hours will be intense. From what I understand, you all have a certain level of experience and expertise, so I won't insult you with any basics.

"I currently have assets working Intel and hope to be able to commence this operation without too much delay. In the interim, you will train. It won't be too hard; you do need to be able to function at the end of it.

"Pay close attention and you will be home with your lady in no time. Slack off and she will be in need of someone new to keep her warm."

Chameleon paused for a moment as he looked the men over carefully, "Alright, Mr. Jones here will show you to your quarters. Fall in here in one hour. Dismissed."

The men turned right in unison, picked up their duffles and followed the man called Mr. Jones to a building nestled behind the barn, out of view of the main clearing.

Chameleon smiled at Kane when they were out of sight, "I must say, Kane, they look far better than I had expected. I was certain your crew would have been high school dropouts from the ghetto or something. I stand corrected."

Kane smiled while in his heart he wanted to punch Chameleon for his insult, "There is far more about me than you can possibly know. You only know what I want you to know. Nothing more."

Chameleon laughed and reached to pat Kane on the shoulder, "My apologies, sincerely. I meant no offence. They are a fine looking group of men and I think our chances are far better than I originally thought. That is all."

Kane smiled, "I could really use a beer. Do you happen to have any?"

Chameleon nodded and led Kane towards a smaller building in the opposite direction of the barn.

The inside of the small building was sparsely furnished. A bed was along the far wall, a table with a couple chairs sat in the middle of the room, to one side was an area that was intended to serve as a kitchenette and a bathroom was on the opposite wall. This was Chameleon's private quarters and it wasn't anything one would consider homey. Kane was surprised by it. "I thought you would have better accommodations for yourself?"

Chameleon smiled, "Oh I do, just not here. Here is all business. My home is far more comfortable."

Kane nodded as he sat at the table. Chameleon pulled two beers from the small refrigerator and sat at the table across from Kane. As he handed Kane a beer he chuckled lightly and pulled down a small flap on the front of his balaclava to expose his mouth and lips.

Kane saw it and laughed hard, "Well, sir, I was not expecting that." He laughed some more.

Chameleon chuckled, "Nothing gets between me and a cold beer." He chuckled as well.

The two men took a few drinks of their respective beers before Chameleon became more serious, "My team has discovered a possible location where the Shea clan may be held. I am concerned though. For someone as good as this Jerome is supposed to be, I am surprised at how easy it was to locate him."

Kane took a few more drinks of his beer as he considered Chameleon's words, "Is it really a surprise or are your people just better than you expected?"

Chameleon thought for a moment, "We were able to track the chopper that was used and were able to determine where it landed. From there, they were able to use the GPS of the rental vehicles to track them to a location just outside of town." Chameleon shook his head, "I find it extremely difficult to believe Jerome would be so careless."

Kane shook his head, "Do you think he created the false trail to perhaps ferret out who may be trying to track him?"

Chameleon nodded, "This is not something I personally would do, but it does make sense. At the same time, why bother? Why not simply plan your movements so there are no trails whatsoever?"

Kane shook his head, "So either he is clumsy and we know where he is, or he is cunning and he has diverted our attention. Or the other possibility is he expects us to think he would be too stupid to leave such a trail and look elsewhere and the whole while he is actually there?"

Chameleon laughed, "You see my conundrum, then?"

Chameleon looked at Kane closely for a moment. Kane ignored it as he drank his beer and appeared uncaring. After a few mouthfuls, Kane casually place the bottle on the table and looked to Chameleon, "Frankly, I would put my money on careless, or a team member that made a mistake. Jerome is very good by all accounts, however, he has never done anything like this before. Rookies make rookie mistakes. I'll bet this is one and a huge one at that. Do we know if Connor has been contacted yet with any demands?"

Chameleon smiled, "I have a fresh wire on their landline, and no, not yet."

Kane nodded, "That seems a little odd, don't you think? I mean, I think I would have been on the horn as quickly as possible to get things moving."

Chameleon adjusted himself in his chair, "Yeah, me too. That is just one more thing that doesn't seem quite right. Why give the feds time to set up? Why take your time? The longer you hold them, the greater the risk becomes and the chances of failure grows."

Kane was silent for a few moments before he rose and walked to the door of the building and looked outside. His team was starting to gather for the beginning of the training.

A smile lit his face as he turned back to face Chameleon, "Arrogance."

Chameleon's tone changed, "Excuse me?"

Kane continued, "Arrogance. This Jerome character is arrogant. He knows the Feds are involved or at least will be involved. He is not the least concerned about them. He believes that since he is the new kid on the block, he is unknown to them and they won't be looking for him, at least not initially.

"The Feds certainly know something about our operations, I would expect. We naturally would be their first persons of interest. I doubt they know where to find you or me but it will keep them busy trying to locate us.

"It wouldn't be until the exchange is in play before there is any real external risks to Jerome's crew. That would be the only time any of the authorities would be in a position to try and trip them up. I believe we will have begun operations long before that point.

"He thinks he is safe and can take all the time he wants. He can make Shea sweat, he can get enforcement chasing their tail all the while he is sitting back patting himself on the back.

"Why would he be so arrogant you ask? As far as he knows, no one saw the abduction, or at least no one that is of any threat to him. He has no way of knowing your man saw that whole thing. That is why you were able to find out what you did. He was sloppy, but he doesn't know it."

Chameleon remained quiet as he considered Kane's words. He had always worked from his own judgement and having another opinion in the mix was more of a hindrance than help. He needed to ignore what Kane has said and look at the situation for himself. After that he could consider what Kane had said and decide which he thinks is more plausible. Only, now that he has heard Kane, he is having difficulty pushing that scenario from his mind.

Chameleon smiled, "My confidence is high. I have a fresh load of weapons arriving this evening. I have fresh transports arriving as well. I think your team will be ready. My team already is."

Kane smiled, "Good to hear. We may be able to work together after all. Maybe."

Chameleon laughed, "Time will tell, Kane, time will tell."

***

Training for Kane's men went late into the night and began again early in the morning. By mid afternoon, Chameleon was satisfied they were ready and dismissed them for food and rest. Tonight would be the night of the assault.

Kane joined Chameleon in the CIC. On the large screen was an aerial photo of the area of operation. It had been taken earlier in the day by Chameleon's own people from a sufficiently high altitude as to not arouse suspicion.

The detail on the images was quite good, and with the various angles of the shots, they had a good look at the layout of the target. Reviewing the photos, Chameleon was able to distinguish a couple areas that could be breached.

Their assault would have to be swift and precise. Mistakes would be costly. Extracting the Shea clan was the most important thing, but doing so and staying alive was always preferred.

Kane and Chameleon worked over the images and devised the best plan given the location and the assets available. The sun was below the treetops when they completed the plan. It was time.

The team leaders were summoned to the briefing room. After a half hour, each returned to brief their teams. With that done, Kane's men were assembled and the vehicles were brought in.

Each squad was sent through the armoury for their weapons and ammunition before going directly to their respective vehicles. The plan required four vans approaching from three different directions.

Two vans would approach from the front, but only after the back two had reached their positions. The front two were intended as a distraction for the back two to move in. The plan seemed simple enough. Kane's men would be doing the assault. Chameleon kept his men as the drivers. They were armed and ready, but would only join in assault if the need arose.

The men sat without conversation as the vans drove. The compound was on this side of town. That would save considerable driving time. That too was of benefit to them.

As they entered the correct section of town, the vans slowed as they made their way to their respective positions. A few minutes before they got there, the radio crackled. The recon helicopter reported the approach for all units was clear. No perimeter electronic detection system found.

The vans turned off their headlights and quietly coasted to the side of the road and parked. A few moments later all team leaders reported ready. The back two units left their vans and approached through the forested area, stopping short of the chain link fence. With their night vision goggles, they carefully scanned the fence line and their side of the building looking for sentries and surveillance cameras.

With none detected the teams moved closer to the fence and pulled out the testing equipment to check the fence for alarms or electric currents. Again, nothing was detected. Each step was reported as they proceeded.

The lack of security was surprising to Chameleon, but at the same time he was grateful. The teams breached the fence and quickly moved forward to the back side of the building and reported ready.

The front teams began their move. With the same checks as they moved, they made their way to the main gate of the complex. The chain that secured the gate was quickly cut. The teams pushed the gate open and moved in, weapons ready.

The main door to the building was in front of them, but no lights inside the building could be seen. The obvious conclusion was that any light was being blocked, but it was just an assumption. Two thirds of the men donned night vision goggles, while the rest remained natural. If there was light on the other side of the door, they would be ready and would give the others time to removed their goggles. If it was dark they were also ready to advance.

With the team ready, a small explosive charge was attached to the front door, and then blown. The lock on the door vanished and the team moved through the door quickly. As expected, the inside of the building was lighted and as expected, the blast attracted attention.

A group of armed men raised their weapons and were preparing to fire when the explosive charges of the back teams detonated. The sound of it startled the men inside the building momentarily.

Within seconds, all that could be heard was automatic weapons fire and leaders yelling to teams. The confusion of the assault lasted about thirty seconds and then all was quiet. Moments later the front team emerged from the building with the grateful Shea clan.

They were quickly loaded into one of the vans and sped away. The teams returned to the building to survey the damage and collect whatever evidence of their operation that may have been left behind. A few moments later all teams moved to the vans and returned to the compound.

The van with the Shea clan proceeded to the Shea house and stopped outside the gate. The van door was opened and everyone got out. When the van was empty, it sped off to Chameleon's compound.

20

Angela, Janet-Elaine, Simon and Elaine walked quickly up the driveway to the house. Connor had already opened the main door and was on his way down the stairs to greet them. The smile on his face was broad and in seeing it, Angela began running towards him and jumped into his arms.

She wrapped herself around him as completely as she was able and Connor chuckled lightly, "Easy, Angela, you are going to break me."

Angela giggled, "Sorry darling, I am just so happy to see you." She gave him a big lingering kiss as the rest of them arrived.

Janet-Elaine looked up at Connor, "We missed you Daddy. It was a fun adventure. It was real loud."

Angela eased herself back to the ground, allowing Connor to bend over and pick up Janet-Elaine, "I missed you too, princess. I am glad you had a fun time. You weren't scared I hope?"

Janet-Elaine shook her head, "No. Grandma told me all about the game we were playing. It was fun to play with the men."

Connor forced a smile, "That is good, sweetie. Why don't you go into the kitchen? I think there is a fresh tub of ice cream waiting for you."

Janet-Elaine smiled broadly as she left them and ran into the house. When she was out of sight, Connor wrapped his arm around Angela and turned to Simon and Elaine, "That must have been a little intense?"

Simon shook his head, "That is an understatement. When the rescue team came, everything happened incredibly fast. It was hard to figure out what was happening until it was all over."

Connor nodded as if he understood. There was no mistaking the sarcasm in his voice, "Sorry I missed it. Sounds like it was a hoot."

Elaine smiled half heartedly, "Indeed. I think I would like a drink now if you gentlemen will excuse me."

Connor chuckled lightly, "That sounds like a great idea, Elaine. I think we should all go in and relax. I am expecting a phone call any minute anyway."

They weren't in the house long before the phone rang. It was Chameleon, "I trust your family is in good health, Connor?"

Connor controlled his voice, "Yes, they are none the worse for wear. Thank you for what you did for them.... for us."

The line was quiet for a few moments before Chameleon responded, "You are most welcome, Connor. I can only imagine how it must have felt to lose your family like that twice in such a short time frame. I can't imagine it was very pleasant."

Connor detected the matter-of-fact tone of Chameleon's voice and didn't like it, "I can tell you quite plainly, Chameleon, it was horrible. Horrible beyond description. I never want to feel like that again."

Chameleon's tone didn't change, "I don't imagine you would. I expect that, if nothing else, you understand the importance of leaving the past behind. Pick up the pieces and push forward, if you know what I mean."

Connor waited before responding. His voice was guarded, "I understand perfectly. I have never talked to you. I have never employed you. I have absolutely no knowledge of you or anything you may be involved in."

Chameleon chuckled lightly, "Very good, Shea. I expect this is the last time we will ever need to talk. I offer you and your family my best wishes for the future. I hope your daughter gets the life we all would like her to have. Goodbye Shea."

The phone went dead immediately. Connor stood quietly for a moment holding the phone to his ear before turning it off and putting it down. When he turned he could see Angela and Elaine staring at him, "It is nothing. He was just making sure everyone is fine."

Elaine wanted to ask questions, but she could see she wouldn't get any answers. Connor could sense the questions within her and hoped she wouldn't ask. He was grateful when she didn't.

After an awkward couple of minutes, Connor smiled and clapped his hands together, "Alright, then. What would everyone like to do for dinner tonight?"

***

After all the weapons were returned to the armory, the men were dismissed for the evening. Most went immediately to the mess for a meal before turning in.

Kane joined Chameleon in his quarters for beers. With the small talk over and a fresh beer in each of their hands, Chameleon became more serious, "Looks like the operation went off without a hitch."

Kane nodded as he took a drink, "Yes. It was far smoother than I would have ever expected. Kudos to you and your team for doing such a good job of preparing my boys."

Chameleon half smiled, "You are welcome. There will be a mess for the authorities to decipher when they come across those remains. How many of Jerome's men were there?"

Kane hesitated a moment before he spoke, "There were eight. They were heavily armed, but surprise is a wonderful thing. We definitely had the jump on them."

Chameleon nodded suspiciously, "Still, it seems odd that your team was able to take them out so efficiently without any injuries to your team, or the hostages. That isn't usually the way these things play out."

Kane took another casual drink. He put the bottle deliberately back on the table between both his hands and after a moment looked up to meet Chameleon's eyes, "I am not really sure what you are driving at, but it was a very well executed plan. Enough distraction and surprise combined with some first class shooting and the whole dance was over in seconds. I don't know about you but I am damn grateful. There are a million things that could have gone wrong, but nothing did... nothing"

Chameleon kept his eyes fixed on Kane's for a few more moments before he suddenly smiled, looked away and took a long drink from his beer, "I am most grateful as well. All's well that ends well and all that."

Chameleon took another drink before returning his attention to Kane, "So, where do we go from here. The Shea family are all back together, happy and cozy. You and your team are alive and well. My people are continuing with their... er, activities. All things are well in paradise. Except for one small matter." Chameleon hesitated for a moment before continuing, "You say there were only eight men guarding the Sheas. Jerome is still out there somewhere and I am pretty sure he is going to be a little annoyed at you and me. That could pose a bit of problem for both of us and our operations, wouldn't you agree?"

Kane smiled as he took a drink, "Yes, I would agree with that. What are you proposing?"

Chameleon stood up sharply and walked away from the table and stood for a few moments with his back to Kane. Finally he turned around, "It is fairly safe to assume that Jerome will see this as us having declared open war on him. He is not going to simply move along. He may be limited in his resources, but clearly, his limit is still significant. That could pose a problem and an ongoing unnecessary expense for us. I suggest we merge our forces... an alliance as it were."

He nodded as he reflected on his own words. "Your men have clearly demonstrated their abilities tonight. Quite frankly I expected a fifty percent casualty rate, thus my surprise.

"My operations are extensive and as such are pulled a little thin to be engaging in a war on a different front. You are in this just as deep as me now and you can be sure Jerome will know you were involved tonight. I could use your men to assist in this war."

Kane chuckled lightly, "Of course you could." Kane paused for a moment before continuing, "I have investments of my own that will be under greater risk as well and I will need my personnel available to me. I can't afford to commit my men for any length of time away from my normal operations."

Chameleon nodded knowingly as he took another drink, "So what would you suggest?"

Kane shook his head as he took a drink. It was several moments before he spoke, "We both do things that could be combined and done together more efficiently. I think that if we took a little time, and we trusted each other, we could combine our operations and together better allocate our respective assets." Kane thought about what he was saying for a few moments before continuing, "Yes. I think together we could be much stronger and the financial rewards would be significantly better. Together we would be a force that Jerome, or anyone else for that matter, would have significant difficulty taking down."

Chameleon stared at Kane without emotion for several moments before finally allowing a small smile and nodded. He finished the rest of his beer and placed the empty bottle on the table before he spoke,

"It has been a very long day. Why don't we just pack it in for the night and revisit this discussion in the morning."

Kane thought for a moment, "Perhaps. It would give us both a chance to think through our options." He finished his beer before standing. He walked over to the refrigerator and took another beer before turning back towards Chameleon, "Good night."

He walked out of the building without another word and headed across the compound to his own quarters.

***

Kane arrived at Chameleon's building early. Breakfast had just been set out as the two man sat. The television was on and the morning news reports were coming through. Chameleon acknowledged Kane's arrival pleasantly, "Good morning, Kane. I trust you slept well?"

Kane nodded with similar pleasantness, "Thank you, yes. Very well indeed." He sat at the table across from Chameleon, "You certainly know how to do breakfast. This is quite the spread."

Chameleon nodded, "Indeed. A satisfied belly frees the mind for more important pursuits."

Kane chuckled and was about to speak again when a story on the news grabbed his attention and he spun to face the screen.

The image on the television was from outside the compound they hit last night and the cameras were pointed towards the building. The slender Asian reporter had just finished her report. Kane had always liked the mannerisms in her reporting, but it was the story this time that had his attention and he focused on her words.

"That is correct, Jim. The police are not releasing many details at this time. It would appear that last evening, after ten p.m. a gun battle with automatic weapons took place at this location. I can confirm that eight bodies have been recovered by the coroner's office. I saw one male dressed in what appeared to be military Special Forces style clothing.

"The police are saying at this time that it was a special tactical assault on a known terrorist cell. They had been observing these suspects for some time and last night they moved on the facility. The police are claiming they have seized a large cache of weapons and explosives. Those are all the details we have at this time. We have been promised an update in half an hour."

Kane's head spun back to Chameleon. His anger was clear and he spoke over the television, "What the hell is that about. That story is a load of crap."

Chameleon nodded and chuckled. He was more amused than upset, "Listen, Kane. The police have eight bodies to explain. They undoubtedly knew of the abduction. I'm sure by now they also strongly suspect these to be the kidnappers.

"They are not about to go around saying they had no idea where the hostages were being held, and the assault last night was conducted by an unknown organization. Can you imagine the heat they would take if that little tidbit got out.

"This little story makes them look like the good guys serving and protecting. They still have no clue who was involved, but I am sure they know why."

Kane looked at Chameleon for a few moments before he too chuckled, "Of course you're right. The last thing they need to do is tell people that highly trained bad guys are running loose, prepared to blow shit up. That would be bad PR." He chuckled again as he began his meal.

The walkie talkie on the table crackled momentarily before a voice came through, "Chameleon, CIC."

Chameleon put down his utensils, swallowed what was in his mouth and quickly wiped his hands before keying up the walkie talkie, "Go!"

"Delta One reports that a marked police vehicle, a detective's car and a black SUV just arrived at the Shea house."

Chameleon nodded with a smile, "Very good. Keep an eye on the place and let me know how long they stay. Chameleon out."

Kane smiled, "Very good. I wouldn't mind being fly on the wall during that conversation."

Chameleon nodded, "Me as well. I'm certain they are happy with how things worked out, but they are going to have a number of questions for our friend and his family."

The smile left his face just as quickly, "As long as Shea behaves, we shouldn't have anything to worry about. He doesn't know much about me or us. However, what he does know could prove cumbersome."

With Kane's belly now full, he leaned back against the chair and took a drink of his coffee, "This is precisely why I mentioned our amalgamation."

Chameleon nodded, "Oh, I understand fully your reasoning and its validity. I am just not one that likes to share. Besides, I would be exposing myself significantly if I gave up information about my operations."

Kane laughed from the belly, "Oh yeah, Chameleon. It is all about exposing your operations. What about my operations, eh? I would be unzipping my fly too. We both have much to lose... but I think what we will gain will far outweigh that...

"I am a businessman, Chameleon, through and through. I seize opportunities I can profit from where ever I find them. I don't care much for ethics or any of that respectable citizen crap. The bottom line is the bottom line.

"Frankly, I couldn't care less about your operations aside from how joining forces will stabilize my operations and help with my profits. Does that not make sense to you?"

Chameleon returned his focus to the meal in front of him without answering. Kane chuckled and turned his attention back to the television. The sports was on now and he watched the various scores and reports of the previous evenings competitions.

The two men sat in silence as they watched the rest of the news program and the beginning of another news based program that followed.

Kane stretched as he prepared to stand, "Well, I guess our business is concluded. I will gather up my people. If you would be so kind as to give us a ride, that would be most appreciated."

Chameleon was about to speak when his walkie talkie crackled again and the same voice came through, "Chameleon, CIC"

Chameleon keyed it up quickly, "Go"

"Delta reports the authorities have left the Shea residence. He reports that from what he could tell, they didn't appear too satisfied with the meeting."

Chameleon hesitated for a moment before keying up the walkie talkie again, "Very well. Thank you. Out."

Chameleon placed the walkie talkie carefully on the table before looking up at Kane. He hesitated again before he began to speak. His words and tone were guarded, "A few years back my organization was geared up for private enforcement, investigation and personal security. I had a number of rather large corporate customers and business was great.

"When Shea decided to retire I lost a significant amount of revenue. Fairly rapidly, some of my other clients also stopped using my services. I needed to diversify even further.

"That was when I learned of the work being done at Xavier. I managed to gain access to the company and the research they were doing.

"Circumstances and memory worked together and allowed me to come up with the operations I am now engaged in. The money has been amazing. I won't allow anything to get in my way."

Kane realized Chameleon had made his decision and he smiled as he sat back down. He looked at Chameleon for a moment to gather his thoughts, "We are both involved in human nature. I tend to provide for the vices of man, while you are engaged in the creation of my market, as it were."

Chameleon allowed a small chuckle, "Well that is one way to look at it." He hesitated before continuing, "What you are proposing makes sense. We both import from the same regions and such, so it makes sense to work together. We both have operations locally that could share resources. I think this will work fine for both of us."

Kane nodded his head in agreement, "That was entirely my point. I doubt it will take long to pull it together either. Both of our operations listen to instructions. This is a good thing."

Chameleon smiled, "Indeed. Well there is no time like the present. We may as well get started on some of the logistics."

Kane smiled, "Works for me."

Chameleon removed his balaclava exposing his face to Kane for the first time. He looked older and more worn than Kane had expected. The hints of grey somehow fit with his accent and the creases in his face. He was a handsome and distinguished looking man; one that people would find easy to trust based on looks alone.

Kane smiled, "That has to feel better."

21

When the authorities left, Connor returned to his family waiting in the living room. As he walked through the entry, Angela spoke guardedly, "Do you think the police are going to be a problem?"

Connor smiled, "I doubt it. It is in their best interest to proceed in this manner. Deviating would only create questions they really don't want to answer. Don't worry Angela, everything will be just fine. You guys are home safe and sound and that is all that matters. Nothing like this is ever going to happen again."

Simon sounded concerned, "That is a guarantee you really can't make, Connor. This Chameleon guy has a long reach. I wouldn't be so quick to count him out."

Connor nodded, "Count him out? I have no intention of doing that, but as long as we are not involved with anything concerning him, he will have no reason to bother us. He is a businessman first and foremost. He will not expose himself to unnecessary risks. It simply isn't in his best interest. Besides, I owe him a great deal. I have to have faith that everything will work out. I have no choice at this point."

Simon nodded, "Agreed. We do have to get on with our lives. We can't just sit around until this all blows over. I have work to do, so do you. We have to put our lives back on track again."

Angela spoke with a shaky voice, "I don't want to be left alone. We have to stay together until this is really over."

Connor sat next to Angela and took her in his arms, "I understand, Angela. Really I do. I won't be going anywhere. At least not for a while. Simon on the other hand, has to get back to life. I really don't think he or your mother are in any danger."

Connor glanced past Angela and looked at Simon and half smiled.

Simon nodded and spoke confidently, "Really, we will be just fine. I have no doubt about that. I would not be doing this if I thought your mother or I were at risk."

Angela nodded through her sniffles as she fought to hold back her tears, "I am just not as strong as I used to be. That is all. I'm worried."

***

Kane and Chameleon talked most of the day. Each revealed one specific detail about their business and then the other. The day progressed back and forth like that until there were no more secrets. At least no secrets about the aspects of their operations that was of necessary interest to the other. Each had answered the other's questions and a loose plan for moving forward was agreed upon.

Kane had assured Chameleon that he would make certain that Shea was not going to be a liability to them. He knew Connor as a man of honor and that was the most important thing; that and his desire to keep his family safe.

Jerome on the other hand was a loose end that needed to be dealt with. They needed to formulate a plan to draw him out into the open where he could then be terminated and his operations brought to the ground. Kane had even joked that when it was over, some of Jerome's people would be looking for work. They could probably pick up some trained assets at very reasonable prices.

Chameleon had not been so amused, "That would be interesting if possible. Loyalties are not that easily swayed however, as I am sure you are well aware. I am more interested in eliminating the risk than looking for new staff."

Kane's smile waned, "Of course. I wasn't suggesting anything different. I was simply trying to add a little levity."

Chameleon half smiled, "Naturally. Let us proceed."

Kane nodded and thought carefully for a few moments, "We should proceed with business as usual. He will be expecting us to do that. He is going to believe that we have freed the hostages and consider him a non-threat and he will proceed on that assumption. I would. Let's use that to our advantage."

Chameleon hesitated before responding, "What do you have in mind?"

Kane was silent as he thought further. He paced back and forth for a few moments before sitting at the table. He sat silently with his fingers interlocked under his chin. Chameleon understood and remained silent.

This was a crucial time in their business association and he wanted to give Kane every opportunity to show his value. He was prepared to terminate him if that need should arise, but would prefer an ally.

Kane understood the look on Chameleon's face, but it didn't concern him, "We know that Jerome was associated with Shea. We do know that. We are also pretty sure that is where Jerome acquired his Intel. From that we can assume that he is aware of you and your connection to Shea. These are all givens.

"We can assume that he is also aware of me. He is therefore aware of our operations and it is probably the result of that information that allowed him to believe he could pull this off. He knows now that he is out of his league. He will not be pleased with that knowledge and I doubt he will let it sit. He will be looking for another overt opportunity.

"I have a shipment coming out; you do as well. Let's work together to bring both out together. We will be a bit obvious in our actions. Not enough to attract federal attention, but enough for Jerome to notice. He will work to position the shipment in a way that would allow it to be intercepted. We will, of course, be expecting that. I think we can pretty much assume exactly where he will make his move. We will take him out then."

Chameleon looked analytically into Kane's eyes. He carefully reviewed Kane's theory. He compared that to his own thoughts and couldn't find any flaws in what Kane was saying.

"I am intrigued, Kane. I like the way you think."

Chameleon smiled, "Let's work out the details. The sooner we take out Jerome, the better I will like it."

***

The CIC was a buzz of activity as Chameleon and Kane entered. Chameleon barked at no one in particular, "Sitrep."

The man that was obviously in charge spoke immediately, "Assets on the move. All green. ETA three hours."

Chameleon smiled at Kane, "So far so good. Let's hope this plan of yours works."

Kane nodded, "I have no doubt it will. We should load up and get to the warehouse."

Chameleon looked at the large clock on the wall and nodded, "Yes, I believe it is time."

Chameleon barked again, "Have the team assemble. We are heading out in five."

The same man as before responded, "Yes, sir."

As Chameleon and Kane walked from the room, they could hear the call over the loudspeaker for the men to fall in.

***

It had taken an hour for the team to make their way to the warehouse. On arrival the majority of them took up strategic positions out of sight. The remaining few milled about looking as though they were busy.

Kane's men intentionally outnumbered Chameleon's two to one. That had been by design. Kane expressed no concern over the one sidedness of the deployment. In fact, he had been very pleased by it. In Chameleon's mind, putting the majority of risk on Kane's assets would be a good way to weed out the weak ones in the firefight he was expecting.

The wait for the arrival of the South American cargo wasn't much longer. The tractor-trailer unit pulled straight into the warehouse and the doors closed behind it. Once it was confirmed that everything was secure, the back of the trailer was opened.

Kane knew what to expect, but actually seeing all those young women climb out of the back of the trailer appalled him. He knew why they were here. He knew what they would be forced to do. His resolve strengthened and he was more determined than ever to see this through.

Chameleon noticed Kane's expression, "You alright, Kane? You don't look too good."

Kane chuckled, "I'm great, Chameleon. Don't worry about me."

He immediately joined the other men escorting the women to a small holding room. Once secured, he returned to the trailer to assist with the unloading of the cases of assorted contraband that formed his part of the shipment. That product was neatly stacked against one wall for later distribution.

When completely unloaded, the area was checked again and the tractor/trailer was permitted to exit the building. As it left, Chameleon walked over to Kane reviewing his stack of cases, "So what do you think, Kane? Why hasn't Jerome showed? Perhaps he isn't coming after all?"

Kane allowed the arm that was holding his clipboard to drop to his side as he turned to face Chameleon.

He smiled knowingly, "He will be here. We just need to be patient. My guess is he is waiting to ensure things are reasonably quiet here. He is probably thinking we will start to feel more at ease as time passes. Naturally we would be on high alert when a shipment arrives and that state of readiness calms with time. I would wait before I made a move if I were him."

Chameleon nodded, "Perhaps you are right. We'll wait. We'll see."

***

Two more hours passed without a sign of an assault. Chameleon was starting to lose patience. The men in their hiding spots were beginning to look uneasy and uncomfortable. Chameleon was about to order them all to move forward with their distributions when a voice for the second floor called out, "Here they come!"

Chameleon's head snapped to look up to the voice as he began running up the stairs. Kane was right behind them. On the monitors in the office they could see three black vans approaching rapidly.

Chameleon smiled, "Perfect." He walked to the railing and looked into the warehouse, "Get ready, show time. Lock and load."

Then he returned to the office to watch the vans get closer. Two of the vans continued directly towards the front and the third turned to circle around back. It was clear they had done their reconnaissance ahead of time and knew the layout.

The vans all came to a halt a few feet from the edge of the building and the men they contained exited rapidly and made their way quickly along the outside wall of the warehouse. Each of them was heavily armed, dressed in black and all wore gloves and balaclavas.

As they approached the main entrance points, Chameleon spoke into the headset he had donned, "Stand by. They are just outside the door. Hold until they are all in. Do not fire until they are all in."

A succession of "Copy" came back to him through the headset as he watched the monitors. His heart was racing and the grin on his face grew. He was certain he had set up the perfect trap. When those men came through the door, they would be turned into hamburger in seconds. They would know very quickly that they had messed up.

Outside the door the groups of men bunched up in a mass formation, with two men holding the doors handles ready to slide it open when the command was given. They hesitated, and Chameleon was visibly gesturing to the monitors, urging them through the door. When all the men outside, front and back were in position, the doors of the warehouse slid open rapidly. The assault teams moved through the door quickly and took position just inside as they scanned the area for aggressors.

Chameleon waited until he was sure all of them were in the warehouse, then he ordered his teams on the outside of the building to move to their offensive positions behind the assault team. As his men approached he ordered the men inside to open fire.

Chameleon was shocked when not a single round was fired. He spun and saw the barrel of Kane's Beretta pointed at his head. Kane smiled broadly and spoke succinctly, "Don't move a muscle, Chameleon. You are done."

The man seated at the monitor turned and stood from his chair and removed the weapons Chameleon was carrying. The stunned look on Chameleon's face made Kane's smile grow, "What's the matter

Chameleon, not exactly what you thought would be happening here today?"

Chameleon's shock turned to anger, "Why you double-crossing son of a bitch. You are screwing with the wrong man. You think you can take over my operations just like that? Seriously? I will see you burn in hell for this."

Kane laughed, "What happens to your operations is up to me and Jerome now, not you. Your threats no longer have meaning. How does it feel to realize the men you have been hunting have been playing you from the beginning. Everything you have done has been part of an orchestrated plan geared to take you down."

Chameleon calmed his voice, "You are a dead man."

Kane's smile left his face, "No doubt. That is what eventually happens to men like you and me. But it won't be today, and it won't be by you."

The visions of all those young women and Chameleon's plans went through Kane's mind as he squeezed the trigger of his weapon. There was a single report and Chameleon's head opened as he fell to the ground dead.

The man that had taken Chameleon's weapons looked at Kane in shock. Kane smiled, "Arm him. He pulled first. Never forget that."

The man nodded as he put Chameleon's pistol back within the loose grip of his dead hand and followed Kane out of the office and down the stairs to the main area of the warehouse. All of Chameleon's men were being gathered in the middle and zip strapped together. Kane smiled as he walked around the outside of the group and up to Jerome.

Jerome was smiling with his hand outstretched. Kane took it and shook it, "That went way smoother than I expected. Very well done."

Jerome smiled, "Indeed. I love it when things work according to plan. That is so rare." He shook his head lightly, "The helicopters are inbound. We need to leave before the local law enforcement arrives."

Kane nodded as he looked around the prisoners again. He was satisfied they were secure and he motioned his men to exit the warehouse. Chameleon's men, the women in the small room and the contraband were all left exactly where they were.

The helicopters arrived shortly after they vacated the building. Kane was the last one to board the last helicopter and he gave a final look into the warehouse as he did so. The helicopter rose from the ground quickly as soon as he was in and headed out as low over the buildings as was safe.

Looking back Kane could see the Special Response Unit arrive at the warehouse as well as a few marked police vehicles with lights and sirens announcing their arrival, as well as a couple black SUV's.

The helicopters had all left the warehouse area flying in different directions. They all flew as low as possible to avoid radar, but if they were detected, it would be individual birds on one specific heading and the rest wouldn't be compromised.

***

When Kane arrived at the Shea's house, the drive was full of vehicles. Some he recognized, some he didn't. It had been a hard few days and he was looking forward to a nice barbeque with family and friends.

Entering the house, Kane was greeted by Janet. She threw her arms around him and squeezed like it had been forever since she last saw him.

Kane chuckled, "Easy, girl, you're going to hurt the old man."

Janet giggled as she stepped back, "I am so glad to see you. I always worry."

Kane nodded compassionately, "You don't have to worry, Sweetie, your old man is too important to get hurt."

They laughed together and walked arm and arm onto the back patio area of the house. Outside nice music was playing in the background. Janet Elaine was running through the crowd. Angela had a drink in her hand and was talking to Davidson and Williams. They too had drinks. Kane assumed they must be off duty.

As he made his way to the bar to get a drink for himself, he saw the faces of many people he knew as high officials from most criminal investigation services, national investigation services and Interpol.

He nodded approvingly to no one in particular as he stopped beside Eric Jerome standing at the bar, "Hi Eric. It looks like a pretty good turnout. With all this brass standing around, one could go blind from the glitter."

Jerome chuckled, "No kidding. They do have their uses though, it is good to stay friendly." He chuckled again as he tapped his glass against Kane's.

Kane nodded, "That they do. I wonder sometimes if they know they work for us and not the other way around?"

Jerome laughed out loud as he turned away from the crowd and leaned on the bar, "It is probably best they don't know. It could be bad for business."

Kane snickered.

Connor approached the two men with his hand out to Kane. Kane took it with a smile, "Hey, Connor. Good to see you."

As the men released Connor nodded, "I'm glad you could make it. It has certainly been an interesting couple of weeks."

Kane nodded, "Jerome and I were just talking about the excitement of the last couple of days, but yes, it has been weeks of this for you and your family. You must be pleased that it is over and you can relax again."

Connor shook his head lightly, "Is it really, Kane, really. How can I be sure that something won't reappear down the road."

Kane shrugged lightly, "There are no guarantees in life, Connor. You of all people should know that. All I can say is Chameleon and his lot won't be coming back... ever."

Connor nodded and smiled, "I know what my part of the whole plan was. My families kidnapping was all part of it, but what was the rest. I never did hear what actually transpired."

Kane looked to Jerome, unsure if he wanted to give up details. Jerome understood the look and smiled to Connor, "Kane doesn't like to speak of these things. There is always security concerns. I, on the other hand, am not quite as worried about such things." He paused for a moment to gather his thoughts before continuing.

"Like Chameleon, we are contractors of sorts. The market we work in is, er, diversified. Much of what we do never happens and frankly, we don't exist. That is really all I can say about that.

"This operation was unique. There were a lot of favors called in from a number of sources. This entire operation was conducted exclusively by law enforcement and only law enforcement. We weren't involved at all, officially.

"Your family was kidnapped to create an urgency in Chameleon and Kane was set up to be recruited as an ally. That went off without a hitch.

"Chameleon's abduction of Kane was also planned. In the heel of his shoe was a GPS tracker. As soon as he arrived at Chameleon's base camp we knew exactly where it was and the tracker was turned off to prevent detection.

"Some of the men Kane took back with him were mine, and some were his. We believed Chameleon's ego would make him want to expend our men rather than his own. Thankfully we were correct.

"From there it was a matter of getting him to trust Kane and to put the rest of the plan in motion. Through his familiarity with Chameleon, Kane was able locate Chameleon's South American operations and his European contacts.

"Then it was just a matter of coordinating the assaults. Typically with this many agencies working together around the world, with time zones and the like, many things can and do go wrong. Amazingly there weren't many issues at all.

"We lost a couple good men in the raids in South America. The local agency messed up a couple of identities… it happens, sadly, but it happens. Overall it was a great operation.

"Local and federal officers also hit the lab and seized all sorts of records. Approximately two hundred people were taken into custody. Most were released and are now back out there looking for work, but the key figures will not likely see the light of day for some time…" Jerome chuckled, "I know for a fact of at least six that had… 'accidents' on their way to booking. Justice is handed out differently in certain places around the globe."

Kane's chuckle didn't go unnoticed as he took another drink.

Connor smiled as he listened. When Jerome was finished, Connor pointed his thumb back over his shoulder, "So all these guys, do they know who you are and what you did?"

Kane laughed, "Well, most of them know us by name. A few know us on sight, but will never admit it. Most of these men have no idea what we did. Most only know their own part of the whole picture.

With luck, they never will."

Connor nodded to confirm his commitment to staying quiet as well, "I heard the warehouse also had received shipments of drugs and guns. I didn't think Chameleon was into that?"

Kane nearly choked on a mouthful of his drink, before he chuckled, "Yeah, who knew, eh? I wouldn't have thought he was into that either."

Connor understood and his nod suggested he would not pursue that question further. "Hard to believe that if I hadn't retired, none of this would have happened. It was because of me that he went in this direction."

Jerome shook his head, "No way in hell is this your fault. Some would also argue that it was that Harrison chick's greed that started it, also a bunch of crap. This is all on Chameleon and only on him. He made the decisions he made in his own interest. Don't ever forget that."

Connor nodded lightly as he cleared his throat, "The food is just about ready. What say we get a fresh drink and join the rest of the party?

Other titles by SM Dougan

The Truth Series

Angela's Truth
Truth and Vengeance
Deadly Truth

Zane Wilder

The Wilder Doctrine

For more information on SM Dougan and his novels, visit
http://smdougan.com

Made in the USA
Charleston, SC
04 September 2013